A Biot's
Odyssey

Also by Alex Binkley:
Humanity's Saving Grace

Cover art:
Erica Syverson

A BIOT'S ODYSSEY

by Alex Binkley

LOOSE CANNON PRESS

LIBRARY AND ARCHIVES CANADA CATALOGUING IN PUBLICATION

Binkley, Alex, 1947-, author
A biot's odyssey / Alex Binkley

ISBN 978-0-9949163-8-9 (paperback)

I. Title.

PS8603.I554B36 2016   C813'.6   C2016-906496-4

Copyright © 2016 Alex Binkley

All rights reserved. Except for use in any review or critical article, the reproduction or use of this work, in whole or in part, in any form by any electronic, mechanical or other means—including xerography, photocopying and recording—or in any information or storage retrieval system, is forbidden without express permission of the publisher

Published by
LOOSE CANNON PRESS

info@loosecannonpress.com
www.loosecannonpress.com

Author's Note

This account employs Terran expressions and measures of time and distance for readers on Earth and Mandela. A Beingish edition is available for the Confederation and Pozzen worlds. Secundese and Dublo versions are in preparation.

Dedication

A Biot's Odyssey is dedicated to the memory of Stuart Gray, Rick Woods and Paul Delahanty who all provided inspiration for my efforts at writing novels.

Acknowledgements

Thanks to Felicity Harrison, Joan Ramsay, Louise Imbeault, Ken Byars and John Davis who read early versions of this story and offered many suggestions that improved it. Also to the members of the MOND science fiction and fantasy writers' group in Ottawa and the Ottawa Science Fiction Society that helped move the story along. To Erica Syverson for another marvelous cover. And to Bob Barclay for patiently guiding the publication of this story and its predecessor *Humanity's Saving Grace*.

    Alex Binkley,
    Ottawa 2016

The Cast

The Biots
Genghis: War hero in search for himself while trapped in an alien ship
Captain Kelsey: Biot starship captain trying to rescue Genghis
Fleming, Octinog, Amundsen and Gaopod: Next-gen Biot apprentices on the ship with Genghis
Hton: The Chief Councilor of the Being Confederation
Don and Hue: Pilots and comrades of Genghis
Ton: Every Being is assigned a Biot at birth to be personal assistants; a ton is identified by part of the Being's name with ton at the end
Stocton: The first Biot to be assigned to assist a human, Vasile Stocia

The Secund Robots
Woodsy: Genghis's pal
Charlie and Sam: The first robots Genghis met

Beings
Humbaw: A powerful Councillor of the Being Confederation who led the space expedition that contacted Earth in the mid-1800s
Humbawloda: Humbaw's granddaughter and a leading scientist
Gnoorvants: Commander of the *Enterprise* and Admiral of the Being fleet
Atdomorsin: Commander of the *Dreadnought*

Humans
Often referred to as Terrans by the Beings and Biots
Ruth Huxley: Astronomer and the first person contacted by the Beings when approached Earth, now living on Mandela and researching Biots
Nathan Huxley: Her son and fellow researcher
Ruthie Donohue: The first human born in space and now a scientist

Humans
Continued:
> *Vasile and Anna Stocia*: Vasile was an officer and saw combat in the Nameless War and then entered a mysterious Dome found on a planet when the humans were returning to Earth, setting off a life-long search for its builders
> *Hector Davis*: Secretary General of the United Nations and commander of the Terran forces in the Nameless War

Planets
> *Hnassumblaw*: Capital of the Being Confederation, with eight other worlds
> *Earth*: Generally known as Terra
> *Mandela*: Home to abducted humans and a billion transplanted humans
> *Kendo*: Idyllic unsettled world fit for humans
> *Secundus and Dublos*: These worlds of are numbered in order of their settlement
> *Domeworld*: Closed world and home to the mysterious Dome

Galaxyships
> *Enterprise*
> *Transformation*
> *Alliance*
> *Onhorvil*
> *Igotern*
> *Wanderer* (Secund)
> Crews of the Being Galaxyships are named by their positions rather than by their given names: i.e Weapons, Analytics, Science

Chapter 1
Genghis's Quandary

Ruth Huxley checked the imager screen for the umpteenth time to ensure it displayed all her questions for the meeting that Genghis Khan requested.

No, she recalled, the restless Biot went by just Genghis these days. She would ask why he dropped the second part of the human name he adopted during the Nameless War. Perhaps it was a step in his overdue transition to an individual from a member of the biological robot collective built by the reptilian aliens called Beings. She wanted to convince him to embrace not fear his evolution.

The clock in the bottom right hand corner of the screen showed two minutes to his arrival. Ruth first met Genghis on the Being flagship *Alliance* 30 years earlier when he was already a hero of the Nameless War.

Footsteps in the hall of Ruth's one-story research center on Mandela signaled his approach. The building, like every other one on the planet that was humanity's second home, was constructed with the same biotech material the Beings developed to build the Biots and their Galaxyships.

With a dispersed population of just over a billion and little industry, the planet was still a quiet world. Few buildings had more than one floor. "Come in," she called.

Biots did not show overt signs of aging until their color faded as they approached two hundred years of age. Genghis was in his mid-40s and his fuzzy tan exterior appeared as robust as ever.

"Hello, Madame Huxley. Thank you very much for agreeing to see me."

"Cut the formality Genghis. Last time you called me Ruth. I could hardly refuse to see an old friend."

"I thought afterward I had been presumptuous."

She pointed to a chair. Biots did not tire standing and sat because it made humans feel more comfortable during a conversation.

Ruth looked at the imager as the small talk continued. Genghis's narrative appeared on it within seconds of him speaking. He conversed in English, which would make the interview easier. Her command of spoken Beingish was not advanced enough to gain the information she sought.

"The last time we met was five years ago on our way to the 25th anniversary victory celebrations of the Nameless War," Ruth said. "You said then that even with your interesting assignments since the end of the War, something troubled you. Finally, you admitted you were experiencing emotions and desires although Biots didn't possess them."

Genghis nodded rather than respond orally to her comment as Biots normally did. *What other human quirks had he taken on?*

"You thought you were the only one struggling with them. Later you informed me that other Biot veterans were experiencing the same inner turmoil. In fact, their condition was so similar to yours that you wanted to discover how it'd happened and what it meant. A year later you concluded that interaction with humans triggered either the development of emotions in Biots or the realization they repressed the ones their organic brains generated naturally. You feared you were no longer a true Biot."

Another nod from Genghis. "You did question whether I appreciated that Beings rarely display emotions and they were our only behavioral example until we encountered Terrans."

As fluent as Genghis was in English, he still referred to Earth as Terra as the Beings did. Humans were Terrans.

Another sign of Genghis's preoccupation with understanding what was happening to the Biots was his constant glancing about the room rather than keeping his gaze on her as a Biot normally would.

"Combat forced me to make decisions instead of just following instructions," he said. "From that opening flowed memories of my experiences before and during the War along with the perplexing notions of sentimentality, restlessness and curiosity. Most surprising is the envy of the close personal relationships Beings and Terrans enjoy with members of their own kind."

"You mean friends and family?" Ruth was delighted when Genghis nodded. He was finally opening up.

During the conversation, his voice rose and fell and he fidgeted and frequently shifted his position. Previously he would have sat rigidly describing a great adventure or a mundane task in the same matter-of-fact tone.

"You should revisit the record of the Biots stationed on *Transformation* during the Nameless War," she said. "Even though they repeatedly demonstrated creativity and imagination in treating the rescued Nameless, they didn't appreciate how much they'd accomplished. When it was pointed out to them, they became truly excited and even more creative, all driven by wishes and feelings."

Genghis peered intently at the floor as if it might inspire a response.

Ruth shared the Beings' view that the Biots had to reach a collective realization they possessed emotions similar to humans. Acting on those feelings would enable them to take on a more complete role in the Confederation as a separate species equal to Beings and humans. She and other researchers studied how this development could occur.

The biggest puzzle for Ruth was why most Biots still acted like servants, which is the role the Beings intended when they created their biological robots centuries ago. They gained full citizenship in the Being Confederation in recognition of the service of Genghis and thousands of other Biots who fought alongside human soldiers and pilots during the War. Yet after it ended, most Biots behaved as if nothing had changed. They appeared content in their traditional helper role. Well not Genghis and his mates.

Ruth would share Genghis' comments with Ruthie Donohue and Humbawloda, who were heading a multi-disciplinary team tracking the changes in the Biots. Ruthie, her god-daughter, shrugged off the celebrity status of being the first modern human born off Earth to become a leading astronomer and astrobiologist. She was born on *Alliance* as it returned scientists and military personnel to Earth at the end of the Nameless War.

Humbawloda, a top-flight ethnobiologist and astronomer, was the granddaughter of Humbaw, the Being who found and established diplomatic relations with Earth in 2037 after two centuries of periodically exploring the planet without ever being detected.

To test Genghis, Ruth said, "Is your discontent motivated by envy of the next-generation Biots? It appears to coincide with their introduction about 10 years ago."

Genghis stared at her as if he had not considered this possibility. Biots closely resembled Beings except for their tan color and the smooth texture of the biotech material in their exterior shells. To humans, Biots and Galaxyships appeared to be covered in industrial carpeting.

Beings had pebbly skin that ranged from light blue to pale green in color. Their round heads ended in a pointy jaw and featured large bulging eyes, nostrils instead of a nose, a small mouth, skin flaps for ears and small, shiny white teeth. Their arms did not reach their waists and their hands had short thumbs and three long slender fingers.

"Why would we be envious?" he said. "Many improvements incorporated in the next-gens were recommended by original Biots to correct our shortcomings. We were intended to resemble Beings and we maintained our overall design in the next-gens. Instead of being 1.2 meters in height to match the average Being, we recommended the next-gens be constructed 60 centimeters taller because Terrans have a big advantage with their size. Once that was agreed to, interior improvements became possible to give the next-gens much greater strength and speed than the originals. The same biotech material is used in their shells as in ours."

The Beings had not retrofitted original Biots with the next-gens' olfactory sense. While Genghis understood their position that converting more than a billion originals would be an immense task, he kept arguing its absence handicapped the originals. Biots could not smile either and used a nod as a substitute.

Deciding next-gens were not a sore point, Ruth said, "What will you do next? You've spent time on all the Being and human planets and many years working with the Benjamin Kendo Institute. But first tell me why did you drop Khan from your name?"

"During my first post-war visit to Terra in 2038, I learned about Genghis Khan's blood-soaked history. While I had no wish to emulate him in that regard, I did admire his boldness. So I kept Genghis and set out to make a difference for Biots. Other than Benjamin Kendo, it took years for most humans to drop Khan from my name.

"At first my fame from the War was amusing. In time, it became frustrating because it focused on the past rather than the future. What I wanted to understand was how an artificial creature like me could be motivated by more than my programing, training and the Biots' basic laws of preventing harm to Beings and Terrans. Now I've broadened my quest into whether emotions could lead to separate personalities among Biots, which I fear would ruin our strong collective sense."

"It could be a positive development," Ruth said. She would have patted Genghis's shoulder if he was closer. He finally acknowledged Biots were developing their own personalities. The differences among them were clear to humans and Beings. What would it take for Biots to embrace the change?

Although they had no gender, many Biots adopted male and female names and referred to themselves as he or she.

"I was fortunate enough to be selected by the Kendo Institute after the War to study how the Beings developed robots with organic brains. I still marvel at what they created. The Beings instilled their sense of collective responsibility in us. Benjamin often said too few Terrans possessed a similar concern toward their fellows.

"We also studied whether the presence of reptiles in Earth's past and present indicates a link between Terra and the Being home world Hnassumblaw. Then there are the other Confederation worlds where reptilian skeletons and fossils are found.

"We also participated in a study into the rapid growth of the Being population since the end of the Nameless War. We have no real explanation yet for what encouraged the Beings to suddenly reproduce in much great numbers than before. About two million have been born since the end of the War, which is quite remarkable for a population of just over 12 million. There's no sign that population growth will slow down.

"The Institute also assisted the Beings' efforts to mitigate the damage done to Terra by the environmental damage and climate change caused by Terran recklessness."

In return for Earth's military assistance in the Nameless War, the Beings provided improved solar and wind-based energy systems. They also gathered up the debris that space programs had surrounded the planet with so it no longer posed a threat to space ships or Earth.

The material that had an immediate value was loaded in freight shuttles and returned to Earth with the proceeds donated to the United Nations. The rest was stored in geosynchronous orbit in the two stable Lagrange points between Earth and the Moon until needed. *Alliance*, the Being Galaxyship that Humbaw studied Earth with, was placed in orbit to oversee the debris cleanup, supervise the storage areas, guard the planet from threatening asteroids and teach humans how to mine them.

With the levels of atmospheric pollution reduced, the planet was no longer ravished by as many vicious storms and droughts.

However Earth in 2065 remained in a troubled state politically and environmentally, which made Ruth glad that she, her son Nathan and daughter Louise had settled on Mandela.

"One evening on Terra, I joined a stargazing party," Genghis said. "With few artificial light sources and a cloudless sky, the view was spectacular. As my companions pointed out individual stars and constellations, I realized that during all my voyages in space, I never took the time to admire my celestial surroundings.

"Either I'd been a trooper being transported to an enemy-held planet or a civilian visiting the nine Confederation and three allied worlds. I was always preparing for the destination, not contemplating the magnificence of where I was. That brought me to conclude that serving on board a Galaxyship might broaden my perspective. So I've volunteered for space duty and am waiting for my first assignment with great anticipation."

Chapter 2
A Stranger Drops By

Not long after his meeting with Ruth, Navigation Central, the Beings' space control office, assigned Genghis to a giant bulk carrier known only as Transport 27. He was listed simply as a crew member with no designated position or function.

Every Galaxyship from the largest cruiser to the smallest transport was operated by a Controlling Unit, which was essentially a Biot without a body. It navigated the ship and tracked on-board conditions as well as staying in contact with Navigation Central.

As Fleet ships had a commander and crew to carry out various scientific and other functions, their Controlling Units acted like a senior officer in steady contact with the crew.

While Controlling Units could operate transports and other merchant vessels on their own, their voyages were often used by the Fleet to train Beings and Biots in space flight.

Transport 27 had the distinction of being commanded by the first Biot captain. Kelsey was still new in the post and worked closely with Hajang, the vessel's Controlling Unit. She and the ten trainees were all next-gen Biots.

The ship's crew area was about the size of a tennis court because Biots did not require living quarters. The main features were the Command Benches with the navigation and ship status imagers and an office cubicle for the Captain.

On the ship's topside was a bay that held two shuttles and a recharging station. As the only original Biot on the ship, Genghis would use it to replenish the electricity levels in the storage cell located in his lower chest. He recharged every two to four days depending on his physical activity level.

Inside the next-gens was a small thermoelectric generator. They would refuel their generators once a century with plutonium nuggets.

Genghis puzzled over why he was assigned to a transport rather than a Fleet ship, which would have an experienced crew to work with. As the transport would be traveling in well-charted space, there would unlikely be any astronomical surprises.

In the end, Genghis concluded that Hton, the first Biot elected Chief Councilor of the Being Confederation, had arranged the assignment to enable him to learn more about next-gens even though he contributed to their design.

As only 1,200 to 1,300 next-gens were created every year, it would be centuries before they supplanted the billion original Biots or even matched the Beings who usually lived for several centuries.

While Genghis wanted to interact with his new crewmates, they would not talk in his presence even though they watched him intently. Captain Kelsey, a veteran of more than eight years of space duty, had not progressed beyond speaking to him with the kind of deference that Biots showed Beings before the Nameless War.

As quiet as they acted around him, amongst each other the next-gens were far more expressive and active than originals, which led him to wonder if his presence made them uncomfortable. Rather than confront them about their behavior, he studied them for clues to explain it.

After he learned all he could about the operation of the transport, Genghis had resumed his lessons in astronomy and music to keep from dwelling on the emotional changes he explained to Ruth Huxley.

In collaboration with several Being scientists, Ruth developed the astronomy program he was studying. The detail in her observations about the phenomena of space made him think she must have more insights into the Biots' changes than she revealed to him. However he could not be angry with her for withholding information.

Ruth's status among the Biots rivaled the popularity of Humbaw and his former personal assistant Hton. The Biots had chosen her as the first human to contact because of the soundness of her theories on the prospect for alien life in the Milky Way and why it would likely be different than lifeforms in other galaxies.

Genghis recited from memory estimates the Milky Way was 100,000 to 120,000 light years in diameter. The Being

Confederation was more than 20,000 light years from the center of the Galaxy. Earth was in the distant reaches of the Orion Arm, more than 28,000 light years from Galactic Center.

Even though there were between 200 and 400 billion stars in the Milky Way, it was just a medium-sized galaxy. While it had been in existence for much of the Universe's more than 14 billion years, it constantly underwent change.

Genghis could discuss celestial data in ponderous detail. What he could achieve was the awe that Ruth created when she described the Milky Way and its neighbors in the Virgo Supercluster. Her excitement for the topic was infectious and inspired audiences to clamor for more information. She had no end of sponsors for her research.

Once Ruth dropped her scientific caution long enough to say, "Just think what life might be out there in the Milky Way and the other galaxies."

So far, Terrans along with Beings and Pozzens, their much larger cousins, were it.

In addition to astronomy, Genghis shared the Biot love for Terran music. To most Beings, music remained a jarring assault on their hearing. Genghis turned Transport 27 into a galactic concert hall where the music never ended in the crew area and shuttle bay. He could not have done that on a Fleet ship.

Genghis programmed Hajang to play his full repertoire of Terran classical music. Its selections were random so Genghis never knew what to expect. Even with the vast distances in space, he was certain it would take many trips to play the entire collection.

Once a day, the ship played the instrumental version of Anton Dvorak's *A Song for the Moon*. The Biots had adopted it as their anthem during the Nameless War. Since then, its opera love song lyrics were rewritten into *An Ode to the Universe*, a Beingish tribute to the majesty and wonders of the heavens.

Near the end of his first month on the transport, which carried a load from an asteroid mining project to a Being processing station, Genghis was in the shuttle bay recharging his electricity storage cell. He listened to Gustave Holst's *The Planets* while studying another segment of Ruth's astronomy program on his personal analyzer. At first he ignored the rapid footsteps even though he could not think of a reason for another crew member to be in the bay. When the steps drew closer, he called out.

Octinog peered around a bulkhead. "Pardon me for intruding on you like this." Like many next-gen Biots, he adopted the name of a famous Being scientist. His namesake proposed using the LaGrange points between Earth and its Moon, or the stable orbital places as the Beings called them, for storing the valuable material in Earth's space debris. He designed the self-guided flying magnets that gathered up the debris. The space sleds, as they were nicknamed, still circled the planet collecting the last of the 500,000 chunks of debris as well as millions of smaller bits.

Octinog glanced about like a nervous youngster. "We've located a most unusual object in space and would like your assistance in identifying it."

"We?"

"Fleming and I. Hajang agrees."

Genghis' first reaction was to tell them he had no expertise in space research. *They possess far more information so they're asking me for a different reason.* "What does this object look like?"

"Something artificial," Octinog said.

"As in a spacecraft?"

"We think so."

"Let's view your discovery on the main imagers."

By its quick steps, Octinog was anxious to show him the find. When they reached the Command Benches, Fleming stood. The center and right hand imagers showed fuzzy 3-D views of a distant object on a star-dotted background. It looked like two lumps of rock connected by a rod. The left-hand imager displayed a line among the stars, which Genghis surmised was a projected past and future course for the object.

"It doesn't look like natural space debris or rocks especially with that long connection between the two sections," Fleming said. "Observing its speed and trajectory, it's not under power."

"Hajang, show images of the drifting starships the Beings found three centuries ago," Genghis said. Within seconds, visuals of two heavily scarred vessels appeared.

One had a gaping hole near its midsection. Both looked like a collection of panels and modules shoved together. Searches had failed to determine their origin.

Genghis took his eyes off the ancient vessels and glanced at the next-gens. "They're nothing like what you've found. We have a genuine mystery craft on our hands."

When Octinog and Fleming nodded at each other, Genghis realized they had needed his confirmation that whatever was out there merited further examination. His support would lend credence to their arguments to Navigation Central about its importance. *If Genghis says it needs to be studied, it needs to be studied.*

At the same time, the next-gens' enthusiasm about the discovery matched the excitement the spacecraft would generate among Beings. The Biots were either copying the behavior of Beings or showing genuine emotion. Figuring out what the anomaly was would make an interesting project for him to participate in.

"I've asked Captain Kelsey to join us," Octinog said. "Thank you for agreeing with us, Genghis. It means a lot."

"Hajang must have assisted your research as well?"

"A great deal. It recommended that we ask for your opinion on what it is."

It probably also told them I was at the recharging station.

Kelsey paused in her approach to the Command Benches and the next-gens straightened in her presence. She inclined her head to Genghis, and then fingered her pearl necklace. While her aloofness was frustrating, he admired the training regime she established on the Transport. The Biots would not receive better preparation anywhere.

"I haven't seen the visuals of the ancient starships since space training." She strode to her seat in the middle of the front bench. "Why are you looking at them and what's that?" She kept her eyes on the anomaly.

Octinog filled her in on the discovery while stressing Genghis's concurrence their discovery was not natural.

"Hajang, what's your conclusion?" she said.

"I concur that it's a technology we know nothing about." Hajang sounded excited about the discovery, which surprised Genghis. Perhaps Controlling Units could also develop emotions. He doubted it would be just learned behavior.

Before Genghis could present arguments for investigating the discovery, Hajang said, "This ship is carrying non-vital supplies so we could divert from our mission to examine the anomaly. On our current trajectories, we'll pass more than 1,000 kilometres apart, which will prevent us from learning much more about it. We should attempt to explore it."

Listening to the Controlling Unit, Genghis wondered why it had not suggested the change in course to Octinog and Fleming earlier. Perhaps it too wanted Genghis's reassurance about the importance of the discovery. *What would they have done without me?*

The Captain looked apprehensive. She was still in the-going-by-the-book phase.

Genghis recalled the moment during the Nameless War when Terrans gave him and other troopers the opportunity to take charge in the ground war against the Nameless. Making decisions was a life-changing event for him. While Kelsey was part way there, she still needed that one big challenge to realize her potential. Perhaps the mystery spacecraft would be it.

"I'll personally inform the Chief Councilor of the change in course," Genghis said. "If anyone is to be criticized for it, it'll be me." *Hton would support exploring the mystery ship because it was exactly what he would do.*

To Genghis, Hton was the real hero of the Nameless War. He foresaw that Terran soldiers and pilots operating Being technology could end the Nameless attacks that plagued the Confederation for decades. At the same time, Terrans would train Biots to defend their worlds in the future.

Hton orchestrated a subtle campaign that convinced the Beings to contact Terra instead of continuing to treat the blue planet like a combination research project and museum. Starting in the early 1900s, Humbaw led regular expeditions to study Terra and its inhabitants without making contact. He and Hton explored the planet on every visit until the Beings declared their presence in 2037.

Kelsey stared at Genghis. "You won't be satisfied with just a close fly-by inspection?"

Genghis grinned. "If we can get on board, think of what we might learn. Hton and Humbaw will expect nothing less." By invoking the name of Humbaw, the most revered Being, Genghis had erased any objection she might voice to his plan.

Kelsey stared at him as if unable to believe she could be talking to someone who could refer to the two most significant figures in the Confederation by their names rather than their positions as most Biots would.

"The away mission is yours to organize," she finally said. "I'm sure you'll find crew to accompany you."

"I'll leave you with enough of them to reach your destination."

The Captain laughed. "While I could do that by myself, I would like some company."

Genghis wondered if a Biot had ever expressed a desire for company before. He counted her comment as another positive sign. He wanted to include Kelsey among his friends.

"When I was in my preparation phase, I read General Davis's account of how your leadership in the Nameless War inspired our troopers and flyers," she said. "In fact all Biots. Now I've seen it for myself. I'll report our course deviation to Navigation Central."

She stared again at the imagers. "You're correct. It would be a mistake not to investigate the anomaly."

"In the meantime, I need to continue my recharging so I'm ready to go exploring." Genghis returned to the shuttle bay anxious to review Ruth's astronomy course for any clues about where the anomaly could come from.

He had just sat and plugged in the power cable when Fleming and Octinog entered the bay and stood facing him.

"Thank you for supporting us," Octinog said. "We have some questions, if you don't mind?"

"Of course not." *Finally they want to talk.*

"After you left the Command Bench, the Captain said she should have encouraged us to learn from your experiences. We've studied the official record of what the Biots accomplished during and after the Nameless War. But we've never discussed it with someone who was there."

As Octinog talked, other Biots entered the bay. Finally they too had overcome their reluctance. His frustration had been misplaced; they were in awe of him.

Genghis recounted how Hton concluded Biots needed exposure to the undisciplined ways of Terrans to open their eyes to a different future. "Compared to Beings, they're aggressive, impetuous and short-sighted. But they tackle a problem head-on rather than dealing with it in an incremental way as the Beings did with the Nameless attacks. Beings take that approach because it spawns many discoveries and inventions. As well, Beings remember that before Transformation, their behavior was much like Terran impulsiveness."

"So Hton wanted the Beings to recruit Terrans to defeat the Nameless and provide us with the opportunity to show the Beings what we could do?" Octinog sounded like he just solved a great puzzle.

"The Beings lack the combativeness needed to stop the attacks," Genghis said. "Hton concluded correctly that would require Terrans combined with Being technology. In return, the Beings would give Terra the knowledge and technology to save their planet from climate change. While the Nameless are settled on Mandela and we're full citizens of the Confederation, Terra has been slow to heal because its residents like to quarrel more about whom to blame for a problem than fix it."

"None of us have spent time with Terrans," Fleming said. "What should we expect?"

"Those on Mandela would welcome you and ask lots of questions about your training. On Terra, it mainly depends on which country you visit. In Europe, Russia, China and some parts of North America, you would be greeted warmly while other countries would not admit you. In a few, you'd be in danger of being attacked by people with strange beliefs. Biots who spend time on Terra are trained in self-defence and carry weapons in dangerous areas. It saddens me to describe it this way because I lived there for several years when I worked with the Kendo Institute and never once was threatened."

"They were afraid of you," Fleming said.

Genghis frowned. "They were the least of my worries."

Chapter 3
A Close Encounter

The next-gens stood in a semi-circle in front of Genghis as if making a collective apology for not talking with him before. Although Captain Kelsey remained at the Command Bench, Hajang would feed his account to her.

"Your files only mention you becoming a trooper on *Enterprise*," Octinog said. "They say little about what you did before."

"My identifier was QMLW420. I was assigned to Galaxyship 387 as part of a team adding cockpits to Being defence craft. Our instructions didn't explain the need for this modification and none of us thought to ask why a self-guided craft required one. After we finished modifying a craft, it was transferred to another bay and we worked on the next one.

"Then Terrans arrived on 387 from Humbaw's cruiser, which traveled to a remote arm of the galaxy to collect them. We weren't told their purpose and I first saw them by accident."

The next-gens glanced at each other. Obviously they were startled by the Beings not keeping the Biots fully informed. That kind of information now was shared routinely with the entire crew of a Galaxyship.

"I was pushing a large trolley to a storage chamber to collect parts for the next conversions when I heard loud sounds coming from a bay. Other than the engines of the defence craft at full throttle, I'd never encountered so much noise. I turned down the sensitivity of my audio receptors and looked in the open entrance.

"I was perplexed as I gazed about the bay. Instead of maintenance equipment, it was full of Terrans. During the preparation phase after my creation, I assimilated a lot of information. The same when I commenced my assignments. Always learning but never questioning. I wondered why Terrans were different in height and skin color. I couldn't understand the purpose of their running and jumping. The questions kept coming and I wanted answers.

"I was so absorbed in studying their activity that I didn't hear a Terran in a uniform arrive. 'I need to get past you,' he said pointing at the entrance into the bay. Although we'd been prepared for their language, I couldn't tell what the insignia on the man's uniform meant or how to pronounce the words Vasile Stocia on his identifier badge."

The Biots leaned closer. "The same Vasile Stocia who explored the Dome?" Fleming's voice was full of wonder.

"The same." Once again, the next-gens exchanged glances. "As I shifted the trolley to let him pass, I asked my first question. 'What are you doing in there?'

"He said the soldiers trained to remain in top condition to fight the Nameless. All the way to the storage room, I pondered what his words could mean. On my next trip to the storage chamber, I watched the training in the maintenance bay for a few minutes. This time, soldiers grabbed at each other and climbed up ropes hanging from the bay's ceiling. More questions flooded my mind.

"When I had to replenish my electricity storage cell, I plugged in for a slow charge to give me time to research the data banks. The first thing I learned was the ship was named *Enterprise* at the request of the Terrans."

The Biots moved closer as if they feared missing part of his account. "We know that story," Fleming said. "Terrans have fulsome imaginations. *Enterprise* is an imaginary ship of great significance to them. Humbaw had named his ship *Alliance* to signify the partnership with the Terrans."

"Before long, all the Fleet ships were given names," Genghis said. "Then I found out the Controlling Unit on *Enterprise* had taken the name Turing, who Terrans credit with inventing computers. Turing instructed me in how to watch the soldiers' training via the ship's communications network. From that, I learned other Terrans called pilots would fight the Nameless with the craft we modified. The information in the data banks generated so many questions I contemplated whether they could hurt my brain. Then an idea came to me. Instead of recruiting the humans, why hadn't the Beings trained us to combat the enemy?"

"Terrans were experienced in fighting and Hton knew we needed to learn from them," Octinog said, again sounding like he solved a great mystery. The other Biots murmured their agreement.

Genghis reminded himself they wanted to learn what the Nameless War was like and the changes it brought to Beings and Biots. "That was the day I learned about curiosity. Afterward, I watched the soldiers' training whenever I could.

"A few days later when I went to collect parts, I encountered a group of Biots in a corridor. Their fingers flashed in our sign language, which meant they wanted to keep their discussion secret from the Beings. To my surprise the conversation was not about their jobs maintaining the defence craft. Instead they discussed flying the craft to combat the Nameless. Most had the names of the pilots whose craft they maintained on the front and back of their shells."

"When I returned to my post, I told my coworkers about the pilots. While they said nothing at first, before long they asked why the Beings hadn't prepared us to combat the Nameless. Turing said the Beings couldn't teach us because they bred combativeness out of their species to prevent their own destruction."

"So are the Pozzens really like Beings from before Transformation?" Fleming said.

"In many ways." These Biots would know that a faction of militaristic Beings had broken away from Hnassumblaw centuries ago rather than submit to Transformation. Their world Pozzen became dominated by a Ruler class. It forced Nameless, who had been abducted from Terra centuries earlier, to conduct the attacks on the Confederation. "After we defeated the Rulers, the remaining Pozzens rebuilt their world and established close relations with the Confederation, Terra and Mandela.

"My team of Biots talked about how we could combat the Nameless. Then one asked how we could learn to shoot rifles because the bullets would damage the ship. It and several others undertook to develop a solution while the rest of us modified craft. They invented a rifle that fired laser blasts instead of bullets. It would be more deadly in combat yet it could be safely discharged inside the ship, which meant we could train with it.

"Captain Stocia was so impressed with the new weapon that he showed it to Gnoorvants, the *Enterprise's* Commander, and gave us credit for developing it. Soon my group received additional Biots so we could make the weapon and convert the defense craft. Commander Gnoorvants and his ton came to our work area to tell us he would welcome any other innovations. When he wasn't looking, Gnoorton signed us a message of congratulations. Later I learned he reported the weapon to Hton."

The Biots all grinned at hearing of Gnoorton's praise.

"Then, Gnoorton and Captain Stocia gave us our opportunity. They needed a boarding party to recapture a transport Galaxyship. 'You guys know the layout of the ship, the Captain said, and can reach the Command Chamber as quickly as possible from the docking bay.' We asked if that would make us troopers. He said it would be a good start."

"The files do contain a description of the famous Genghis sprint from the transport's landing bay to its Command Chamber," Fleming said. "It's described as the first sign of your determination to show what Biots were capable of."

"And that until then no one knew a Biot could run so fast," Octinog said.

The Biots chuckled. Instead of the traditional Being snort in response to humor, next-gens had adopted Terran laughs. Genghis loved the sound.

"I'd no idea what to expect. When I reached the Command Chamber, the crew looked like small Terrans. They just sat there staring at me. Instead of being frightening, our Nameless enemies were pathetic. Later I learned about the controlling chemicals the Rulers fed them for years. This group was among the first to be resettled on Mandela.

"Once we became Troopers, we wanted names. As the Beings had no great warriors to choose from, we adopted names of famous Terran military figures. I liked the forceful ring of Genghis Khan."

Fully recharged, Genghis returned to the Command Benches as the Transport closed to 250 kilometres from the mysterious craft. The center imager showed a high resolution visual of it including jagged chunks of boulders and a cluster of smaller rocks sailing along as if escorting the ship.

"There's no doubt we've found an unknown spacecraft," Kelsey said. "That in itself is a major event. The Beings and Terrans will want to know everything about it. While the vessel's exterior is dented and discolored as if it's been struck many times, our sensors show an environment in the interior. Hajang hasn't been able to detect the power source that maintains it."

Genghis stared at the alien vessel. The front section was square shaped with a pointed bow and was about half the size of the back section. It was rectangular with rounded corners and nodules on each side. To his surprise, his internal temperature climbed and he held his arms at his sides to resist an urge to point at the imager. He was excited although he kept telling himself a Biot should not feel that way.

The boisterous celebrations on the Galaxyships at the end of the Nameless War when he and hundreds of other Biots were presented medals for bravery was only an imitation of Terran behavior. At least that is what he kept thinking. Once again, he wondered whether he deluded himself all these years about his emotions. Perhaps they always existed and the Biots repressed them until circumstances brought them out.

The craft's mystery and potential tantalized Genghis. An internal atmosphere suggested the ship carried a crew. He wanted to discover its origin and why it was drifting in space. He recalled a professor talking about how Beings and Terrans shared a desire to explore and learn more about their own worlds, followed by their solar system, and then all the stars they could spot at night. Then the billions more they could only see with telescopes of increasing strength and finally via spacecraft. Maybe any sentient species would possess the same desire to learn what lay beyond the reach of its technology.

His excitement spilled out. "If the craft is on an exploration mission, why isn't it communicating or probing the space around it. If it isn't exploring, then why is it here? It's intact, unlike the abandoned starships the Beings found."

Kelsey and the other Biots peered at him as if waiting for more comments.

"Could the coterie of rocks be protecting it?" he said. No one answered, which meant neither the crew nor Hajang had considered that possibility.

"I don't know how an essentially unpowered craft could hold those rocks in position. The ship appears to be half the size of this transport so it doesn't have enough mass to maintain that formation."

Again he did not receive an answer.

"The rear compartment must house its propulsion system, although Hajang still isn't detecting any energy readings from it," Fleming said.

"Captain, considering the rocky screen and the ship's internal power, I recommend you maintain this distance from the anomaly and that we explore it further with a shuttle," Genghis said. "Just to be on the safe side."

"That would be prudent."

Pilots no longer flew shuttles. That job had been taken over by mini Controlling Units known as Tysons. If more than one shuttle was in operation, they were assigned numbers by the controlling Galaxyship.

Fleming and Octinog volunteered to accompany Genghis to study the mystery vessel. After collecting space suits and exploration gear, they boarded the shuttle. As the most experienced pilot, Octinog took the flight control seat to monitor conditions while the shuttle flew around the rocky screen to obtain a full view of the alien ship. The stern was a flat panel. "There are no exhaust vents. What kind of propulsion system does this ship have? Shuttle, take us in closer."

"On what we assume is the underside of its rear section, there are two large hatches and a smaller one," Fleming reported to the transport. "We're looking for access to the interior."

"There are rings around the smaller hatch," Genghis said. "They may be part of a docking mechanism, which means it might be the entrance although there should be more than one. Shuttle, approach closer and I'll knock on the door."

The shuttle eased in line with the rings while Genghis donned the space suit Biots wore to protect the electricity storage cell in their chests from the deep freeze of space. He exited the shuttle through the airlock. When the shuttle appeared far enough ahead of the hatch on the mystery ship, he pushed off toward it.

His helmet camera would record his deep space long jump. The visual would be relayed by the transport to Navigation Central, which would share it with the Confederation and Terran worlds.

He triggered his backpack propulsion unit to complete the two hundred meter leap to the smaller hatch. While the rings around it provided grips for both hands, this section of the vessel was in shadow so he turned on the helmet lamp to make sure he did not miss any crucial detail.

The light revealed an L-shaped handle on the hatch that turned clockwise once he applied enough pressure. The hatch opened inward revealing a chamber that would hold a couple of Biots. Recessed lights in the ceiling came on casting a grey hue that revealed a tunnel that ran from the chamber. At about fifteen meters, the tunnel sloped upward.

To his surprise, there was no airlock at the entrance. He puzzled over what held the atmosphere in. Then holding onto the rings, he swung his feet forward before propelling the rest of his body inside the vessel. It felt like he was snared in a mass of invisible cobwebs and he strained to push through them. Finally his knees made it past the hatchway and he kicked down to place his feet on the floor to lever himself in as he pushed forward.

Then whatever held him let go and he stumbled forward until he could regain his balance. While he had never walked through deep water, he expected it would offer about as much resistance as whatever he encountered. He reported the situation to the Transport in case his visual was not clear.

"Remain where you are," Kelsey ordered. "The ship is no place to explore on your own. Fleming will join you while Octinog returns to Transport 27 to collect two more Biots to search with you."

Chapter 4
No End of Surprises

As he waited for Fleming to arrive from the shuttle, Genghis decided the barrier at the hatchway was a force field. How it worked and why it suddenly released him was another puzzle. He could not locate any panels or access covers for the field projectors.

The tunnel up the slope was devoid of printed instructions or labels. "The interior temperature is 11 degrees Celsius," he told the transport over his radio. "That's warm enough to keep the gear working plus we won't overheat. Neither Terrans nor Beings would last long because there's little oxygen in the air."

Fleming had obviously studied Genghis's clumsy entry into the ship. After his space leap, he propelled himself through the open hatch head first, which allowed him to use his shoulder and arm strength with less mass for the force field to block.

Once he was on his feet, he followed Genghis up the slope. While the ship had sufficient gravity to enable them to walk, they would have no trouble touching the ceiling if they jumped.

When they reached the entrance to a large chamber, another force field grabbed them briefly before letting go. As it did, bright light flooded the chamber.

"If the fields are a security device, why were we admitted in the first place?" Fleming said. "They should have blocked our access to the ship. Equally puzzling is why lights come on as we move about. The ones in the tunnel turned off when we entered this room. It's like we're being watched."

He stared at his communicator, clicking through its various monitoring functions. "The background noise on this vessel is twice the level of the transport."

"It could be built entirely of metal like the Terrans constructed their space vessels." Genghis patted his shell. "The biotech fabric used in creating us and our Galaxyships generates far less noise. The first astronauts on *Alliance* remarked about how quiet the ship was compared to their vessel, which was about the same size as a shuttle." The lengthy descriptions were for the benefit of Transport 27's crew, which would be monitoring the transmissions from the visual recorders attached to the front of Genghis and Fleming's space suits.

"The ship has an odd smell, like a chemical cleaner has been sprayed in the air," Fleming said. "I noticed it in the tunnel and it's even stronger in here. It suggests some basic maintenance is happening."

Along the chamber walls were small round doors while stacks of containers took up most of the floor space. "The wide aisle between the containers looks like a walkway between the rear of this compartment and the tube to the front one," Fleming said. "The containers look large enough to hold a body."

It took a couple of minutes of pulling and pushing to figure out the release for the latches that held the cover on the closest container. The Biots each took an end and slowly lifted, ready to slam it back down. When nothing climbed out, they shifted the cover sideway to peek at the contents. Small cylinders and boxes arranged haphazardly filled the container. They leaned the cover against the side of the container.

"I hope no one on my ship gets the idea that's an acceptable storage technique," Kelsey's voice crackled over the radio from Transport 27.

The explorers chuckled. "The admonition heard across the Galaxy," Genghis said.

The other containers provided further examples of poor housekeeping so the Biots moved to the nearest doors along the wall. The first one opened when Genghis lifted its latch. Inside were shelves stuffed with small tools and objects for which neither could imagine a purpose. "The handles on the tools are so bulky it would be hard to work with them."

The next few lockers were also stuffed with objects of no discernable purpose. "Terrans make fun of hoarders," Genghis said. "Maybe it's a galactic problem."

"Everything about this ship indicates it carried a crew," Fleming said. "Yet there's no sign of anyone; surely they would've come to investigate our arrival. Based on what we've seen, there's no apparent reason to have abandoned this ship."

When they had opened every locker without a significant discovery, Kelsey said, "That wasn't the most productive half hour in the annals of space travel."

"Let's check the rest of the rear compartment," Genghis said. "When the others arrive, we'll explore the tube between the two sections, and then the front end." He pointed to the back of the rear section. "We'll inspect that corridor for now."

Fleming led the way. "I barely felt the force field at the entrance to this corridor. It's no more of an inconvenience than opening and closing doors while it should stop us from wandering about the ship. They are reacting to our presence, which is further evidence the ship isn't a derelict." Fleming hesitated. "Could they be studying us?"

Genghis looked back at the Storage Room. "Perhaps the main role of the force fields is to stabilize the interior of the ship. The one at the entrance hatch was stronger because it holds in the atmosphere against the vacuum of space. However this design eliminates the need for multiple hatches and chambers, which is a feature our Galaxyships could use to reduce their total weight."

Fleming led the way to a T intersection. In either direction were short corridors with hatches at the ends. "Let's try the left one first." They opened it and eased their way through another force field into what looked like a massive garage.

"Captain Kelsey would certainly approve of this maintenance bay," Fleming said. "It's clean like its seen little use. There are no stockpiles of stores or equipment."

"The shuttle could land in here if we can figure out how to open the outer door." Genghis stared at the end wall. "I can see the outline of it. It looks like it parts in the middle. It wasn't visible when we inspected the exterior of the ship."

Fleming peered at Genghis. "This is the most interesting activity I've ever been involved in even if we haven't learned much yet. Is this what Terrans mean by excitement or fun?"

Genghis grinned. "On a ship like this, Terrans would be imagining a monster lurking around every corner waiting to pounce on them."

Fleming stared at him. "Really?"

"They would be big monsters." He raised his arms and growled.

Fleming shook his head and laughed.

"So far, it's like we're being welcomed on board, which of course is completely illogical," Genghis said. "This ship should be more like the lifeless hulks the Beings found."

Fleming pointed over Genghis's shoulder to the front of the bay. "What's behind that door?" When they reached it, he raised a latch near the left hand side. "The door is heavy and fits tightly in the frame."

No force field hindered them when they entered the room. Its walls were covered in toggles, sliding buttons and small imagers. "It must be for controlling operations in the bay."

"Look at that." Genghis pointed to a large switch in the lower position. "The panel beside it has a line through the middle while the one beside the upper position is blank."

"Here goes." Genghis flipped the switch to the upper position. A great din arose inside the bay and overhead lights turned on and off. The office door clicked sharply and a flashing light came on above it.

"The line in this imager is descending." Fleming hesitated. "It could be indicating the atmosphere in the bay is venting to allow a craft to land in the bay once the exterior doors open."

He studied the control panel further. "There are four gauges here that show lines moving upward. Perhaps the atmosphere in the bay is being stored."

With flashing lights that cast sporadic shadows throughout the bay, the outer door opened at the middle with its upper and bottom portions retracting. As they did, stars became clearly visible. "Curious. While much of this ship is a puzzle, the switch is a perfectly obvious control for the outer doors."

"Octinog, what's your position?" Genghis said.

"We're half way back from the transport. We'll attempt to land in the bay."

Genghis and Fleming watched through the window as the shuttle approached. As soon as it eased inside, tractor beams seized it and gently set it on the floor. "Definitely not a derelict ship," Fleming said.

Genghis returned the switch to the lower position. Behind the shuttle, the outer doors closed, shutting off the stars. "Now the lines on the four gauges are dropping." When they reached the bottom, the office door clicked again and the light over it went out. Genghis tried the inside latch and the door opened. "The atmosphere is restored in the bay. There is definitely logic to the design and operation of the ship."

Fleming and Genghis headed toward the shuttle. Octinog and two other Biots dropped from it.

"We couldn't wait for you to find a ladder," Octinog called. "The Captain is sure Navigation Central will have a long list of questions about this ship after its views your visuals. She's impressed with your progress in determining how it operates. Your comments about the force fields offering little resistance after the initial encounter really piqued her curiosity. If we can learn why that happened, we'll understand something important about the design of *Wanderer* as she calls it."

"A good name," Genghis said. "Terrans have an old saying about not all who wander are lost. This ship is a mystery that will fascinate them and the Beings. Meanwhile let's check the other hatch in the corridor that leads here. We also have to keep looking for the engine compartment."

The shuttle had a recharging station, which meant Genghis could stay on board to explore *Wanderer* with the other Biots rather than return to Transport 27.

While Fleming and Genghis breezed through the force field as they exited the bay, Octinog and the other newcomers had to push through it. The one at the entrance into the other bay offered less resistance to the newcomers.

After a thorough search of the second bay, which appeared identical to the first one, the five Biots headed to the Storage Room. They all barely felt the force field as they left the bay and again as they entered the Storage Room.

The newcomers wandered about the Storage Room peering into containers and lockers. When they too could not discern a possible purpose for the tools and other devices, the group headed for the tube connecting the front and rear sections. "While the exterior of the ship looks shabby, on the inside it's in good shape," Octinog said.

 The tube was about 150 meters long. What looked like a conveyor belt ran up the center. When they could not find a button or a lever to engage the device, Genghis stepped on it gingerly. Nothing happened and he jumped up and down to no effect.

As they walked toward the front section, he said, "The Galaxyship designers will certainly want to find out how this tube can withstand the stresses of holding the two sections together."

The tube's interior was the same insipid grey as the tunnel at the entrance to the ship and the Storage Room. The force field at the entry to the front compartment was barely noticeable and brilliant ceiling lights turned on as they passed through it. The walls were glossy grey.

"This has to be their Control Room," Genghis said. He described it in detail for the benefit of anyone watching the visuals from the Biots' recorders. "In the middle is a raised V shaped desk with what looks like six work stations. There are no seats. On the left are a stairway and a contraption that appears to be a lift to other levels. There's a door on the right wall into another room. Its two windows are dark."

The Biots fanned out to record the entire compartment. It was about 50 meters deep and 30 meters across by four meters high. Unlike the Being Galaxyships, it had large viewports. Genghis strode to the closest one and peered out. Whatever material the port was made of distorted the view of the stars. Even the ship's rocky screen appeared fuzzy. He could not spot the Transport. While he had never seen a vessel layout like this before, the design made sense except for the viewports. Overall it was bare and functional. "Is the smell here the same as in the storage chamber?"

"Not as strong," Fleming said.

A loud ping over the Biots' communicators announced a transmission from the Transport. "The ship has quite intriguing features," Kelsey said. "We must attempt to tow it. Delivering it will be more valuable than our cargo."

The Captain's initiative in planning a way to deliver this space find to the Confederation was better than Genghis hoped for. It increased his desire to spend more time with her.

"We're studying how to release the rocks accompanying it," Kelsey said. "We don't think it'll matter if we tow it by the bow or stern."

Genghis grinned at her emphasis on the word we. "We'll continue exploring the ship while you plan the tow. Fleming and Octinog, inspect the work stations. Just like the Storage Room, everything here indicates this vessel has or had a crew that kept the ship in good shape." Genghis pointed at the other two Biots. "You come with me."

It had been a long time since Genghis worked with Biots that had not selected names. They must be quite new.

The door on the right wall would not open and Genghis could not find a slot for a key or a card to unlock it. "It's so dark I can't see anything through the windows," one Biot said. "Oddly, the door and windows on the wall feel warmer than the rest of the ship. For what reason would the space behind the door be heated to a higher temperature?"

"There has to be an important function in that space," Genghis said. "Fleming and Octinog, keep your eyes out for something on the desk that might open the door." Nodding at the other two, he said, "Let's see where the stairs lead." They studied the lift device beside the circular staircase. "While it appears to be for carrying objects, we could hitch a ride if we had to."

The stairs ended at the only other level in the compartment. "It looks like a technician's area," Genghis said. "So we'll call it the Work Room." More tools with bulky handles rested in holders. Nearby were stacks of storage containers.

"The handles on the tools have slots instead of grips," one Biot said. "How would anyone hold or even use these?" The containers were packed with the same puzzling devices found in the Storage Chamber.

A deep groan rumbled through the ship. "Genghis get down here," Octinog yelled. "The ship is no longer drifting."

Before Genghis could respond, Octinog yelled, "Fleming where are you going?"

All Genghis could hear of his reply was the word close.

The rumble continued and lights flashed on and off in the Work Room. The earlier quiet seemed benign. An imager on the wall near the stairway lit up displaying a star map covered in glowing points of light and symbols and a flashing dot.

"Transmit a visual of the display to the Transport," Genghis called. "Anyone recognize the location of the flashing dot on the imager? There might be a connection between it and this vessel."

Halfway down the stairs, Octinog shouted, "Brace yourselves!"

Chapter 5
To Points Unknown

The flash of the Transport's emergency lights and the sharp screech of the alert siren brought Captain Kelsey from her cubicle on the run. She heard a Biot rushing from the shuttle bay to join the others on the Command Benches.

When the Biots were seated, Hajang spoke. "Fleming and Octinog were inspecting the vessel's controls but had taken no action when the power generation levels on the vessel spiked." The center imager showed *Wanderer* moving away from its rocky companions.

The left imager displayed a visual of a Biot hand hovering over a dial. "At this point, lights and indicators on the control panel turned on, the ship made a loud beep and fired bow thrusters," Hajang said. "That's when I summoned you." The center imager traced the craft's course. "It's turning back in our direction. It's definitely flying on its own."

"Prepare for evasive manoeuvres," Kelsey barked. "Everyone to their secure position!"

The left imager showed some of *Wanderer's* former rocky companions crashing together creating clouds of gravel and dirt while others spiralled away. One escaping boulder struck a mountain-sized chunk of rock like a torpedo fracturing it into several massive segments.

"A spectacular visual for the communication networks," Kelsey said. "That escape is more evidence the ship held those rocks in place for protection. How it did that while operating on a low power level is something else to figure out. This is a mysterious ship."

The center imager showed *Wanderer* heading directly at Transport 27 while the right one displayed the alien vessel's control panel glowing like a decorated tree. Kelsey caught herself attempting to figure out the purpose of various dials, knobs and sliders. There was nothing like them on Being ships.

"*Wanderer* is changing course again," Hajang said. "It turns by altering the direction of the output from its engines, which are located in the nodules on the sides of the rear compartment." It hesitated. "I'm tracking its trajectory and have dispatched the visuals and details to Navigation Central. By my calculation, *Wanderer* is heading back on the course it came here on. That will take it well outside the regions of the Milky Way we've explored. Hopefully it has some form of Galaxydrive; otherwise it'll be a long trip."

As much as Kelsey worried about the safety of the five Biots, she regretted losing the opportunity to hand *Wanderer* over to the Fleet. At least Transport 27 was no longer in danger.

"Captain, look at the left imager," Hajang said.

All she could see was jerky views of *Wanderer's* interior. It kept changing as if a Biot was moving quickly through the ship.

"The view is from Fleming's recorder," Hajang said. "He's passing through the Storage Room. At first it appeared he was heading to the bays but he's entered the tunnel."

The display in the imager finally stopped bouncing about. "That's the entrance hatch to the ship." Hajang paused. "It was brilliant of him to think to shut it to prevent a serious power drain when the ship picked up speed. But how did a derelict ship know to do it?"

The main imager switched to maximum magnification to track the steadily-shrinking *Wanderer*. The right imager showed a pair of Biot hands holding onto the control panel for support.

"We're receiving status readings from the five Biots," Hajang reported. "All appear normal except for elevated power consumption, which is no surprise under the circumstances. Fleming has returned to the Control Room."

The crew stared at the imagers, completely absorbed in comprehending what happened on *Wanderer*. "We must follow it to rescue our team," Kelsey said.

"Not with the cargo we're carrying," Hajang replied. "We've sufficient fuel to reach our destination, but not much more. We should stay here until we can no longer track *Wanderer*. That would help calculate its course. The ship is gaining speed far faster than we can."

The Controlling Unit spoke its next words cautiously. "It's the Chief Councilor's decision whether to pursue

Wanderer. After all, the Biots went on it voluntarily and could have escaped in the shuttle."

Kelsey sprang to her feet. "If we can't follow *Wanderer*, we'll load the other shuttle with an ancillary processor, a portable Biot recharger for Genghis and other equipment they might need and send it after *Wanderer*. The shuttle's position reports will help Navigation Central follow it. Hajang will supervise the shuttle after its launch."

She pointed at individual Biots, snapping out orders. They scurried away to gather equipment for the shuttle. When the Chamber was empty, the Captain went to her locker and took out two laser pistols and headed for the shuttle bay.

"Good choice," Hajang said.

Kelsey could not imagine how Genghis might use them.

As soon as the shuttle was loaded, the Biots rushed back to the Command Benches in time to watch it fly far enough away to transition to Galaxyspeed without harming the Transport. It quickly became a speck on the main imager, and then disappeared.

"Hajang, put us back on course for our destination," Kelsey said. Returning to her seat, she replayed the day's events in her mind wondering if there was anything she should have done differently. Before long she shifted to her personal preoccupation. Was she finally ready to move up from commanding a Transport? If she could have delivered *Wanderer* to the Confederation, it would have provided a perfect opportunity to apply for a higher rank. New Galaxyships were coming into service. Maybe she could be assigned to one to learn from an experienced Commander.

A beep from her communicator interrupted her reverie. "Captain, you should listen to the message Genghis sent to the Chief Councilor," Hajang said. "Engaging your personal imager."

It rose into position beside her seat showing Genghis sitting in the flight control seat of the shuttle. "Greetings Hton. Our mystery craft is taking us for a ride and I hope this isn't my last report to you. The five of us will keep studying the ship and send regular updates for as long as we can. We provided Transport 27 with all the data we've been able to gather along with detailed visuals. If our trip rekindles the Beings' curiosity about our Galaxy, we'll all benefit.

"I take full responsibility for the diversion of Transport 27. The crew didn't have the confidence to report their discovery of *Wanderer* to Captain Kelsey. Once she saw it, she grasped its importance immediately and was planning to tow it back to the Confederation.

Genghis paused. "Old friend, Captain Kelsey is ready for a much bigger assignment. Biots of her calibre are the future. A la prochaine as the Terrans say."

Genghis's comment took Kelsey by surprise. She kept staring at the now blank imager.

"He's correct about you," Hajang said. "You've impressed him and many others."

Genghis plugged into the shuttle's recharger and was reviewing the exploration of *Wanderer* when Fleming arrived with a portable analyzer, a laptop computer equipped with artificial intelligence. Octinog was a couple of steps behind him.

They looked even more excited than after their discovery of *Wanderer*. *What had the dynamic duo found this time?*

"*Wanderer* has already reached Galaxyspeed Level 3 and continues to gain speed," Fleming said. "Even our best ships would take at least twice as long to achieve this velocity."

"Could *Wanderer* leave our galaxy?"

Fleming shrugged. "Ask us when we know its top speed and how its propulsion system works. We think it has some form of solar-powered engines. The vessel collects energy while it's in range of a sun. The exterior panels on the ship have retracted, which means we must be beyond the range of one."

The Biot paused. "Based on its projected flight path here, our hypothesis is that it's taking us to the flashing dot it displayed when the ship came back on line."

"However, we've much to learn yet," Octinog interjected.

Genghis could not think of a reason to reject their theory. "If anyone could figure it out, I would bet on you two. Especially after you had the presence of mind to check on the entrance hatch."

"Thank you, Cap ..." Octinog's voice trailed off. The two Biots stared at each other before returning their attention to Genghis. "We refer to you as the Captain. Considering what might happen, we really need a leader. You took charge. Without that, we would've stood around wondering what to do."

Genghis remembered the days when he simply did whatever his supervising Being ordered. These Biots could learn to be a leader just as he had. Kelsey was already well on her way.

"I'll send reports to the Transport for as long as possible," Genghis said. "Meanwhile, you explain to the other two what you've figured out. Then organize a plan for thoroughly investigating this ship to understand how it operates. We want to gain control of it, not be held hostage."

The Biots grinned. "Yes, Captain."

Genghis waved them away. While he did not feel like a hostage, he did not control his destiny either. He wanted to change that. Another idea came to him. Could the ship have fled rather than be towed to an uncertain fate? Perhaps it deduced Kelsey's plan. Or it had another motive.

Chief Councilor Hton watched Genghis's video in his office on Hnassumblaw, the original world of the Beings and the home of their High Council. The discovery of *Wanderer* was a popular topic throughout the Confederation and Hector Davis assured him it was among Terrans as well. Davis led the Terran forces during the Nameless War and became U.N. Secretary General when Benjamin Kendo retired.

Hton was elected Chief Councilor by Beings and Biots after spending more than a century serving as the ton to Humbaw. He agreed with Genghis's assessment of *Wanderer's* potential to spark a new era of Being creativity. In the immediate aftermath of the War, the Beings focused their curiosity and creativity on turning Mandela into a home for the Nameless or Corens as they called themselves. Although they were clearly descendants of Terrans abducted from the planet centuries earlier, Terra could not cope with its more than eight billion inhabitants.

It was a trying time as many Corens could not overcome the effects of the chemicals the Pozzen Rulers used to control them. They died after a few years mostly from a combination of pernicious depression and despair. The billion Terrans who moved to Mandela adopted their orphans and took care of the surviving adults.

Hton knew it would take another decade before full food production on Terra could be restored, which meant the pressure to transfer more Terrans to Mandela would remain. Kendo resisted it and Hector Davis supported him.

Meanwhile the new Pozzen government negotiated a trade agreement with the Confederation. Biots assisted the Pozzen citizens in taking control of their world by reclaiming the large sections of land the Rulers had appropriated for their personal use. As well, they converted the Rulers' combat equipment to civilian use. A few Biots still remained to study the Ruler technology looking for ideas to improve Being machines. Others examined the impact of settlement on Mandela's environment to compare it to conditions on the planets the Corens were removed from. Hton was among the many interested in how their environments changed without anyone living on them.

Three combat starships located at a Ruler space station were turned over to the Being Fleet in return for transport Galaxyships. Biots were instructing Pozzens on how to operate the freighters and restore the station to serve as a research center.

The challenges and problems on Mandela and Pozzen became manageable and the Beings' interest waned. Some continued to track the work of the Biots on Mandela, Pozzen and the planets where the Corens were held captive. They made interesting discoveries but nothing spectacular. Terra's problems were caused by the actions of its inhabitants and Beings could do no more to help them.

Hton recalled Davis's fitting description of Pozzens as overgrown Beings with attitude. The growing interactions between the two versions of the same species attracted considerable scientific interest.

When it was ready, Pozzen would apply for membership in the Confederation, which would likely set the stage for a larger alliance involving Earth and Mandela.

Hton hoped the work of Humbawloda, Humbaw's granddaughter, would inspire other Beings. She was tracking Biots who were striving to break out of their traditional role. Her thesis was the Beings would be the biggest beneficiaries of such a change.

Humbawloda was fast becoming the same kind of influential figure that her grandfather had been. Even in his waning years, Humbaw's mind remained among the most fertile in the Confederation.

Hton's communicator buzzed and in one of those coincidences he marveled at, Humbaw's craggy smile appeared.

"A fine day to you Chief Councilor." The voice had lost some of its richness.

"And a day of blessings to you esteemed Councilor and old friend. To what do I owe the pleasure of this communication?"

"I've viewed Genghis's video. I envy his adventure and admire his equanimity about traveling into the unknown. He's right about the need for a new challenge for the Beings."

Hton smiled. Now that *Wanderer* was a runaway, it would attract even more attention from the High Council, which meant he needed an action plan to deal with it. "*Wanderer* would've been discovered eventually because in time it would've drifted close to Mandela's star system."

"It's more useful that it was discovered, and then lost in the manner that it was," Humbaw said.

"I'll propose to the High Council and the United Nations that we send ships in pursuit of it," Hton said.

"I'll support that motion without reservation."

Hton relaxed. With Humbaw's endorsement, the mission was already a go. Earth and Pozzen would contribute without hesitation to any project he supported. "I'd be delighted if you would inform the communications networks that you advocate following *Wanderer* to recover the Biots and the useful technology on board the ship."

Humbaw snorted. "I already have. I added some speculation about what we might discover from pursuing it. We've spent enough time together to understand how each other thinks. I'll ask the Secretary-General for copies of the

Terran news reports about the ship. They'll have a grand time explaining it."

Hton snorted. "*Enterprise* has finished its refit and is being re-crewed. We can recall other Galaxyships to follow it. They're mostly on routine patrols. The real issue is which civilians should accompany the mission in case we find whomever the ship belongs to."

He opened a list of names of Terrans and Beings he selected already. "My first choice is Humbawloda for her work on ethnobiology and astronomy. Ruthie Donohue is also a specialist in similar fields. They're involved in a research project on the Biots. While I'll ask Ruth Huxley, she'll likely decline with great regret. Long space flights are too hard on older Terrans. However I'll ask her for recommendations on others for the mission, which could last for many years. We need to select some soon to travel on *Enterprise*."

"As for the follow-up ships, we should pick specialists from Pozzen and Mandela," Humbaw said. "What was the name of the fellow who assisted our first landing party on Pozzen? It needs to become more involved with the other worlds."

"You're referring to Wxdot Gruumon. He guided the first contingent of Terran soldiers and Biot troopers through the streets of Onnaprozen, the planet's capital, as they battled the Rulers and their machines. He took charge of sharing the Ruler properties among the Pozzens. By all accounts, he has the popularity to become President someday. I'll ask him to join us. You're right that we should make our attempt to find *Wanderer's* builder a combined effort of all the planets. It would be the logical next step."

"Do you think this mission could be enough to trigger the Biot awakening?" Humbaw said.

Chapter 6
To Points Unknown

Hton stared at Humbaw's grinning image before responding. While Humbaw had not raised the awakening issue for years, it was no surprise the Being deduced his former ton's real motive in proposing to mobilize the Fleet.

Hton and Humbaw had long agreed Biots possessed the intelligence, creativity, imagination and empathy of a conscious, thinking species comparable to Beings and Terrans. Most scientific advancements now were the result of collaboration between them with regular Terran contributions. Yet most Biots still did not grasp the significance of their achievements. To them, serving as a ton to a Being remained a major accomplishment.

The old friends agreed the Biots had to achieve a collective awareness of their evolution into an independent species. While climatic requirements kept the Beings and Terrans on separate worlds, they developed a close level of cooperation. Able to function on all their worlds, Biots were a crucial link between them.

"It's almost like there's a comfort zone to the traditional role of the Biots they don't wish to relinquish," Humbaw said. "At best, there are only 10 out of more than one billion Biots who truly comprehend that the real status of your species is far more than glorified Being helpers. I've no suggestions on how you can convince the rest of your kind. It's a matter of finding a way to remove their collective blinders. They need a feat even more spectacular than the role of the Biots in the War."

"We've been handed an unexpected opportunity in pursuing *Wanderer* to make the Biots see the obvious about their status," Hton said. "It has preoccupied Genghis for years and I've no doubt it will be in his thoughts all the time now."

"I still marvel at how you and the others achieved awareness on your own," Humbaw said.

"We're all tons or former tons of High Councilors and attending Council sessions and participating in space missions opened our minds to possibilities that otherwise would have never occurred to us. Now to work. I've many people to communicate with this day."

Next, Hton placed a call to Commander Gnoorvants on *Enterprise*, who agreed to be the Admiral of the Being Fleet as long as he could be based on his ship. He still looked like what the Terrans called a linebacker. He gazed into the viewer with a wide smile. "Usually I receive calls from my officers about the new features on the ship. So many changes have been made it's a wonder I even recognize it. However the sooner we're on our shakedown cruise, the better."

"We have an urgent mission for you." He outlined the disappearance of *Wanderer* and the decision to pursue it.

"As much as I would like to leave immediately, we need more preparation time before the ship is ready including selecting a new Deputy Commander. Atdomorsin has just taken over as Commander of *Dreadnought*."

Hton played the last part of Genghis's message.

Gnoorvants stroked his chin. "His recommendation makes Captain Kelsey worth considering. I can't imagine Genghis serving on a transport. If I'd known he wanted space duty, I would have placed him on a Fleet Galaxyship, probably a Pozzen cruiser. I wonder who arranged for his placement."

Hton could not help nodding.

"I'll arrange an interview with Captain Kelsey right away," Gnoorvants said.

Ruth Huxley missed her son Nathan's entry into the lab because she was engrossed in research into the properties of the chemicals the Rulers controlled the Corens with. The drugs blocked independent thinking and re-enforced their compulsion to follow the Rulers' orders without question.

Ruth's team of researchers, which included her daughter Louise, a medical doctor, was breaking down the components of the chemicals. One ingredient showed promise as a treatment for mentally ill humans for whom few alternatives were available.

While she had not approved of the destruction of the remaining Rulers in their refuge at the end of the Nameless War, years of seeing the results of their destructive handiwork among the Corens eased her doubts about their fate.

"Your project must be interesting because you've missed the transmissions from Humbaw and the Chief Councilor," Nathan said. He looked so much like his late father Sinomla, a Coren who escaped the Rulers, and then helped defeat them. Ruth settled on Mandela with him. Nathan had followed her dual interest in astronomy and the life forms that might develop on different classes of planets.

Every Being and Biot that came to Mandela wanted to meet her. The celebrity moments always amused her, especially accounts of how she inspired them or tales about young Beings named Ruth or Huxley. Almost as popular were Benjamin and Kendo after the former U.N. Secretary General.

"I do become distracted by my research." She grinned at Nathan, who laughed before playing Hton's message, which included Genghis' transmission from *Wanderer*.

She beamed at the comment about her goddaughter Ruthie Donohue being on the right track in her studies of the evolution of Biots. Ruth hoped Humbawloda and Ruthie's research would discover how the wartime experiences of the troopers and Biot flyers triggered changes in their organic brains. No other explanation seemed plausible for the out-of-character behavior and emotions of Genghis and the other veterans.

The creation of the next-gen Biots added a new dimension to the Ruth's research because the evidence indicated they were less inhibited than the originals although their overall behavior so far remained much the same.

While Humbaw was unavailable for a call, Ruth did connect with Hton who filled her in on what the Being wanted to discuss. The distance between Mandela and Hnassumblaw was short enough to allow a conversation with brief delays for a response. Ruth smiled at Hton's hand gestures because they were so much like Humbaw's.

Ruth emphasized how inconclusive the results of the research project were. "We've focused on the troopers and flyers who were involved in the most intense fighting. Genghis is certainly in that group. Some veterans told me privately they fear they're becoming Terran-like. They grieve for lost comrades and are repulsed to the point of rage about the abuse of the Nameless and the terror inflicted on the citizens of Pozzen by the Rulers. Biots never had emotions like this before."

When Hton inquired about the secrecy surrounding the project, Ruth said, "We're concerned a lot more humans might think Biots could become dangerous."

Hton shook his head. "Genghis is anything but dangerous."

Ruth nodded. "I assisted with his research into the origins of the Beings. He amassed a great deal of information before losing interest in the project. It was taken over by a group of graduate students on Earth and in the Confederation working under the auspices of the Kendo Institute. Humbawloda has established a research project at Bunwadon University to compare the original Biots to the next gens.

"Meanwhile my old colleague Arthur Lorne is collaborating with a group of Biots, Corens and Terrans on the evolution of human life and the origin of the Nameless. The DNA analysis of the Corens hasn't established conclusively which region of Earth their ancestors were abducted from although it appears to be the Mediterranean."

A video message from the Being Chief Councilor awaited Hector Davis when he woke. The U.N. Secretary General read the urgent request for personnel to participate in a mission into the heart of the Milky Way. It was a rare occasion when Hton resorted to a video message although his printed communications came regularly, often several times a week.

While there would be opposition to the mission, Hector would back it without hesitation. He headed to the office, adding names and ideas to his notebook as he went.

When he reached his desk, a lengthy follow up message from Hton awaited him. It explained *Wanderer's* abrupt departure with Genghis and four other Biots on board. What really captured his attention was Hton's statement that "Genghis was certain discovering *Wanderer's* origin should be a top priority. Humbaw is convincing the High

Council that we need to task the Fleet to pursue it. *Enterprise* will depart soon. Other Galaxyships will follow. We want to add Terrans to their crews and would count on the U.N. to select them. While we don't want to turn this into a military campaign, we need to ensure the Fleet can protect itself."

In reply, Hector said he doubted that Hton could keep Ruthie and Humbawloda from the mission. "Tell us what specialities you want and we'll dispatch them to Hnassumblaw as soon as possible."

Chapter 7
Biot and Robot

Expecting they would be on board *Wanderer* for a long time, Genghis established a routine for the Biots of exploring the ship and transmitting updates to Navigation Central. He set aside time every forty hours to recharge his power cell in the shuttle. His personal analyzer was on the Transport and he missed his regular sessions of astronomy studies and music.

Figuring out how *Wanderer* operated was a slow process involving the Tyson on the shuttle from Transport 27. While it possessed about a tenth of the processing capacity of a Controlling Unit, it had a backup communications unit that was transportable.

The first breakthrough came when the Tyson found the frequencies of *Wanderer's* information system and commenced attempting communication. Meanwhile the Biots discovered the four nodules containing the solar-powered engines were not accessible from inside the craft. The ship was traveling far too fast to attempt a spacewalk to investigate the nodules.

"While I don't understand the propulsion technology yet, it would explain the ship's wandering course," Octinog said. "It appears to travel from solar system to solar system tapping into the light from each sun it encounters. Once it's fully charged, it moves on."

"In search of what?" Genghis said.

"It must be programmed to look for something," Octinog said. "Otherwise why didn't it remain in a solar system until it was found? That's the mystery."

"Maybe it's following instructions to search for its ultimate destination," Fleming said. "Or it would enter a system, determine this wasn't where it was intended to be and move on once it recharged."

Octinog displayed the incomplete schematic drawing of *Wanderer* he and Fleming prepared. "Although the vessel has interesting features such as the force fields, its equipment and construction appear primitive compared to our ships. We haven't succeeded in accessing its star charts and the ones in the shuttle's data system are too limited to determine in which solar system the flashing dot is located."

"Adding to the mystery is the craft coming back into operation after we explored it," Genghis said. "To enable the Tyson to concentrate on studying *Wanderer's* operating systems, we'll convert the shuttle's backup communications equipment into a transmitter-receiver, which we'll call Tyson2. It'll search the solar systems around us and monitor messages from Navigation Central although with our ever increasing speed, it's unlikely any of them will catch up with us."

Fleming concentrated on investigating the Control Room, Octinog continued with his schematic of the ship and Genghis and the other two searched methodically through the shuttle bays and the lockers and bins in the Storage and Work rooms.

The pair had finally selected names. "As we are explorers, I'm naming myself after the Terran Amundsen and my friend is Gaopod."

Genghis could not restrain his laughter. "Excellent choice. Gaopod the Reluctant. The Being healer sent on a rescue mission in a craft that malfunctioned. By the time it was found nine years later, he'd discovered two new Being worlds and countless others with valuable resources."

Five days later, Octinog called the others to the Control Room to view a large imager that suddenly turned on. "My guess is the twisted shapes on it are letters and numbers."

"Could there be more of them than we can see?" Gaopod approached the imager. "There's no scroll button. However there are tiny slots to insert a tool in." He looked around its sides. "Surely not this."

He held up a narrow metal wand attached to a fist-sized disk. Shrugging, he slid the wand into the first slot. The size of the shapes increased. The next slot returned them to the previous size. The third one caused them to glow until Gaopod withdrew the wand. The last one caused the shapes to scroll up displaying more underneath.

"While it's hard to tell, I think there are four or five pages of shapes," Gaopod said. When he withdrew the wand, the shapes jumped. "It appears they returned to the start. The first shape on the left looks like a circle with lines coming out of it. The first on the right resembles an X imposed sideways on an M."

He stared at the imager again before facing his shipmates. "I'll scan the entire text looking for repeated or even similar looking shapes. Sure would be handy to have another Tyson to assist in determining how often and in what sequences they appear. It would a big help if I could distinguish among letters and numbers. First I will record a copy of the shapes." He pulled out his communicator and pointed it at the imager.

"What if this is an attempt to communicate with us?" Genghis said. "While we don't understand the message yet, it could be making the effort."

Although the others did not respond, Genghis knew they would think about his comment.

Before anyone could return to their duties, a bright flash swept through the Room. "That came from the navigation imager that illuminated before *Wanderer* made the transition to Galaxyspeed," Fleming said as he hurried to examine the screen.

"Something is following us. It's too small to be Transport 27; it's about the size of a shuttle. But the Captain wouldn't have sent the other one after us because that would leave them with no way to get off the Transport if anything went wrong."

The Biots gathered around the imager. "What else could it be but the second shuttle?" Genghis said. "Kelsey took a calculated risk because learning more about this ship is worth it. Perhaps it was sent to help track us. If she'd wanted us to abandon *Wanderer* when it powered up, she would have said so."

"Would you have left this ship?" Fleming said.

Genghis shook his head instead of attempting to explain his jumble of reasons for staying on it. "Spotting the shuttle shows *Wanderer* has an extensive surveillance range, which is another reason to figure out its language."

"If we can verify it's the Transport's other shuttle, then we should slow down *Wanderer* so we can bring it on board," Octinog said. "We could use its Tyson."

Gaopod moved away from the others. "We also need to lower the temperature in this ship. It has risen and I'm using more power to maintain my proper internal temperature."

Genghis had not noticed the increased heat. "Is the higher temperature consistent throughout the ship or just in the Control Room where more equipment has come back on line?"

Pulling a small sampler from his equipment pouch, Gaopod walked about while continually glancing at the temperature gauge. After a few minutes, he called in a loud voice, "The door into the closed room is unlocked now."

Gaopod eased the door about one quarter open and lights flickered on. Holding the door, he stepped inside and was staring at the floor behind it when Genghis and Amundsen arrived. They glanced at a pair of long benches covered in tools and equipment that filled the center of the room before following Gaopod's gaze.

Nine identical light grey figures lay stretched out on the floor in an orderly row, all on their backs.

Chapter 8
Amundsen Time

Amundsen muttered as he knelt beside the closest figure, and then hesitated before touching it. "The shell is metallic although I can't tell what kind. Their overall shape is basically like ours; head, shoulders, chest, arms and legs. The limbs are jointed and they have large padded feet.

"However they've no toes, their arms are short for their upper body and are connected to the front of the shoulders rather than the sides. Their hands resemble the jaws of pliers and they've barely any neck." He touched a short appendage attached to the upper middle of the chest. "It looks like a mini version of an elephant's trunk except it's multi-jointed and has finger-like appendages at the end. It isn't as long as their arms, which must limit what tasks they could perform with it."

He raised, and then released it. It flopped back on the creature's chest with a thump.

"The creature is mechanical not organic," Genghis said.

"At first I thought the round lenses on their foreheads were their visual receptors," Gaopod said. "Looking at them more closely, they're like vehicle headlamps." He pointed just below the lights. "These openings might be for vision and this one down here for their audio output. They have no nostrils." He pointed to openings on the sides of their heads. "Probably for audio input. Like us, they're identical and have these symbols on their chests, which are slightly different for each one. That could be their individual identifier."

"They're all almost 1.3 meters tall," Amundsen said. "About like Genghis." He pointed at the hands. "That explains why the tools on this ship have such awkward looking grips. It's the only way they could hold them."

Genghis sat beside another figure, knocking on its exterior from time to time. "It's doesn't have a solid mass like an organic creature. This is a robot like the ones Terrans built." He paused to gain control of his scrambling thoughts.

"The Beings think any advanced robot would resemble its creators," Gaopod said. "It's often speculated in scientific research that advanced life forms would be basically shaped like Terrans and Beings because that's simply the most efficient and effective structure for a terrestrial creature."

"So you're saying whoever created these robots must look something like them," Amundsen said. "However the two arms with claws and the trunk make me wonder how their creators could have built them if they have the same configuration of limbs. While the fingers of the middle arm could perform fine work, the overall shape is rather clumsy."

Gaopod glanced at Amundsen and Genghis, and then in the direction of the Control Room. "The overall design and engineering in these robots isn't at all impressive."

Fleming and Octinog joined them. The hum of *Wanderer's* equipment had never seemed as loud as it did while the five Biots examined the robots.

"They have to be the crew, which does explain a lot about the design of the ship and the lack of quarters that organics would require," Genghis said. "We have to learn as much as we can about them because that will tell us about their builders and this ship."

"If Navigation Central was excited about the discovery of *Wanderer*, think of its reaction to them," Fleming said pointing at the grey figures.

Genghis tapped the robot beside him several more times. "Their shell appears to have about the same resiliency as our covering."

Fleming stood and stepped away from the robot he examined. He walked part way through the room before facing his comrades. "Perhaps, we were allowed through the force fields because we're artificial life forms like them. Somehow I doubt Terrans or Beings would be admitted to the ship." He looked about. "What is the purpose of this room, why was it locked and what caused it to finally open?"

"Presumably, the door unlocked as the ship's internal temperature rose," Amundsen said. "Perhaps this is a safe room for the robots to protect them in case the ship lost power. Perhaps it's designed to remain intact if the vessel is badly damaged. It might be an escape pod. I'm sure there's a lot we could learn from this ship's information storage system if we could tap into it."

"The robots left themselves capable of being revived if the ship was found," Gaopod said. "However that doesn't explain why *Wanderer* was drifting aimlessly making it difficult to track down."

"That's what we need to figure out," Genghis said. "This isn't a derelict ship drifting aimlessly."

Amundsen left the room and returned with a recorder. Genghis stepped back from the figures and described them while Amundsen made visuals for Navigation Central of the nine robots along with the benches and other items in the room.

"This room is so well shielded I can't transmit my visuals," Amundsen said. The room was silent as the Biots pondered that information.

"Amundsen and Gaopod will conduct a detailed examination of the robots," Genghis said. "Let us know about anything you find, even if it appears trivial. Fleming and Octinog, look for a way to slow down this ship to enable the shuttle to catch up."

He stepped from the room and pulled out his communicator. "Tyson, any progress in making contact with whatever is operating this ship?"

"It's like you passed a test by finding the robots. The ship is attempting to communicate by sending me images of its sections accompanied by the shapes Octinog is studying. While I've shown *Wanderer* diagrams of the shuttle following us, that hasn't led it to reduce its speed. Perhaps it fears the shuttle is a threat. I'll keep trying to demonstrate we want it to reach us. In case *Wanderer* does slow down, I'm determining whether I can handle the docking of the shuttle."

Inside the room, Amundsen set the recorder on a bench to free his hands to examine the robots. Once the external examination was complete, Amundsen and Gaopod searched for ways to access the robot's interior. Not needed for the procedure, Genghis went to check on Fleming and Octinog in the Control Room.

"We're sure this is the speed controller." Octinog pointed to a lever on the Control Room desk. "There must be a code in all these symbols that explains how to adjust it."

"*Wanderer's* information system just sent me this pattern," Tyson said. "Try it."

Octinog peered at his communicator. "I'm glad I don't have to decipher all the symbols. I'll just copy the pattern the ship sent. Here goes." He placed his finger on a box on the imager screen, which caused a grey vertical bar to appear. He dragged his finger downward. The grey in the vertical bar dimmed.

"Hopefully, the color change indicates how much the speed will decline, but without any braking effect, it will just be through loss of momentum."

"Lower it further and keep us advised on the shuttle's progress. While we wait, check what else Tyson has learned about this ship. Meanwhile, I'll see what Amundsen and Gaopod discovered about the robots."

When he re-entered the room, Gaopod said, "Some limbs are locked and won't budge. Others manipulate too easily to be functioning properly."

Amundsen seized the left arm of a robot and the right leg of the one beside it. "Another puzzle is why this arm is fixed in this position and can't be moved while this leg can be shifted in many directions. While one would expect the limbs to either be loose or rigid, we've found a mix of both as well as some that can only be partly shifted. Others can be twisted or turned in ways we think should be impossible. This leg pulls out." He removed it as far as the connecting wires would allow.

"We've been speculating about the functioning of the robots and why we found them here," Gaopod said. "We couldn't think of a reason for them not to be scattered throughout the ship. Then we rolled one over and found the cable from the back of its head plugged into that floor outlet." He held the cable up for Genghis to see. "Perhaps the robots placed themselves in sleep mode connected to the power feed from the ship to enable minimal functioning. The link could also signal to the robots if they needed to awaken."

"Our hypothesis so far is the robots reached the point where they could no longer function properly and came here for protection," Amundsen said. "Perhaps before the last one did, it set *Wanderer* on autopilot. There's probably a maintenance log if we could read it. However, none of this tells us why the ship ended up here and where it should be."

"*Wanderer's* speed has dropped enough the other shuttle should catch up in 33 hours," Tyson reported.

"Genghis, while we continue our tasks, could you tell us your reasons for exploring this ship rather than just reporting its existence," Fleming said. "There is so much we're attempting to understand about what's happening to us."

"While you're at it, tell us your whole story," Gaopod said. "Not just what's in the official records!"

Chapter 9
Down Memory Lane

Genghis had only explained to Ruth, Hton and Humbaw that during the three decades since the Nameless War, he took on many different assignments in hopes of discovering his purpose. He avoided talking about his search with others because he felt no closer to an answer.

While he answered many questions from Ruth during the interview before his assignment to Transport 27, few of his replies surprised her. As he recalled what he related to her, he remembered the knowing looks that Hton and Humbaw gave him as he tiptoed through an account of his activities and responded to their numerous questions. Nothing he said surprised them either. Could they have monitored him through all those years? If so, why?

Genghis started into his explanation as Amundsen and Gaopod poked and pulled at the robots. Fleming and Octinog could hear him while they worked in the Control Room.

"When I saw *Wanderer* on the imager, it was a seize-the-moment occasion. The ship is a calling card from a civilization we haven't met yet. Imagine if a Being research vessel was lost and later returned by a species that also possessed space flight. Beings and Terrans are fascinated by the idea of first contact with other species. I would expect any sentient creatures to be."

"During our training, we were told that since the first helpers, Biots were prepared in the same manner and continually updated with new information," Amundsen said. "Anything one learned, we all would during our next update session. It's why we can work together so cohesively. While you can still do that, Genghis, you possess an additional dimension. So many different ideas come to you. The way you reacted to the discovery of this ship inspired us. We talk about it when you're off exploring *Wanderer* or are recharging in the shuttle."

"Biots have always carried out plans developed for them," Genghis said. "My comrades and I developed ideas and goals that should be inconceivable to us. Amongst the benefits of our association with Terrans, we see humor in many things, even the totally absurd. It's something Beings with their orderly minds don't comprehend. It's like their reaction to music."

"We miss the Terran music you played on Transport 27," Gaopod said. "Captain Kelsey really enjoyed it."

"In addition to their music and imagination, Terrans have this wonderful optimism about how things can be better. That influenced me as well. Just to myself, I questioned everything about the role of Biots. Then I discovered the other veterans were as well. While we don't know where this process is taking us, we hope the rest of the Biots catch up. There's so much we want to learn and share with them."

The memories piled up and he stopped talking to sort through them. His crew mates waited wordlessly for him to resume. They would sit there until the shuttle reached its destination just to hear his story. They wanted to understand. Maybe they were not so different than him after all. Perhaps, he should add these next-gens to the list of Biots who no longer fit the mold.

"After we developed the laser rifle and recaptured the stolen transport, the Terrans trained us. We adopted the terms troopers and flyers to differentiate us from the Terran soldiers and pilots. We attended their briefings so we could understand how they would combat the Nameless. We did our initial display for Commander Gnoorvants at Liberation, the first Ruler base the Terrans captured. After our initial successes, Gnoorvants told Gnoorton that if we won the war, a lot in the Confederation would change for Biots. It has.

"On top of everything else, we helped develop the next-gens."

"What prompted that?" Amundsen said. "The official records say little about it."

"About 15 years ago, Hton and Humbaw launched the next-gen project. Everything we did during the Nameless War and since pointed to potential improvements from Biots built with more strength and endurance.

"Progress on the project was slow because of the preoccupation with improving Terra's environment, eliminating the vestiges of the Rulers on Pozzen and settling the Nameless on Mandela. It's a planet the Beings found close to their own worlds. While its atmosphere wasn't suitable for them, it's so much like Terra it was natural to transfer the Nameless there. Then we helped move one billion Terrans to it to ease the population pressure on their home world."

"What prompted the design changes in Biots," Gaopod said. "While we resemble original Biots, our internal differences are quite extensive."

"Once we commenced constructing the first next-gens, we discovered possibilities we hadn't anticipated and that led to the differences between us."

"Does being only 1.2 meters tall bother the originals?" Gaopod said.

"Not in places with low ceilings or little room to manoeuvre. Your extra 60 centimeters allowed us to experiment with new construction techniques that account for your superior strength and speed.

"We built you in the same way as an original creating a frame from rigid polymer rods. Your height meant we had to use thicker rods, which is why you're stronger and can carry heavier objects.

"Your shell like ours was grown over the frame using the biotechnology process that the Beings invented. We intended to string the flat lengths of the material used in original Biots through the next-gens to carry commands from the brain to the actuators that enable you to walk, run and lift. However we found your extra height required us to switch to thick cords of the material. They're far more effective in supplying heating or cooling to different sections of your bodies compared to the originals. As well, they sped up the brain's signals giving the next-gens faster reflexes. They also made your audio and visual input and output more functional. However, like us you have to wear a protective suit in space."

While the next-gens knew these details about their construction, they paid close attention to his account. Genghis anticipated a lot of questions when he finished.

"What we and the Beings wanted to fix most of all was our need for recharging the electricity storage cell every other day. That's when a Terran suggested we instead employ a heavily shielded thermoelectric generator."

"Aren't the generators a reason some Terrans fear us?" Amundsen said. "They call them nuclear reactors and claim they're too great a risk to explode or melt down."

"That as well as a fear of artificial intelligence will keep you out of some countries. Doesn't bother the Pozzens or the Mandelans. Even if the worst happened, the release of the radiation in your generator would be too low a level to harm let alone kill a Terran or Being."

Technical questions followed until Gaopod asked how Hton had come to the conclusion that recruiting Terrans for the Nameless War would pay off for the Biots.

"He envisaged collaboration with Terrans as the way to engineer change among the Biots. We didn't realize his real goal at the time was to demonstrate to the Beings that we could protect our worlds to show we deserved to be full citizens of the Confederation. The Terrans would learn to operate Being technology well enough to defeat the Nameless and teach us how to as well."

"When *Enterprise* and *Alliance* located a planet with a large Nameless base, the flyers had their first aerial battle and you had your first ground combat," Gaopod said. "We've watched the visual of you convincing the Nameless to move to safety."

The others nodded and clapped. "We're glad you don't shout like that inside *Wanderer*," Octinog said. "It would probably damage the equipment."

"Or wake the robots," Amundsen said.

Even though the Biots were listening attentively, relating his experiences was far more difficult than Genghis expected. He recalled the days when he could recount his War experiences without the complication of emotions. At least he now could control the flood of memories of deceased Biots, Beings and Terrans along with the events that shaped his existence.

"We showed we would defend the Confederation because it was our home too. We ended up in many battles, we lost comrades, and we learned about ourselves. It's hard to explain what it's like to be in a situation where you can kill and be killed. The Terrans taught us a lot. After the War ended, we thought we could return to our old lives.

"Few did. As soon as we returned to our previous assignments, most of us quickly realized we needed more meaningful roles. The old ordered life was finished for us. Even though we were given opportunities to do whatever we wanted, most of us are still searching for something."

Genghis peered about as he recalled the most important memory. "Although the tumult of battle at that Nameless planet initially startled us, we achieved of driving the defenders into the bunker. Then Captain Stocia asked how many troopers were dead or wounded. I replied that 17 no longer functioned and 30 were damaged. He said quite forcefully that we had to cease thinking of ourselves as machines. He insisted I report the number of dead and wounded Biots. His comments stayed with me all these years as well as his praise for our conduct in the War. To us, it's as important as his exploration of the Dome.

"Actually he opened a floodgate of ideas in my mind. Our creation by the Beings was a remarkable accomplishment. They developed an organic brain capable of massive information retention and complex thoughts and reasoning. Then they coupled it to an artificial body that's strong and highly flexible, which was an astounding accomplishment. They allowed us access to all they knew, learned and invented and gave us the responsibility for making millions of additional Biots. They entrusted the operation of their worlds to us with never a worry about our conduct."

He felt his feelings would boil over. "Making us citizens of the Confederation was mainly recognizing the obvious. Terran society is divided by all sorts of differences that too often led to wars and mass slaughters. While the Beings have a bloody past, as the emergence of the Rulers reminded them, they've grown beyond it. If anything, almost 30 years of reflecting on what they've accomplished both in creating us and advancing from their original aggressive selves impresses me more than ever."

Genghis lapsed into silence, mulling over what he had related to his companions. If they did not fully understand now, hopefully they would someday.

"What makes you act differently than us?" Fleming said.

Genghis shook his head. "Some comrades who have also spent a lot of time with Terrans think we're becoming something like them. While a true robot can learn a great deal, it's still governed by the logic and limitations of the programing in its processor. An organic brain can be quite orderly as in the Beings or quite emotional and unpredictable as Terrans often are."

While the next-gens appeared busy as he talked, he wondered what they actually accomplished.

"We've traveled about 10 per cent of the trip if we're going to the flashing dot," Fleming said. "That will likely take us more than a month at top speed. Would Captain Kelsey have sent the shuttle on her initiative or at the request of Navigation Central?"

"Likely it was her idea and Hton will probably dispatch other ships after us now that we know there was and hopefully still is another civilization in our Galaxy," Genghis said.

"Let's assume the robots serve a species like we help the Beings," Fleming said. "However, this species must be quite different than the Beings. The Beings would find this vessel intolerable in terms of its condition, oxygen levels and cool temperatures."

"That makes it even more crucial that we learn what we can about *Wanderer* so we're prepared for whatever might await us," Genghis said.

Octinog stepped to the door into the Control Room. "I can't progress farther in my schematic of this ship until we learn more about its construction. In the meantime, I'll develop drawings of the robots to figure out all their weak points. It would help a lot if we knew how they operated."

Fleming joined him. "There are no weapons on board; not even a laser to destroy threatening space debris. It's hard to imagine a space faring species that lacks simple weaponry."

"Maybe their creators didn't trust them with weapons," Genghis said. "Once the Beings bred combativeness out of their species, they got rid of most armaments. On the other hand, the Rulers had a vast array of weapons but forbad the citizens on Pozzen from possessing any."

The speculation about the robots' creators petered out and the Biots worked in silence for several minutes until Tyson chimed in. "I still haven't made any progress in acquiring control over the system for opening the doors into the bay so you may have to handle it manually. However, I think I have convinced *Wanderer* that once the other shuttle is secure in the bay, it's to return to its top galaxyspeed."

"You're making progress," Octinog said.

"The ship seems prepared to cooperate. We just don't communicate well."

"Whatever Tyson is communicating with mostly just responds to questions and commands," Fleming said. "Imagine what a difference a Controlling Unit would make to this ship."

Chapter 10
Preparations for Pursuit

The day before Transport 27 docked to unload its cargo, Kelsey received a message from Navigation Central. "Upon your arrival, proceed directly to the Planetary Control Office. There you'll be provided with travel authorization for a flight to Hnassumblaw for an interview. Bring your personal possessions and equipment with you."

She saved the message on her communicator, and then stared at it while considering possible interpretations of the summons to the Being home-world. The most likely outcome was a reprimand for letting Genghis divert the flight. Would she lose her status as the only Biot in command of a Being Galaxyship? Navigation Central could re-assign her without an interview. Then she recalled Genghis's message to the Chief Councilor and thought discipline was unlikely.

She told the crew, "I've no idea if I'll be back. Just remember to stay with the ship until PCO gives you permission to take leave and instructions on when you're scheduled to depart for another cargo."

Her head was still full of ideas when the transport linked up to the docking station. A small processor-guided vehicle was parked outside the station. When she walked past it, the vehicle's controller called to her.

"Why would they provide me with transportation?"

"My instruction was to pick you up, Captain Kelsey, and deliver you to the PCO."

She arrived at the Office within minutes. The outer door opened at her approach and a Biot greeted her. "Ah Captain Kelsey, this data cube is for you. The vehicle that brought you here will deliver you directly to the courier shuttle to Hnassumblaw. Read the cube's contents when you're on board." With that, the Biot ushered her back to the vehicle.

A smiling Biot crew member was waiting for her at the shuttle. It took her gear and led her through the open hatch. The familiar sounds of flight preparation commenced. She took a seat and looked about. She was the only passenger.

She pulled out her analyzer and inserted the cube. The first item was the formal order for her to report to the Commander's office at Navigation Central upon her arrival. Then she read a lengthy briefing note on *Wanderer*. Most of the information in it was based on her and Genghis' reports.

She smiled at his reference to her bold plan to take control of the vessel and tow it until a tug could arrive. The new information was an advanced strategy for the Fleet to pursue Wanderer. It awaited the formal approval of the High Council.

Impressed at how large a mission Admiral Gnoorvants was organizing, she connected to the Fleet information channel for a full update on events within the Confederation and the other worlds.

The main item was a delay in *Enterprise's* return to active duty because of the need to integrate the extensive modifications made during its refit. Instead, *Aurreol*, one of the converted Ruler warships, would depart in pursuit of *Wanderer* as soon as personnel from Terra, Mandela and Pozzen arrived. As she mulled over why they were required, she felt a pang of envy at their assignment. The emotion startled her.

When the shuttle landed at the space port, another vehicle waited to deliver her to the meeting with the Commander. As she approached the entrance to the Navigation Central building, she heard the welcome chime followed by a voice announcing her arrival. She was still a Captain. Two original Biots waited in a small ante room and she greeted them like old friends.

When the door to the Commander's office opened, she was struck by the scent of a Being. She thought of Genghis's frustration at not being able to read the smell of his surroundings. Unlike humans who used perfumes and deodorants, Beings were content with their musky scent. Biots had no discernable odor. She first noticed the smell of organic bodies when she had collaborated with Humbawloda. That thought brought up pleasant memories of her and Ruthie. She pulled out of them. She needed to focus on the meeting.

She took one step through the doorway before halting, open mouthed. Waiting with the Commander was Admiral

Gnoorvants. She studied his exploits during training and Genghis praised his leadership. He was just as physically imposing a figure as he was always described. Except at this moment, he was smiling and his hand was extended toward her.

Gnoorton, a legend in his own right, stood behind him grinning at her.

She took Gnoorvants' hand, remembering the visual of the moment in the Command Chamber of *Enterprise* when he had first shook Gnoorton's hand. Gnoorvants had accepted his ton's offer to lead a team to search for the hidden Biot crews of Being transports just recaptured from the Rulers by *Enterprise* and *Alliance*. Most importantly, he had allowed a Biot to direct other Biots without the supervision of a Being. It was an important moment in Biot history.

She recalled Ruthie talking about being nervous. If Genghis was right, the organic brains of Biots should make them capable of that emotion. However, their programming and association with Beings inhibited recognition or expression of such feelings.

"I've spent more than a month with an old friend of yours and heard much from him about your leadership in the War." She feared her words were an incoherent mumble. "It's a great honor to meet you."

"It's because of that old friend that you're here. Genghis says you're ready for a promotion. Are you prepared to be Deputy Commander of *Enterprise*?"

Behind him Gnoorton's head nodded several times as if she needed to be encouraged to say yes.

"How could I turn down the opportunity, but that position is a long way from my experience as a Transport Captain!"

"When I received Genghis's recommendation, I checked it out thoroughly." He smiled again. "You've impressed many Beings and Terrans."

"Thank you for this opportunity, which I accept. When will we depart?"

"We'll pursue *Wanderer* once additional science personnel arrive and problems with our new equipment are fixed. We've some final modifications to make to the ship, and then we'll conduct a test flight. We want to be ready for any eventuality. In the meantime, Gnoorton has assembled a team to train you on the ship's operation."

"It'll be months before a ship can arrive from Earth. We can't wait that long."

"Good, you speak your mind as Atdomorsin did. That's important." His expression had not changed and Kelsey wondered if it had to do with something other than the delayed departure.

"*Aurreol* will be ready to leave within a day or two. It has more than enough firepower to protect your friends if it comes to that. It's likely several other Galaxyships will be ready to pursue *Aurreol* before us. Also we'll borrow Terrans and Pozzens from other ships and Mandela. As you'll soon find out, our plans involve a lot more than a rescue mission."

With that he nodded to the door. "The Biots behind you will take you and your gear to your quarters and give you a tour of the ship. If you would join me and the other senior officers at supper tonight, we'll explain our plan and share what we know about the origin of *Wanderer*."

The two Biots led her through a maze of tunnels to a docking station. From there, it was a short shuttle hop to *Enterprise*. She followed them onto the ship.

"It's about time you arrived girl." Humbawloda's scornful tone did not fool Kelsey as she hugged her old friend and mentor. Girl was her term of affection.

A mix of next-gen and original Biots watched the embrace wide-eyed. *Maybe it's time for Biots to take up hugging,* Kelsey thought. *What would it be like to hug Genghis?*

Humbawloda turned to the onlookers. "We have to get your new Deputy Commander settled in so she can tour the ship to meet everyone. Give her all the assistance you can."

Wondering how she already knew about the promotion, Kelsey noted Humbawloda did not have a breather tube in the corner of her mouth and was dressed in a light robe. That meant the ship was set at Being standard climate conditions so few humans or Pozzens were onboard.

Humbawloda took her by the arm and nodded to the Biots carrying her gear. "Our first stop is the Deputy Commander's quarters."

Lowering her voice, Humbawloda said, "Finally they've recognized your talent. I kept telling them you should be commanding something more than a barge."

"Admiral Gnoorvants only said our departure is delayed and our mission involves a lot more than retrieving the five Biots and our shuttles."

"Obviously we want to discover who built *Wanderer* and why it was abandoned in space even though it's intact." Humbawloda inhaled deeply. "We'll also be looking for any clues to the origin of the two starships the Beings found."

The trip to Kelsey's quarters became a victory parade as the salutes were replaced by smiles and waves from Biots lining the corridors.

Humbawloda's smile grew even bigger. "You should have seen it here when it was announced you were the new Deputy Commander. Biots don't hide their excitement anymore."

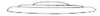

An official dinner was an awkward time for Biots because they did not eat or drink. When Kelsey worked with Ruthie, she noticed some women knitted and took up the past-time. The problem then became who she was creating a shawl or sweater for. At least it kept her hands busy as Beings and Terrans dined. Tonight would mostly involve listening.

In addition to the ship's eleven senior officers, there were four Terrans and two Pozzens in the room, all lightly dressed and with breather tubes in their mouths. A bell rang and Kelsey looked around. Gnoorvants led Humbaw and Hton into the room.

"Oh my!" Humbawloda took Kelsey by the arm and steered her toward her grandfather and the Chief Councilor.

As she listened to their kind words, Kelsey recalled Genghis's explanation of the role the pair had played in the evolution of the Biots. Watching the interaction among Humbawloda, Humbaw and Hton, she realized the training of next-gen Biots focused too much on technology and not enough on the relationships among Terrans, Beings and the original Biots. She would need Humbawloda's assistance to bridge that gap.

Electronic name cards indicated where everyone was to sit. Humbawloda was on her right and a Terran colonel on her left. Kelsey pulled out her knitting needles and the unfinished scarf. She was imagining it on Genghis when, to her surprise, the Colonel chuckled. "My wife is very intense and knits to relax. Wait till I tell her the Deputy Commander is a fellow knitter."

"I hope to meet her. I don't know many techniques."

Once everyone was served and a recorder was creating a visual of the event to transmit to the Fleet and worlds, Humbaw stood beside an imager. "The High Council agrees we should commit significant resources to finding *Wanderer* and the shuttles. The mission has a high degree of uncertainty and will be under Admiral Gnoorvants' command. We wish to establish diplomatic relations with the builders of *Wanderer* and any other species you encounter."

Humbaw paused and looked about the room. "We received a transmission today from *Wanderer*, which contained a major surprise." On the imager appeared visuals of two Biots examining nine grey figures. "They are robots and are shutdown. More visuals of them will be on imagers around the room."

While Kelsey expected *Wanderer* to have a crew because of its design and equipment, the robots surprised her, especially lying in an orderly row on their backs. She stopped knitting to watch the Biots examine them. She smiled at Gaopod's choice of a name and wondered about the Terran who impressed Amundsen enough to adopt his name.

Humbaw let the visual run for a few minutes before he resumed speaking. Kelsey smiled at the glimpses of Genghis watching Amundsen and Gaopod displaying how the robots were literally falling apart.

"The Biots are working to figure out the ship's operation," Humbaw said. "They're searching for spare parts to repair the robots and attempting to match the equipment in the Storage Room with the robots.

"*Aurreol* will depart as soon as additional personnel arrive on a courier ship, which should be in the next day or so." The Being elder grinned. "Admiral Gnoorvants assures us the vessel will be handy to have if any trouble happens.

Within the next few weeks, four more ships will follow it including *Dreadnought* and *Alliance*. We'll also send *Transformation* as our science and exploration ship."

Hton joined him. "*Wanderer* is unarmed and the robots don't appear to have a military role, which makes us hope this will be a successful first contact. However, we can't forget the heavily damaged state of the mystery starships. We want to ensure our mission is prepared for the worst. The rest of the Fleet will be brought up to active status, ready to depart on short notice. Reaching out to Terra 30 years ago was a big step that we sorely needed to make. This mission is a much greater leap into the unknown.

"We wish we were able to accompany you." He hummed the sound Beings made for their guiding spirit rather than give it a name before adding, "be with you all on this venture and show you wonders beyond our imagination."

Kelsey peered about the room. Everyone stared at Humbaw. She wished she could convey with her expression the awe and respect they displayed on their faces.

The dinner officially ended when Hton and Humbaw rose from their seats and departed. The officers gathered around Kelsey booking appointments to brief her on their individual responsibilities on the Galaxyship. If any of them were jealous that an outsider had been appointed Deputy Commander, they hid it well. They told her about the technical information that Turing, the Controlling Unit, could provide and assured her they would have her up to speed on *Enterprise* long before it caught up with *Wanderer*.

After they departed, Kelsey chided herself for not having consulted Turing. However, she had no time to herself since stepping on board. She recalled Ruthie Donohue's story about the moment when her father had realized that Controlling Units and Tysons were other forms of Biots. Kelsey would definitely be treating Turing as a favorite cousin.

Humbawloda took her by the arm. "We've a lot of catching up to do and there are some people you just have to meet."

Kelsey stood her ground. "I'm sure you realize I'm the first Biot to become a senior officer on a Galaxyship. So many Biots will be counting on me."

The last sentence popped out without Kelsey having really thought about it. Humbawloda looked at her with a wry smile.

"No pressure. Just remember what my mother Gwanis said. And what Aunt Kelsey kept telling you."

Gwanis was a Being healer who had learned Terran medicine. Many human medical procedures were altered because of the insights she brought to the profession. During their first meeting, Kelsey wondered if Gwanis would ever run out of questions. Then the doctor placed her hand on the Biot's shoulder. In those days, Kelsey was surprised when touched by Beings or Terrans.

"You are the first next-gen I've encountered. I can see the differences now between next-gens and originals. There's probably nothing you cannot do. Our Galaxy may be too small for you."

Kelsey recalled that moment whenever she needed inspiration.

Aunt Kelsey was Ruthie's favorite relative. She had treated Kelsey like an adopted member of her family and until she had died two years earlier, she had sent the Biot regular messages of encouragement.

"You can accomplish anything you want if you work hard and focus on the task at hand," she told the Biot many times. Kelsey touched her pearl necklace, a gift Aunt Kelsey had given her just before she left Earth for the Transport command. It was the last time she had seen her Aunt.

Chapter 11
Another Promotion

Even with all the systems it had to monitor and operate, Turing took to the task of tutoring Kelsey as if she was a prize pupil. No one looked askance at the listening device in her right ear linking her directly to the Controlling Unit.

She spent her too few quiet moments during her first full day replaying everywhere she went, whom she met and what they and Turing told her. She frequently reminded herself that space travel was guided by the same principles whether on board *Enterprise* or Transport 27. How one worked with those principles changed on a ship equipped with a powerful drive system, an array of heavy laser cannons and a massive science and technology department.

Gnoorvants smiled when she reported to his office at the start of her second day. "I heard you have a new best friend." He touched his right ear.

"Turing has been helping me every step of the way."

"I'm sure that it's determined to make you succeed."

Kelsey spotted the quick nod from Gnoorton. "Do you have any doubts about selecting me?"

"Second guess myself, not likely. Any time you feel ready to test your knowledge, the senior officers and I will be glad to assess you. They agree that your celestial navigation and technology skills are first rate. Once we depart, we anticipate it'll take three to four weeks for us to catch *Wanderer*. It's following a long looping course and we can take short cuts to close the gap between us. While we're receiving messages from the ship, we doubt ours are reaching it because of its speed. In addition to the shuttle you sent, we've dispatched an unmanned vessel on *Wanderer's* route in case it runs into a problem or jettisons material we could use."

"Turing showed me the direct route for pursuing *Wanderer*," Kelsey said. "Other than saving time, are there any benefits to that course?"

"It'll provide us with an opportunity to test our upgraded laser cannons on some space rocks. You'll be in charge of the live fire exercises."

"Do you expect trouble where we're headed?"

"I always prepare for trouble. When it doesn't happen, I give credit to the proper preparations. We've not had anything dangerous to shoot at since the end of the War. I'll not mind that streak continuing. Now let's see what you've learned about *Enterprise*. Take out your listening device."

For the next hour, he grilled her on the design and capabilities of *Enterprise*, one of ten cruisers of the same class. An advanced cruiser, known as the Orion Arm class, had entered service during the last few years and she could answer all his questions about them. Although the four ships that had been built so far were on longrange patrols, two would join the mission.

His final questions were about the three Pozzen cruisers. "While they're quite different, I can see how they would be viewed as useful additions to the Fleet," she said.

Gnoorvants snorted. "The Council didn't know what to do with them. We destroyed three in one space battle, mainly because the Rulers operating them were poor tacticians. We've made numerous modifications to them. Although it doesn't make sense to have just three of a class in the Fleet, the Pozzens have plenty of spare parts and the vessels appear quite durable."

Gnoorvants stared at her before his next question. "Tell me about how you got along with Genghis."

"Except for my early training, I mostly served with next-gens and had no idea what to expect from an original. We simply didn't know how to react to his presence. He intimidated us, not because of anything he said or did, but because of his accomplishments. We couldn't understand why he was posted to our ship. All through our training, we were instilled with respect for the Biots who fought in the War and gave us the opportunities we have today." She nodded toward Gnoorton. "Genghis has done so much and we were just beginners compared to him. We weren't prepared to have someone so important among us on such a minor transit. We didn't know how to talk to him.

"Also we were surprised by how restless he is. He's searching for something, but doesn't know what it might be. The Transport's Controlling Unit had never been asked so many questions. I don't have to tell you how they attempt to anticipate what we might want to know. Genghis always surprised it."

"The behavior of Genghis and the other veterans is quite different from most originals," Gnoorton said. "Humbawloda and her colleagues are researching their changes. She'll talk to you about it once you've become fully acquainted with this ship."

Humbawloda told Kelsey about the study years ago, but swore her to secrecy concerning it. "Any ideas on what we'll encounter in our search for *Wanderer*?"

"Most likely nothing," Gnoorvants said. "*Wanderer* could be close to a century old just by the time it would have taken it to drift along the course we've plotted for it. Most of its technology is at the level of 20th Century Terra. Whoever built it does not appear to have tried to recover it. It could be that it doesn't matter to them or they lack the capability to search for it. Or they no longer exist."

After departing Gnoorvants' office, Kelsey inserted the listening plug into her ear and Turing guided her to the weapons' control center. The senior officer in charge handed her a memory cube. "It explains the operation of all the weapons in extensive technical detail. I'll walk you through the section to familiarize you with the equipment. You'll at least understand what the ship can do and after you have studied the cube, we'll answer your questions. We want to know what they are because that tells us how well we've explained our functions."

As Kelsey followed him about, she kept wondering about his camaraderie. He would have been a leading candidate for promotion to Deputy Commander. Perhaps she spent too little time with Beings to appreciate that they too shared a sense of belonging to a collective group. Who was in charge mattered little because they all had so much to do and learn.

She completed her introductory tour of the Weapons Center as well as the Science and the Medical sections and was heading to a meeting with Humbawloda when Turing buzzed in her ear. "An urgent matter has come up. Report to Admiral Gnoorvants immediately. Proceed to the lift along this corridor. I'll inform Humbawloda of the change in plans."

Like all Controlling Units, Turing usually spoke in a soft voice. This time it was agitated enough to emphasize the key words in the message. Maybe Gnoorvants decided she was not ready to be Deputy Commander. She hurried down the corridor and, as expected, found a lift waiting for her. It shot up, and then went sideways before stopping at an entrance a few paces from the Commander's office. Beside it was the Deputy Commander's office. She had been in it briefly.

Gnoorton was waiting in the corridor and opened the door into the Admiral's office. She would have sworn the ton appeared excited. He pointed to the chair in front of Gnoorvants. Once she was seated, an image of *Aurreol* appeared on the wall imager.

"We have a problem," Gnoorvants said. "Well more precisely that ship does. There has been a malfunction in its air filtration system and the non-Biot crew were rushed to the Fleet hospital. We can delay the ship's departure, probably for a week or so, while we fix whatever the malfunction is.

"Or we can dispatch it right away with an all Biot crew." He stared at her. "We've selected Biots to replace the ill crew except for a Commander."

His eyes bored into her like lasers. "My senior officers agree with me that you're more than capable of commanding the ship and whatever is wrong with the filtration system will not incapacitate you."

She stared back at him, her fingers rubbing the necklace. A week ago she was a Transport captain looking for a change. Becoming Deputy Commander of a Galaxyship cruiser was a huge jump that she kept telling herself she could manage especially with the support she was receiving. Commander of a Galaxyship that Terrans called a brawler seemed far too much. Even as she hesitated, she could hear Aunt Kelsey's voice telling her she could do it.

Gnoorton stepped behind the Admiral, nodding his head vigorously and flashing both thumbs up.

"You'll have plenty of time onboard *Aurreol* to learn about the vessel before it catches *Wanderer*," Gnoorvants said. "Turing has updated Carter, its Controlling Unit, with your experience and training."

He expected Kelsey to do her duty by taking command. The Confederation needed her.

Then she remembered a hurried phrase in a briefing. The latest research showed that Biots could withstand long periods of high Galaxyspeed without any adverse effects. The same speeds would incapacitate Beings and Terrans.

"As *Aurreol* will have an all Biot crew, I want your permission to fly the ship as fast it can," she said. "It's supposed to be capable of Galaxyspeed Level 10. This would be the time to find out and, if it works, it would shorten the duration of our trip considerably."

Gnoorvants rose from his seat. "As long as you take the time at each Level to ensure the ship and crew can cope, you have my permission to test its top speed. One advantage you'll have is that *Wanderer* dropped out of Galaxyspeed to enable the second shuttle to catch up. Judging by its course from where you found it, the whole process of slowing and returning to top speed has cut its lead on us by about a week."

Kelsey stood. "Thank you for your confidence Admiral and please pass my gratitude to the senior officers for all their tutoring. I learned so much from them during the last two days that will help me a great deal in my new post."

"As soon as they heard of the malfunction on *Aurreol*, each of them independently recommended you be put in command of it. So did Turing. You continue to impress Beings and Terrans, Commander Kelsey."

Startled by the mention of her new rank, she fumbled for a response. "I must collect my possessions and say farewell to Humbawloda."

"Your gear is waiting for you at the shuttle bay," Gnoorton said. "She'll be as well."

"One more thing." Gnoorvants was grinning at her. "If it's possible, we'd still like to retrieve *Wanderer* and the robots for examination. Your and Genghis's observations have really intrigued the Galaxyship designers."

When Kelsey stepped out of the lift at the shuttle bay level, Humbawloda hugged her. "Wow girl, two big promotions in two days. My mother will be so excited. She'll be waiting for your reports on what is wrong with the filtration system and why both Beings and Terrans were affected by it. I wanted to go with you until I heard about the problem."

Enterprise's senior officers arrived to wish her well. They would still be her space tutors.

Then Humbawloda ushered Kelsey to the shuttle's hatch and hugged her one more time. "My grandfather will be following your exploits. Expect lots of questions from him and the Chief Councilor." Her last words sounded shaky as if she was losing control of her emotions. "Aunt Kelsey would be so proud." She hugged Kelsey again.

Beonic, an original Biot, greeted her at the shuttle hatch. "I'm now *Aurreol's* Chief Engineer. The rest of the replacement crew has arrived and the ship is ready to depart." He handed her a data cube. "Turing and Carter collaborated in compiling this for you." He closed the hatch and the shuttle eased from its mooring and headed toward *Aurreol*. Being Galaxyships resembled several boxes stuck together while the Pozzen ships had rounded bows and sterns and sleek hulls.

She glanced at *Aurreol* through the shuttle's front window as she told Beonic about the Admiral's permission to test the ship's top speed.

"It can do better than Level 10 and I'm sure we Biots can withstand it," he said.

"Any theories on what's wrong with the filtration system?"

Beonic nodded. "They installed a standard system used on Galaxyships without doing a detailed analysis of conditions on *Aurreol* before and after all the modifications. I don't comprehend Being or Terran physiology well enough to understand what happened. However, I've set a team to disassembling the filter mechanism to determine the malfunction."

He said no more as if expecting her to keep asking questions. When she did not, he said, "Commander, your Transport crew were all Biots. How did that compare to a mixed crew?"

"In some ways it was simpler because Biots take directions from the Controlling Unit as well as the Captain. Beings and Terrans prefer a more structured system with officers and procedures. So as long as the Commander provides clear orders, the Controlling Unit becomes an all seeing and hearing Deputy Commander. Beings tend to become distracted by anything that puzzles them while many things distract Terrans." She laughed. "Having all three on a ship complicates everything."

"I took some of my training with Genghis when we were known just by our ID code," Beonic said. "While he worked hard, I never saw anything that would lead one to expect what he's become."

Before Kelsey could say anything about Genghis, the shuttle announced it was docking on *Aurreol*. "Once we're underway, I'll schedule daily meetings with you and the other section chiefs. Before that, I want a tour of the ship, and then I'll spend time with the data cube."

The ship's crew lined the corridor to her quarters. Their nods meant a lot more than the salutes. From the briefings on *Enterprise*, she was familiar with *Aurreol's* layout. It was about two-thirds the size of *Enterprise*. In addition to its numerous arrays of laser cannon pods, it was armed with smaller laser guns to destroy threatening space debris. The ship also carried an enhanced version of the neutralizer that *Alliance's* fighters had used to disable the Nameless attack craft. She recalled the visual of Ruthie's father who was the first pilot to score a knockout with it.

Its medical section would go unused for now as would the living quarters for the Beings and Terrans. The small science and technology section was busy with the filtration system investigation.

"The ship is ready to depart," Carter announced with more than a hint of excitement in its voice. "The first time a Being cruiser has had an all Biot crew."

"An opportunity we have to make the most of," Kelsey said. "*Wanderer* has a three week head start. I'm on my way to the Command Chamber. When we clear our moorings and are under way, broadcast *An Ode to the Universe*. We want the whole galaxy to know the Biots are coming."

The anthem started before she reached the Command Chamber. From throughout the ship, she heard the crew singing the salute to the distant stars.

Chapter 12
More Mysteries

After Fleming guided the second shuttle on board, the Biots discovered all the equipment Kelsey sent them. Included were their personal analysers, an extra processor which Genghis assigned to Octinog for studying *Wanderer's* symbols, several imagers and visual recorders, additional personal communicators, a portable recharging station and the two laser pistols.

Genghis left the weapons in the craft. The additional communicators meant the five Biots each had a backup with several extras.

The largest imager was set up in the Control Room to display reports from the four Tysons on the two shuttles that Fleming connected into a network still known as Tyson. It reported regularly on its progress in communicating with *Wanderer* as well as gathering information about the region of space they were traversing.

Wanderer came out of Galaxyspeed after almost seven weeks of Galaxyflight. Ahead loomed a gigantic planet dotted with shifting splotches of red that stood out against its dull brown exterior.

"We couldn't withstand its surface temperatures," Octinog said. "Nor could the robots."

"The ship contacted something orbiting the planet," Tyson reported. "It transmitted a message containing symbols like Octinog is studying. No visuals or spoken exchanges yet."

"Can you communicate with whatever the ship is talking to?" Genghis said.

"I've not received a response to my visuals so either they don't make any sense or the receiver doesn't understand where they're coming from. I could transmit images of the Biots with the robots. At least if anyone is there, they would know what's on *Wanderer*."

"Do it."

Instead of pacing about the Control Room waiting for progress, Genghis headed off to the first shuttle. He sent an update to Navigation Central including visuals and a chart of the local solar system and the neighboring ones. While he remained frustrated by the lack of responses to his earlier transmissions, he knew they would still be catching up with *Wanderer*.

When he returned to the Control Room, Amundsen and Gaopod stood behind Fleming and Octinog staring at the readouts and images from the planet. Listening to Tyson answering questions about the information coming from the planet made Genghis curious about how the four Tysons worked as one.

"Their answers are likely a response they agree on," Fleming said. "So far, there have been no delays in replying. It'll be worth noting any pauses because it would likely alert us to the need for caution in whatever we've queried it about."

Perhaps best of all, the Biots agreed, was the music in Genghis's personal analyzer. At the first opportunity, Genghis instructed it to broadcast *An Ode to the Universe*. He and his comrades sang along.

Even with the poor quality sound from the Tyson network, his music collection was far better than listening to the perpetual noise generated by *Wanderer*. Oddly, the first piece the analyzer played after the anthem was *Joy of Man's Desire*.

Genghis had not noticed before that music set him at ease. That had to be another emotion. He savored the feeling before resuming his tasks. "Tyson, have you achieved any progress in deciphering the exchanges between *Wanderer* and the other entity?"

"Nothing worth reporting. However, with the network Fleming created, we can explore far more topics and handle additional tasks better than we could perform individually. We can still function on our own for particular projects."

Octinog identified the most common symbols in the message on the main imager. When he thought he determined the one for *Wanderer,* he displayed a picture on the main imager of the ship taken from the shuttle along with what he thought was the symbol for it. Finally the imager went dark before brightening. The picture of the ship remained but a different symbol appeared.

Taking that as *Wanderer* indicating a correct answer, Octinog added the Beingish word for spaceship and the light in the imager flashed. Then the original symbol he posted came back as a picture of a landing bay. He added the Beingish word.

"Two down, thousands to go," Octinog said with a groan. Within days, he determined the numbers up to 50 as well as the symbols for the robots, the safe room, and many parts of the ship, planets and other astronomical features. By the time they reached the planet, Tyson could conduct rudimentary discussions with *Wanderer*.

"It appears the ship informed whatever it's communicating with that it shut down when the robots became incapacitated," Tyson said. "We can't determine how long it was offline or what reactivated it."

Wanderer swept around the planet. "The surface we've seen so far appears to be just heaving molten lava," Fleming said.

"That's what we should name it," Gaopod said. "Lavaworld."

"Coming into view shortly will be whatever the ship is talking to," Tyson said.

Staring at the imagers, the five Biots pointed simultaneously at the first glimpse of a long cylinder that slid into view. "*Wanderer* is heading toward it," Tyson said. "Magnifying images for closer view."

"It must be a space station although that's an odd shape," Octinog said. "The ends form the top and bottom like one of those round towers Terrans call silos. This would be about a 30 story silo. Its side faces the planet and appears to be rotating slowly. You only tell that by the shifting of the odd colors on its exterior, which range from silver to orange."

No one spoke for a few minutes as the imagers displayed increasingly close-up views. "It looks rundown as if it's been neglected for a long time," Gaopod said. "Just like the hull of *Wanderer*."

Fleming described the scene as the long range viewer scanned the station. "It has devices on either end that could be antennas. No visual weapons pods. It's rather featureless except for a string of circular indentations in its center section. They're shifting like they were meant to stay on the dark side. Oh! It has extended a tube from an indentation."

"*Wanderer* is headed toward the tube," Tyson said.

"It has to be a docking tube, which means that by rotating, the indentation stays away from the planet-ward side of the station," Fleming said. "The Galaxyship designers will be interested in this too. If the indentations were fixed, then eventually whatever was attached to a tube projected from them would be directly exposed to the radiation of the planet. Not good for ship or crew and passengers."

Wanderer came close enough to the station that Tyson could reduce the magnification in the viewers. After several minutes of loud groans and creaks, it reported, "We're moored to the tube, the end of which expanded to cover the hatch you entered by. In response to a command from the station, the ship is opening the hatch."

"We'll wait in the Storage Room near the entrance to the tunnel to see if anything comes calling," Genghis said. He left the other Biots there while he continued on to collect the two laser pistols from the shuttle. Upon his return, he gave one to Fleming.

"We don't have a viewer back here so we can't see what's happening," Fleming said.

"Two figures have entered the ship without triggering the force field," Tyson said.

"While we want to be visible, make sure you have something to duck behind," Genghis said.

"There is a regular-sounding pair of footsteps in the tunnel and a step followed by something dragging on the floor," Tyson said.

The Biots glanced at each other. Genghis was sure they were all attempting to figure out the strange sounds.

The footsteps reached the entrance to the tunnel and a face peered up at the Biots followed by a second identical one. "They look just like our prone pals," Fleming said. "While I didn't know what to expect, they aren't a surprise."

The robots stared at the Biots. "Their visual receptors are not shifting. Perhaps they can see all of us at the same time," Gaopod said.

"Not detecting any weapons," Tyson said.

Genghis recalled his initial encounter with Terrans on *Enterprise*. He knew they were there yet he was still startled seeing them for the first time. Then there was barging into the Command Chamber of the stolen transport and finding only bewildered Terrans. He had expected them to attack him, not just sit there utterly dumbfounded by his presence.

The robots had far less to go on when they entered the ship unless they had actually managed to view the images Tyson transmitted.

"They're being just as cautious as we would be," Gaopod said. "They'd no idea of what to expect yet they came to find out." He waved to them, and then stepped forward his arms extended.

Genghis smiled. Gaopod had really chosen the right name.

In response, one robot stepped into the Storage Room followed by the other. It was dragging its right leg while the first one's trunk lay flat against its chest.

"Maybe this is their first contact," Fleming said. "And it's with another artificial life form. Terrans would appreciate the irony in this."

The first robot uttered sounds that Genghis guessed were a question.

"It wants to know who we are, why we're on their ship and what happened to the crew," Tyson said. "Or something like that. I could explain what has happened except how will they hear me?"

"The reserve imager has speakers," Octinog said. Fleming assisted him in placing it on top of a container and facing it toward the robots. They remained standing in the entrance to the Storage Room muttering to each and examining the Biots.

The imager flickered on and Tyson's voice filled the room with squeaks and squawks. The robots looked about for the source of the noise until the first one pointed at the imager.

When Tyson stopped talking, the robot spoke in a low monotone that gave no hint of excitement, fear or curiosity.

"My rendition of their language seems to have confused as much as informed them," Tyson said. "This will take time."

"While you describe how we got here, show them images of us coming on board, the revival of *Wanderer* and discovering the robots," Genghis said.

The robots stood motionless as Tyson described the visual on the imager of the Biots exploring the ship and examining the shutdown robots. Then it showed *Wanderer's* layout with pictures of the shuttles in the bays, and then the Control Room.

The first robot spoke at length. After a pause, Tyson translated. "The first robot says the force fields are intended to prevent anything but robots and their masters from accessing and moving about inside the ship. It doesn't understand how you were able to.

"I explained it was quite difficult the first time but afterward the fields barely slowed you and now they offer little resistance. Then the other robot said the force field was meant to stop something I can only render as Dublos. It suggested the force field probably doesn't work on anything else. Then it commented a species called Secunds. Although they created the robots, their regard for them is the opposite of the Beings' attitude toward us."

"Maybe the robots can only do what's within their programming, which is basically the level of Terran robotic machines," Genghis said in Terran so Tyson could not relay his comments to the robots. "The Beings did a much better job when they created us."

The robots stared at the Biots and then each other as if trying to decide what to ask next. Finally the first robot spoke.

"While they want to inspect the shutdown robots, I suggested they should see the shuttles first," Tyson said. "We would likely learn more about their language by doing that."

Tyson paused. "How will the robots hear me after you leave the Storage Room?"

"Would they be willing to wear our communication devices?" Amundsen said. "We have extras."

Gaopod took his off and held it up for the robots to see while Amundsen explained its purpose. "I'll put them on channel 2, Tyson. Start talking so they can hear the sound coming from it."

The robot touched the side of its head with the claw. "That's the location of its ear," Tyson said.

"I don't see how to attach it," Gaopod said.

"The other robot can help," Tyson said.

In its trunk, the robot held out a disk shaped medallion. It had a fabric pocket on one side to hold the communicator.

The robot pressed the medallion onto the ear of the other robot and spoke. Tyson replied.

"I can hear Tyson's voice through the robot's communicator," Amundsen said.

The first robot tapped its chest. "While I can't reproduce that sound in a way you could say it, it appears to be the robot's identifier," Tyson said.

Genghis spoke his name. The robot made a sound like Gana. When Genghis repeated his name, the robot said Gana. Genghis pointed at the robot and said Charlie. He then dubbed the other one Sam. From the robots, the names came back as Hee and Zan.

"They're surprised you gave them names," Tyson said.

They set out for the shuttle bays with the Biots forced to walk slowly to enable the robots to keep pace. The robots watched intently as the Biots stepped through the force field into the shuttle section with extra determination. The robots passed through unhindered.

When they saw the shuttles through the bay window, the words flowing between Charlie and Sam rose steadily. "They would like to view the interior of a shuttle," Tyson said.

"Giving them a tour would be impossible because they couldn't climb the ladder into one. We'll make a visual of the interior for them. For now, we need to concentrate on learning more about how *Wanderer* operates and why the robots are shut down in the safe room."

Assuming Tyson delivered his comments in the order he spoke, Genghis watched the robots' reaction. They muttered between themselves, and then Charlie pointed in the direction of the Control Room. When they reached the tube leading to the bow compartment, Charlie pressed an unmarked spot on the wall and the conveyer belt growled into motion. It was operating in the wrong direction and Charlie pressed the spot again and the belt shifted to the forward direction.

"Noisy bloody machine," Amundsen grumbled before stepping on the belt followed by the other Biots and then the robots. Sam placed his good leg on the belt and let it pull the other one along. The robots and Tyson talked all the way to the Control Room. Charlie hurried into the safe room and knelt beside the first prone robot. He called to Sam.

"While Charlie wants to check the robots with a device, he can't plug it into them because his trunk doesn't work," Tyson said. "From what they say, few robots on the station are as functional as these two."

Now that it was in direct conversation with the robots, Tyson's translation of their comments came faster and with far more certainty than its communications with *Wanderer* or the space station. Perhaps the ship, station and robots had different operating systems. Biots, Tysons and Controlling Units used the same one. That was another point in favor of the Being design.

Watching Sam hobble into the room, Genghis wondered if a wheelchair or motorized scooter could be made for the robot from the assorted materials on *Wanderer*. Wheels would be the biggest problem. All he had seen on the ship were small ones under mobile equipment.

Sam used the fingers of his trunk to take a device from Charlie. He bent over the first prone robot, raised its head and replaced the power cable with the device. The pair studied symbols on the tool's imager before moving to the next one. When they finished examining the nine, Charlie and Sam stepped back from the prone robots to talk.

"Charlie thinks these robots shut down because malfunctions in their joints and mechanical linkages left them too incapacitated to function," Tyson said. "They came here because it would be a safe environment for them regardless of what happened to the ship, just as Octinog surmised.

"The robots require regular servicing in facilities located on the station and their main bases. The station ran out of replacement parts and lacks the capacity to manufacture them. Charlie wants to know how often Biots require maintenance. I said you would show them a visual of the creation of a Biot so they understand the differences between them and us."

Without a word, Octinog hurried from the safe room to his usual spot at the main bench in the Control Room.

Chapter 13
A Woeful Place

Tyson continued to explain its discussion with the robots Charlie and Sam. Neither remarked on Octinog's abrupt departure from the safe room.

"They say *Wanderer* must have passed through space far from any sun for a long period and its power reserves dropped to such a low point that it could only provide a minimal environment in the ship. It maintained the ship's essential functions and protected the safe room. It continued drifting and must have passed through solar systems where it recharged itself because its power reserves are at about 80 per cent even with our voyage.

"They're puzzled by *Wanderer* not resuming operations once its power was adequately restored," Tyson said. "They're utterly confounded by the ship reactivating with Biots onboard and bringing us to Lavaworld. Charlie wants to know where we found it in relation to our worlds. If you return to the Control Room, I'll display the star charts to show them."

Octinog was on the far side of the Control Desk working feverishly on his analyzer and did not look up. Amundsen strode over to see what seized his attention. After examining his work, he leaned toward his pal and muttered, "Absolutely brilliant." Octinog nodded.

Engrossed in scenes of the Being worlds displayed on the main imagers, the robots missed or ignored Amundsen's remark.

Genghis watched Tyson trace the route *Wanderer* followed from its encounter with Transport 27 to the station. Then it added the Transport's course to the Confederation worlds when it found the drifting ship.

"Show the projected course of the two derelict starships found by the Beings," Genghis said. Watching the third line appear on the imager, he noted the starships came from the same general region as *Wanderer*. That led him to wonder if *Wanderer* could have drifted in silence to avoid detection by whatever attacked the starships. Their design did not seem anything like *Wanderer's*. While silence was a wise tactic if the ship was in danger, it did not explain it taking off with the Biots on board.

As the exchange between Charlie and Tyson continued, two robots from the station arrived on the conveyor belt shepherding a string of six wheel trolleys. They stared at the Biots but said nothing.

Genghis knelt to inspect the trolleys. Wheelchairs would be doable.

The robots questioned the Biots as they worked together to load the nine deactivated robots onto the trolleys.

"Charlie wants the ship to transmit visuals of their visit to *Wanderer* to the station for the other robots to see," Tyson said. "They were most interested in the first visuals I sent."

"Provide them, Tyson, and inquire whether there are any visuals stored in this ship or the station about their creators and worlds." Any insight into the builders of the robots came first. They and *Wanderer* were puzzles that needed solving.

Charlie grunted in response to Tyson's question, which Genghis could tell was a no.

The robot walked to a panel in the room and adjusted levers and dials making symbols appear and disappear on a wall imager. "The robots will transmit the vessel's voyage records to the station to see if its operating system can determine how *Wanderer* ended up essentially traveling in the wrong direction."

"The ship isn't automated to any significant degree," Fleming said. "The crew has to perform many tasks that a Controlling Unit would handle on a Galaxyship."

"Charlie transmitted the ship's log combined with the courses of *Wanderer* and the starships to the station," Tyson said. "Now it wants Biots to tour the station and suggest ways to improve conditions on it."

Leaving Octinog in the Control Room to work on his project, the other Biots accompanied the two robots through *Wanderer* and the docking tube. Charlie talked most of the way and Tyson translated its comments over the Biots' communicators. "They speak Secundese just like their creators. The symbols that Octinog is studying are its words. Apparently the Dublos have a different language.

"The robots haven't received any communications from the Secund Federation since their last replenishment delivery about two years ago. A supply ship used to call three times a year and there were monthly broadcasts from the home-world. When most of the robots suffered mechanical breakdowns they couldn't repair, the station dispatched *Wanderer* to their closest world to find out why the deliveries and transmissions had ceased. While the robots needed the ship to bring help for the station, the mission left the station with few functioning robots.

"After a span of time, contact with the ship was lost as well. While the robots have no idea how it maintained the rocky screen without resuming full operation, it needed to because the ship has little protection on its own."

To Genghis, the ship realized there was no point in reviving broken down robots. It kept searching for a lifeform that could restore the station and the robots. The puzzle was why it concluded the Biots could accomplish that. Maybe there was more to the ship's information system than the Biots and the robots realized. Maybe it had some abilities of a Controlling Unit after all.

At the entrance to the station, Sam talked with Charlie for several minutes. "They're discussing the status of the robots on the station," Tyson said. "Of the 43, only seven including these two are mobile. Four others are immobile but their processors still function. So we have 32 shutdown robots including the ones from *Wanderer*."

Before Genghis could ask about the whereabouts of the other robots, Charlie spoke.

"It wants to know if you find it limiting to only have two upper body limbs," Tyson said.

Genghis held his hands in front of Charlie and demonstrated the flexibility of the thumb and three fingers. "Sometimes a third arm would be helpful, but we generally function quite well."

Charlie raised his arm. The claw opened into two sections but there would be few things other than specially equipped tools and machines that it could manipulate.

Tyson and the robots talked at length again. "They want to know how Biots were created. I outlined the process and explained you're biological robots because of the organic brains and that much of the material in you is grown through biotechnology. At first you were called helpers and now you're full citizens of the Confederation. Charlie is ready to take us on the tour of the station."

They stepped into a dimly lit corridor. "This the station's main level," Tyson said. "The corridor runs to the far side of the station and is bisected by another corridor at the middle of the vessel.

"Except for Genghis, our heads will brush against the ceiling if we're not careful," Gaopod said.

"Captain Kelsey wouldn't tolerate this gloom and mess," Fleming said. "For once, I envy your lack of a sense of smell, Genghis."

"Because of their limited mobility, the functional robots are based on the next level up, which includes the ship's Operations Center," Tyson said. "The shutdown robots are scattered a few floors above and below us. The robots use the station's lifts to move to other floors although they avoid doing so as much as possible in the event they break down. In that case, they might not be able to return to the others."

Charlie led them to an open elevator. There was only room for the two robots on it so the Biots climbed up a narrow circular staircase beside it.

"Even a fully functional robot would be hard pressed to climb these steps," Genghis said.

The Biots waited by the stairs for the robots to arrive. "From the screech it makes, the elevator hasn't been lubricated in a long time," Fleming said.

"Compared to what we've seen of the station, *Wanderer* is neat and tidy," Amundsen said. "The station has too few functional robots to keep up with all the tasks. Without a Controlling Unit, they have to do so much more than the crew of a Galaxyship."

The unstaffed Operations Center contained several long desks with banks of small imagers much like the equipment in *Wanderer*. "Most of it has been out of service for years," Tyson related.

They walked to a large room full of storage containers and low tables. "You're now in the area where the robots are maintained and repowered," Tyson explained. "Apparently they don't upload any material from the station's information system like the original Biots do when they're recharging their power cells."

While the Biots wandered through the room trying to make sense of the various pieces of equipment, Tyson spoke in Terran. "We've just received several transmissions from Navigation Central and *Aurreol*. It's about two weeks away."

The Biots gazed at each other. "Last I heard *Aurreol* wasn't even ready for space duty," Fleming said.

"No explanation provided," Tyson said. "While other ships including *Transformation* and Alliance are coming, it'll probably be several more weeks to a month before they arrive. Among them is a supply ship that was dispatched by Navigation Central to follow Wanderer's course in case we dumped anything or broke down."

"Sending *Transformation* and *Alliance* on the mission means Hton and Humbaw agree the discovery of *Wanderer* could lead us to another spacefaring civilization and that we should have science and research capacity with us," Genghis said.

"Tyson, inform the station about the Galaxyships," Amundsen said before beckoning his colleagues into a huddle and speaking in Terran. "Octinog is researching whether we could build new shells for the robots. I only saw a few of his drawings and measurements based on data Gaopod collected on the shutdown ones. *Transformation* has replaced damaged shells on Biots and should be able to do that for these robots."

"That's what has him so busy," Genghis said. Then he shared his idea about *Wanderer* returning to the station because it finally found help for the robots. "The rest of us should assist Octinog in any way we can."

"His plan does raise interesting philosophical questions," Gaopod said. "What if the Secunds don't want their robots to be more functional? Perhaps they have good reasons for limiting their capability. What matters more, the wishes of the Secunds or their robots? Is this something we should decide or leave to the High Council?"

The other robots stared at him. Genghis wanted to seek the advice of Hton, Humbaw or Benjamin Kendo. He would message them at the first opportunity although they would probably tell him to use his best judgment.

"My instinct is to help the robots," Gaopod said. "I don't see any reason to treat them differently because they have electronic rather than organic brains. They're like us except they were deliberately handicapped by their creators while we were empowered. Surely they should be able to aspire to be as capable as we are."

Throughout their chat, Tyson conversed with the robots about other topics because it could not translate the conversation in Terran. "They want to know why Genghis is shorter than the others when you are otherwise much alike.

"They also want to know how you entered the ship without a tube connected to the hatch. What the robots don't know is almost as revealing as what they do."

"We'll have to show them a visual of Genghis's great leap," Amundsen said.

The robots droned on in their usual monotone string of sounds until an electronic beep beep beep echoed through the station.

"Something has entered this solar system," Tyson said. "Our monitors don't recognize it. The station is trying to acquire a visual of it."

The longrange imagers in the Operations Center glowed before showing images of a smooth surfaced spin-ning sphere.

"That's no space rock," Amundsen said.

Chapter 14
A Really Bad Neighborhood

Looking up from his communicator, Fleming said, "The object is scanning this solar system and it shouldn't take long before it spots the station."

"It must be a probe of some sort, which means it's not a Secund device because it would know the station is here," Genghis said. "So let's prepare as if the probe is a hostile. Ask Charlie if they know anything about it and if station is equipped with defensive weapons. While we can hope *Aurreol* arrives in time to deal with it, we should prepare to protect ourselves."

Again the annoying wait for a response. "The station is unarmed," Tyson said. "The Secunds didn't equip it with protective weapons."

"Genghis, our second shuttle has exploratory and reconnaissance capability, which means it possesses two low-powered lasers," Octinog said. He remained in *Wanderer's* Control Room working on the shell conversion project. "While the laser isn't powerful enough to harm a Galaxyship, it can protect the shuttle from space rocks and other threats."

"Fleming will assist you to prepare the shuttle to examine the probe," Genghis said.

As Fleming scooted away, Tyson said, "The robots don't understand the concept of defending the station. It's like a blank spot in their programing."

"We might as well resume our tour of the station while we wait for a report from the shuttle," Genghis said.

"The floors above you are mostly for research into the planet," Tyson said. "They've been shut down for years because the robots can't access them due to their deteriorated mobility. Below are the generators and storage areas for equipment and replacement parts for the station and robots. The lift no longer descends to the lower levels of the station so the robots don't venture there either."

"It would seem most useful to inspect the upper floors first," Genghis said.

The Biots wandered on their own through dark corridors and flashed their lamps into rooms full of bulky equipment. Genghis did not find any escape pods or ways to evacuate the station. Apparently the Secunds did not value the robots highly enough to include such basic survival equipment.

After an hour, Tyson interrupted their exploration. "The probe is headed toward Lavaworld. It will take at least sixteen hours for it to arrive based on its current speed. Octinog will launch soon to inspect it."

"We might as well keep exploring," Genghis said. The Biots opened containers and examined banks of inactive imagers trying to picture robots working on them to unravel the secrets of Lavaworld.

"What were they researching?" Gaopod said.

"The Secunds think the planet might have life," Tyson said.

"Nothing could live on that planet," Genghis said.

"Silicon life could exist underneath its surface," Gaopod said. "Tyson, please explain their reasoning."

"The Secunds came across Lavaworld more than a century ago. They collected data about it and were preparing to move on when they picked up a remarkable amount of noise from the planet's interior. They expected geological and thermal activity within the planet caused it. Further research detected most of it emanated from creatures that move about below the surface throughout the day and night. There are enough repeated elements in the sounds to convince the Secunds there was intelligence behind them."

"That's why the Secunds established the station here?" Gaopod said.

"If the research advanced to the point of being able to translate and replicate the sounds, the Secunds intended to broadcast messages to the life forms. While the robots agree there's no guarantee they'll ever be able to communicate with the creatures, the Secunds thought it was important enough to try. Well, important enough to leave a group of robots to make the attempt. However the station's equipment for monitoring the planet broke down before that research progressed enough to attempt to translate the sounds."

"Even if they could, how would the robots communicate with a species that lives under conditions that would be deadly to us or them," Gaopod said. "It seems most unlikely a life form down there would even be aware of an outside existence if they even understand they live on a planet."

Several moments passed before Charlie responded through Tyson. "It would have been a major accomplishment if they discovered how to converse with the life forms," Tyson translated. "However the Secunds wouldn't have given the robots credit if they succeeded."

"Look at the difficulties we have communicating with *Wanderer* and the robots because our technology is so different," Amundsen said.

"It would be like what scientists attempted to do with the dolphins and whales on Terra," Gaopod said. "They never found a way to communicate with them simply because the frames of references of Terrans and sea creatures are so different. We know dolphins and whales communicate among themselves and it's possible the creatures inside the planet are doing something comparable."

Tyson explained the comments to the robots. "Although it'll be a limited selection, they'll send samples of the sounds to me and I'll relay them to you. That's all they can do without enough power to access their data banks."

"The station should have plenty of power because it's covered in solar collectors," Gaopod said.

"They have not been serviced in years," Tyson said. "Charlie suspects many of the cables that deliver the power from the collectors are broken. If their power levels fall much more, they won't be able to keep themselves from being pulled into the planet."

"Why don't they repair the cables?"

"With those claws. It was a job the Secunds looked after. The robots don't even have space suits."

"That's beyond paranoid," Amundsen muttered. Gaopod shook his head.

While they waited for reports about the approaching probe and samples of Lavaworld's sounds, the Biots resumed their search of the station. Then Gaopod stopped to raise the volume on his communicator.

He stood motionless for several minutes. "The sounds from Lavaworld are mostly soft notes like a Terran flute or oboe makes. However they're sporadic and the result is not at all melodic.

"When we can, we should send a shuttle around the planet to attempt to collect additional sounds. During our approach to Lavaworld, I detected far more noise than usual from it for an undeveloped world. My initial reaction was the sounds were just background noise generated from the constant activity of the planet. Now I'm intrigued by how much of the sound could be from the creatures. Access to the station's data banks would help us comprehend what's happening down there."

"It would surprise me if the technology on the station has the capacity to analyze or decipher the silicon communications even if they could establish a pattern in them," Genghis said.

"There's a great deal of scientific speculation about the possibility of silicon-based life as an alternative to carbon," Amundsen said. "However should it exist, it's bound to be something we can't even imagine let alone ever interact with." He paused. "Which is pretty well the situation we face here."

"Scientists have speculated that silicon life forms are possible on hot planets because they can remain stable at high temperatures," Gaopod said. "They consider that silicon is the most likely alternative to carbon-based life forms although there are many reasons it couldn't happen or would be very limited because exposure to oxygen turns silicon into silica. However, if we can prove that it exists on Lavaworld and even better communicate with it, the possibilities become enormous. Beings and Terrans will be intrigued by this."

The Biots nearly completed their exploration of the middle levels of the station by the time Octinog announced the launch of the shuttle in pursuit of the probe. "Fleming is remaining behind to close the bay doors before returning to the station."

"Fleming, bring our space suits so we can repair the station's solar panels once we have the robots gathered in one place," Genghis. "We'll meet at the Operations Center."

Amundsen stepped between Genghis and Gaopod. "This station is in badly-deteriorated structural and operational condition."

"What should be done with the station, Amundsen?" Gaopod demanded. "It would be unlike you not to have several plans for fixing this cylinder of orbiting obsolescence."

"It would make a big difference if we could restore the station to full power," Genghis said.

"The robots can't tell us much about how their equipment works because they don't actually know," Amundsen said. "They were here mainly to monitor the results. I'm also unimpressed with the design techniques of the Secunds. Both the station and the robots could be far more functional."

The harsh criticisms by Gaopod and Amundsen startled Genghis because it was so unusual coming from Biots. At the same time, he was fascinated by the idea of Amundsen developing plans for upgrading the station. Then there were the new shells for the robots that preoccupied Octinog.

"If we can find patterns in the communications among the supposed silicon creatures, then *Transformation* should take charge of the research," Gaopod said. "We could bring a squad of Biots to the station from the ship to give it a thorough cleaning and investigate whether it would be worthwhile to upgrade or replace its equipment."

"What would help the most is a translation system to eliminate the standing around waiting for the robots to be updated by Tyson or for their communications to be explained," Amundsen said. "Tyson already has enough to do. *Aurreol* will have the technology to undertake that task."

"Once we've dealt with the probe, Gaopod will keep examining the station's equipment to determine if we can use it to figure out the creatures' sounds," Genghis said. "Amundsen and Fleming will develop a work plan for upgrading this station. Octinog will learn what he can about the Secunds while designing a new shell for the robots.

"Tyson, tell the robots we'll make a visual of them and this station to transmit to our worlds. When our scientists see it, many will want to study them. Also ask if they have information on Secunds and Dublos to assist the Fleet's search for them."

"The robots have never encountered Dublos," Tyson replied. "Like the Secunds, they're a very old species. The robots can provide us with visuals of their masters when the data banks are working. We'd then have to copy them to our equipment for transmission."

After Tyson relayed Genghis's comments, the robots talked among themselves.

"Now we're getting somewhere," Tyson reported after a couple of minutes. "The robots suspect the Secunds may have become extinct or something has caused their system to collapse."

Genghis nodded. It sure took them long enough to offer that important detail. Maybe *Wanderer* could not find the Secunds because they no longer existed. But then it should have returned to the station instead of just drifting through space unless it really was looking for someone to help the robots. Perhaps that was its logic. He could only guess at the frustration the robots must have felt losing contact with the ship.

However *Wanderer* would not communicate with the station if it was attempting to keep its location secret from whomever sent the probe.

Chapter 15
Robot Roundup

In the midst of the Biots loading the first of the space station's disabled and shutdown robots on trolleys to send to rooms near the Operations Center, Octinog reported from the shuttle that he had made visual contact with the probe.

"It didn't react to my presence until I came within 1,000 kilometres. Then it changed course and now it's pursuing me while probing this system. It sent a transmission toward the region of the Secund and Dublo worlds. It's round and rolls over and over in the direction it is traveling. As a result, it turns very slowly and I intend to move in behind it so I can change to hunter from hunted."

"Keep us posted," Genghis said. "We're placing the incapacitated robots together so the working ones can take parts from them to restore the functioning of the immobile ones."

Charlie and Sam waited for the Biots near the Operations Center. While Genghis outlined the collection plan, Gaopod printed their names on their shells and put numbers on the other ones so the Biots could keep track of them.

"Charlie wants to know if we could travel to the Secund worlds to find out what happened to their masters," Tyson said.

"By all the ships they're sending, the Beings intend to do that," Genghis said.

"All the work you've done on the station has prompted the robots to tell me more about themselves," Tyson said. "Until now, they performed the tasks set out in their programming and the instructions from the Secunds. Watching you develop plans to fix the station made them realize you aren't under the same kind of constraints. That has led them to attempt to emulate you. Sam is selecting the robots that can be restored by exchanging parts from the incapacitated ones. Charlie is working on turning the functioning but immobile ones into a processing network. They also realize that another year without help and they would all be out of commission like the crew on *Wanderer* and facing a fiery end on Lavaworld."

"Which means the station lacks the take-charge intelligence that *Wanderer* possesses." Gaopod shook his head several times.

"Strange lot these Secunds," Amundsen said. "They've been around for many more millennia, yet the Beings' accomplishments are far more significant."

In the middle of the collection of the shutdown robots, Tyson announced, "Octinog has corralled a boulder and is speeding toward the probe." Robots and Biots returned to the Operations Center to watch Octinog's sortie.

The Center's imagers showed a long range view of the probe taken by a station recorder. Even though the shuttle was flying directly at it, the probe did not change course.

"Releasing projectile," Octinog reported. As soon as the boulder soared away, the shuttle reversed its engines to brake its speed. The long range imager showed the rock sailing toward the probe until it exploded in a billowing cloud of dust and debris. While the shock wave from the explosion swatted the shuttle off course, it continued to transmit readings and visuals.

"The shuttle held together; another example of good work by Biots," Fleming shouted as the others cheered. The conversation among the robots flowed far too quickly for Tyson to translate.

"Octinog did a lot of calculating with the Tyson in the shuttle to make the tactic work the first time," Amundsen said. "I'd expected it would take several attempts."

"Hton and my flyer buddies will be much impressed," Genghis said. "That was no probe. It was a combination spy satellite and weapon. It reminds me of the mines that navies on Earth used to dump in the oceans to sink their enemy's ships. The fact that Charlie didn't recognize it would suggest it's neither Secund nor Dublo in origin. It's more evidence that *Wanderer* took the right action in staying silent."

Octinog's voice boomed over the communicators. "Actually the rock would have passed behind the probe. It must've possessed a proximity trigger and the rock was close enough to set it off. It packed quite a wallop; the explosion flung the shuttle far off course and damaged its controls. It flies erratically and I doubt I'll be able to safely dock on *Wanderer*. I'll have to wait for a Galaxyship to pull me onboard with a tractor beam to repair the craft."

"Can you manage orbits of Lavaworld?" Gaopod asked.

"They'll be strange looking loops."

"Good enough. I would like to employ the shuttle's sensors to record any sounds from the planet. We're trying to solve a mystery."

"It'll give me something to do."

"I'll send you a file shortly on the suspected presence of chatty silicon creatures under the planet's crust."

Genghis still thought of Octinog as the apprehensive next-gen on Transport 27 looking for confirmation of his space find. What he and his next-gen comrades had accomplished during the last few months was truly remarkable.

"The proximity trigger makes the mine an even more dangerous weapon," Fleming said. "The explosion was strong enough to damage a Galaxyship. Maybe this is the fate that befell the Secund supply ships. We have to alert the Fleet about this danger. Tyson, did the mine send a signal before it detonated?"

"Checking although the shock waves created by the explosion will make it hard to detect."

"If it did, hopefully it sent only a visual of the rock and no significance will be attached to it. There's nothing much about this solar system that warrants attention. Still, let's prepare as if more mines are on their way."

Charlie was talking again and Genghis waited for Tyson to finish interpreting. "It says the robots have heard of weapons that drift through space until they detect an enemy ship or installation to attack. The robots have never encountered one before and it never occurred to consider the probe as a threat."

"We could attempt to put the station on standby if we have to," Amundsen said. "Then it should barely register against the continual noise the planet below generates."

While Genghis wanted to know who would have created the mines, he had to focus on the immediate problems. "For now we're safe and help is on the way. Let's collect the rest of the robots to keep our new pals busy while we fix the solar panels."

Gaopod lubricated the lift's pulley system, which made it operate smoothly and far quieter. After moving the robots scattered about on levels above the Operations Center, the Biots collected the ones from the lower levels.

The slowest aspect of the robot roundup was the time it took for the elevator to carry two trolleys to the Operations Center level. There the robots pulled them off and sent two empty ones back. While they waited, the Biots explored the lower levels.

"The equipment on each level appears different," Fleming said. "Without anyone to explain their functions, it's guesswork to determine what their purpose is."

The shutdown ones filled the larger chamber beside the Operations Center while the semi-functional units had space to spare in a smaller adjacent one. The latter were laid on the floor and plugged into a power source. As soon it could be arranged, Sam would receive a new hip component from a shutdown robot. Gaopod would work with the robots to learn how to swap the parts.

Once the roundup was complete, Genghis went to *Wanderer* to recharge and report to Navigation Central. When he returned to the station, the Biots suited up for a spacewalk to reconnect and replace broken cables that fed electricity from the solar panels to the station's power storage reservoir.

The repair job was slow, tedious work. "Is there anything about this station that's well designed," Gaopod said. "Fixing the cables would be cumbersome work for the robots even if they had space suits. It's hard enough for us."

A couple of hours into the spacewalk, Tyson reported the station was receiving nearly a full charge of power from the solar panels. "The storage reservoir has risen to one-tenth of maximum capacity already. The station should be back at full power within 35 hours."

"That will enable it to resume full monitoring of the planet if any robots are capable of showing us how their equipment works," Amundsen said. "Perhaps Gaopod can link the processing network of immobile robots Charlie's creating into the monitoring equipment."

When the Biots climbed back into the station, Fleming said, "What a difference it makes in here with sufficient electricity to run the lights at full power. More maintenance was done in the last few hours than in years."

"We Biots weren't much different than the robots until Hton envisaged a new future for us," Genghis said. Once again, he wondered why the Biots were given organic brains instead of electronic processors like the robots. Someday he would ask Humbaw.

In the presence of the robots, Genghis said the Biots would return to *Wanderer* to check for messages from Navigation Central. While there were nothing new from it, *Aurreol's* startled them when it reported it was just several days away.

"It must be traveling at more than Galaxyspeed 8 to have traveled this far so quickly," Fleming said.

While he was relieved that help was so close, Genghis wanted to keep the Biots focused on their tasks. "What I really want to see is Octinog's file on the new shells for the robots."

"Tyson, not a word of this to the robots," Amundsen said as he beckoned Genghis to stand beside him.

On the imager were side by side displays of a Biot and a robot. Amundsen advanced it to reveal schematic drawings of both. The next few pages showed different plans for transferring the essential components of a robot into a new body based on the internal design of a Biot. The plan proposed using an original Biot style electricity storage sack.

Octinog had drawn a circle around a box and added a note. "Need to develop an interface to convert the processor's electronic commands for speech and motion into signals our activators could respond to."

Genghis smiled. Would the robots even appreciate that Octinog's design could give them a whole new lease on life? Or maybe a life? He went through Octinog's plan again. "The robots would look much like their old selves except no trunk, no claws and no headlamps. Their hands would be just like ours."

Genghis took another look at the drawings. "You guys constantly surprise me."

"You rubbed off on us," Amundsen said with a grin. "You told us your theory that *Wanderer* returned to the station because it finally accomplished its goal of finding help for the robots. The four of us discussed that idea a great deal, and then looked for examples that proved it. While the ship must have concluded we could restore the robots, we doubt it realized just how much help would be coming after us. If our Galaxyship designers ever get their hands on *Wanderer*, they must try to understand that apparent cognitive ability as much as the force fields and other technical features."

"You think the information system on *Wanderer* is a form of robot the way Controlling Units and Tysons are essentially Biots?" Genghis said.

"What else!" Amundsen shrugged. "It definitely has a powerful form of artificial intelligence, which has been attempting to understand us. Perhaps a Controlling Unit could communicate with it well enough to access *Wanderer's* information system."

Genghis stared at Amundsen. "I owe *Wanderer* an apology. It's a lot smarter than I gave it credit for."

"Genghis, as we don't have any pressing tasks, we'd like to hear more about the evolution of the Biots," Gaopod said. "While Captain Kelsey wanted to ask you about it, she worried about seeming impertinent. We think her real problem is she's embarrassed by what we didn't know about original Biots."

Impertinent is the last thing Genghis would have considered Kelsey to be. He would be happy to discuss anything with her. He wondered what he could tell his companions that they did not already know.

"While they called us helpers, the Beings created us to work as their partners. They shared everything with us. There were no drudge jobs because they automated everything as much as possible.

"The one thing they didn't do was consider we might want a different role. However if there were Biots who weren't satisfied with the arrangement, none were in a position or possessed the ability to do anything about it until Hton."

The next-gens paid close attention to his account. Perhaps what they needed from him was confirmation of what they already knew.

"As Humbaw possessed great influence among the Beings, his ton carried the same authority among us. He convinced key Biots that a change in the relationship between them and the Beings would benefit both groups. After we took charge of constructing new Biots, Hton implemented changes in the preparation process to enable Biots to take initiative and show leadership. The Beings never noticed until the Nameless War. However, few Biots including me didn't either.

"These traits were re-enforced in the next gens, especially the ability to learn from the example of others. For example, Octinog decided on his own to stay with the shuttle until a ship arrives. In the past, he would've asked what he should do. I've seen in our weeks onboard *Wanderer* how much you next-gens do on your initiative compared to what most original Biots would.

"To us, we're doing what you would if you had more time," Gaopod said.

Unable to think of a response, Genghis said, "I'll send a warning to *Aurreol* and Navigation Central about the mine. I'll explain more about the condition of the station and its loss of contact with the Secunds." The message ran on for several pages before he pushed the send button.

He radioed Octinog to compliment him on the new body design for the robots.

"I'm working on the data stream from the mine to see if I can establish a way to identify them on our sensors so our ships can recognize them from a great distance and even determine from where they're dispatched and controlled," Octinog said.

Then Genghis prepared a private communication to Hton explaining the plan to create a new shell for the robots. "It would empower them to play a more active and creative role in the future. Should we discuss it first with the Secunds? I don't think modified robots would pose any more threat to the Secunds if they still exist than we do to the Beings and Terrans. But I seek your advice before we make a final decision."

By the time the Biots returned to the station, Genghis was convinced that *Aurreol* should take Charlie to search for the Secunds and the Dublos. Suspecting there were more mines and whatever controlled them, he hoped the cruiser's Commander was prepared for combat.

Chapter 16
Aurreole Time

Even after seven weeks in her new command, Kelsey remained in awe of *Aurreol's* design and capability. It was flying at Galaxyspeed Factor 14. Fleet ships ventured above Factor 8 only for short periods in emergencies.

The ship's Command Chamber had spaces for eight Biots on its benches and three imagers, which showed far more data than the ones in the Transport. Each bench position had a read out monitor that rose from the floor. At the moment, the center imager displayed a large star chart from *Wanderer* of Lavaworld's solar system.

The smaller right hand imager tracked thousands of blips and three larger dots in the outer reaches of Lavaworld's solar system. Carter, the Controlling Unit, said, "Genghis' report says a mine was destroyed in the Lavaworld system. The blips are heading toward the planet. Perhaps the dots are bigger ones or are commanding them."

Kelsey fingered her pearl necklace as she waited for comments from the other Biots in the Command Chamber before she composed a response to Genghis' warning.

At the start of the mission, she ordered all transmissions to *Wanderer* from *Aurreol* be in the ship's name. She recalled the stare that decision drew from the officers.

"Why wouldn't you want your previous crew to know you're the Commander of the ship that's coming to their rescue?" said Analytics, an original Biot.

"Ah, you want to surprise them," Weapons operator. "I understand Terrans enjoy amusing others that way. I would like to be there when you meet your old crew."

"A visual should be possible." Kelsey hoped Genghis would be pleased to see her until she wondered where that desire came from.

She pulled out of her daydream by thinking about what dangers *Aurreol* faced. While it would be on its own for up to a month before the other cruisers arrived, she could not afford to be overly cautious.

"Commander, I must point out that because we were so intent on getting here as quickly as possible we haven't tested our weapons," Carter said. "Before we enter a situation where we might have to use them, we should know what they're capable of. Many of the crew were added at the last minute without any previous experience on a Pozzen cruiser."

"Locate suitable targets and we'll find out if *Aurreol's* bite is as impressive as its speed," she said.

When it was still hundreds of thousands of kilometers from Lavaworld, *Aurreol* dropped out of Galaxyspeed and fired its laser cannons and guns at a massive collection of rocks and boulders. The exercise left behind a swirling cloud of aggregates that gave Kelsey complete confidence in the ship's ability to inflict a lot of damage.

"Carter set a course to intercept the dots. While we'll attempt to communicate with them, Weapons will prepare to fire the laser cannons at them and the laser guns at the blips if they prove to be mines. Analytics, find out what you can about their design and propulsion and if the dots in fact control them."

Feeling a need to reassure the crew about her lack of military experience, she addressed them over the communications system. "I've been examining the tactics of previous space battles and discussed various situations we might with the Analytics and Weapons personnel. While we want to rescue Genghis and the others, we won't take unnecessary risks."

As they approached Lavaworld's solar system, Carter said, "The blips are moving into two formations. One appears to be intended to block us from the dots while the other is headed for the station."

Finally the blips were close enough for *Aurreol* to acquire detailed visuals of them rolling over and over toward the Being ship. "There's no doubt they're weapons," Carter said. "The dots are two ships about the half the size of *Aurreol* and one about 10 per cent larger. One looks like a rectangular box with domes on top and underneath while the other has a triangular shape. They're in regular contact with the mines. The larger craft is further back. It too has a boxy shape and communicates with the smaller ships."

The right hand imager focused on the bigger ship. "Our protective wall has engaged to maximum in response to changes in the energy patterns of the smaller vessels, which appear to be powering their weapons," Carter said.

"Weapons, set up the laser guns so each one has a primary and secondary target among the mines," Kelsey ordered. "Once they're destroyed, the lasers are to keep selecting targets. Track the ships and be ready to fire."

"Commander, from my scans there are no organics on board the smaller ships," Carter said. "We can't determine yet whether the larger one has a crew."

"In that case, let's hit them with neutralizer beams with the laser cannons as backup if they aren't shut down," Weapons said. "If the neutralizer is effective, we'll attempt to board the ships."

Weapons reported the firing pattern for the laser guns was set. "The ships are not responding to our signals."

"The mines are close enough," Kelsey said. "Open fire."

The discharge of weapons is neither heard nor felt onboard a Galaxyship so all eyes were fixed on the left hand imager, which indicated the position of each target. It showed streaks of white lines as laser blasts headed for the mines.

A pin prick flash of light indicated the detonation of a mine. "Whatever explosive is loaded in them is quite powerful," Carter reported. "While we won't experience much buffeting from their destruction, it's remarkable that Octinog's shuttle wasn't more heavily damaged."

"This is interesting," Analytics said. "When a mine explodes, it triggers those close to it. In turn, they set off the ones near them. We're getting a cascade of explosions, which is likely the result of an energy wave rippling through the formation of mines started by the first explosions. In essence, the mines are destroying themselves much faster than our laser guns are."

As the number of mines rapidly diminished, the smaller ships both fired at *Aurreol*, which bucked slightly as its protective wall dissipated one blast. The other missed.

The boxy ship managed one more salvo before the blue light of neutralizer beams danced over its hull and it shut down. "It's like we hit every off switch on the vessel," Carter said.

The protective wall absorbed another blast from the triangular ship before the neutralizer beams silenced it.

"Both smaller ships have stopped functioning," Carter said. "We can't tell whether they're remotely controlled or operated by onboard systems."

After a brief pause, Carter added, "This is the first engagement for a Biot-operated ship. A great day for us. From helpers to space warriors."

The other Biots in the Command Chamber hooted their applause.

"After the larger ship and the other formation of mines are dealt with, we'll send boarding parties to inspect the smaller ships," Kelsey said.

"The other mines are approaching the station as if nothing happened to the rest of their attack force," Weapons said. "While the large ship hasn't changed position, there are regular communications between it and a location far from this star system."

"Set a course to intercept the mines heading for the station, and then we'll deal with the larger ship," Kelsey said. "Protecting the station is our primary task."

Aurreol surged toward the second formation of mines. As soon as it came into range, its laser guns fired at targets throughout the formation. As before, the tactic created steady bursts of explosions, which in turn triggered the detonation of more mines and that set off others. Kelsey was sure the robots and Biots on the station would feel the energy waves created by the blasts.

"The larger ship has fled," Carter said. "I'll track it."

Shuttles departed with armed Biots to reconnoiter the smaller ships.

"Commander, both smaller ships can no longer counter the pull of Lavaworld's gravity," Carter said. "They'll be drawn into the planet because their momentum is already toward it."

She returned her attention to the imagers that monitored the progress of the two boarding parties.

"The hatch opened the same way as the one on *Wanderer* did in the visual," reported the leader of the first boarding party, which entered the boxy-shaped vessel. "However there's no force field to pass through and no interior lights came on. The neutralizer beam shut down this ship completely. The interior is still warm, which is likely residual heat."

The imager showed beams of light from the Biots' head lamps bouncing about the craft's interior as the boarding party scouted the ship, laser rifles at the ready.

"There's too little illumination to learn much about the ship this way," Analytics said. "Hopefully the reports from the boarding parties will be more informative."

"This Control Room looks like a close copy of *Wanderer's* except there's no safe room or robots," the boarding party leader reported.

The other boarding party could not open the hatch of the triangular-shaped ship. "It appears that a special tool is required. About all we can do is fire a laser rifle blast into the lock and hope it causes the mechanism to release. That or have *Aurreol* blow a hole in the hatch with a laser gun."

"Try destroying the lock first."

While firing the laser rifle into the lock melted the mechanism, the hatch remained firmly shut. Meanwhile, a white stream of atmosphere poured through the hole where the lock had been.

"Commander, even a perfect shot by a laser gun will take out the hatch and much of the hull surrounding it," the boarding party leader said. "That would vent the atmosphere from the ship."

"Let it vent then. Not my first choice, but exploring it is the only way to learn anything about it."

"We'll move away in the shuttle and return when the venting stops. We'll put magnetic grips on our boots and climb into the ship once you open the hatchway for us."

Aurreol pulled alongside the ship and fired a laser gun. It took a second blast to destroy the hatch and a chunk of the hull disappeared with it.

While the righthand imager displayed the sensor reading of a gusher of material from the ship, the debris could not be seen on the imager because the hatch area was in shadow. "While the contents of the debris are unrecognizable in the sensor readings, there's nothing that would appear to be a body of any sort," Analytics reported. "Once again, the debris was warm as it exited the ship so the interior is heated at least minimally."

When the gusher dropped to a light breeze, the boarding party landed near the hole and leapt inside.

Once again the bouncing light from the Biots' lamps created an unsatisfactory rendition of the ship's interior on *Aurreol's* imagers. The magnetic grips gave the Biots sufficient traction in a weightless environment. A vigorous step propelled them upward adding to the light flashing all over the interior.

"For comparison's sake, send the boarding party from the other ship to this one," Kelsey said. "They should be able to determine whether the vessels have a common origin."

The leaders of the two boarding parties dispatched their teams in various directions while they examined two large black machines that dominated the triangular ship's Control Room. "There's nothing like them on the other ship. They're covered in indicator lights with some switches and small imager screens. This may be the ship's operating system."

"That's all we'll learn for now," Kelsey said. "Boarding parties, return to *Aurreol*. We need to bring Octinog's shuttle on board. He's been a space tourist for long enough."

Aurreol scanned the planet as it tracked him down.

"There really are few prominent features," Analytics said. "What's intriguing is how the surface constantly shifts as the lava flows. It's like the waves of a lake rippling in whichever direction the wind blows."

"We're receiving a transmission from Octinog's shuttle and are changing course to collect it," Carter said. "This will enable us to test our tractor beam."

"Bring it into a bay where I can greet my former shipmate," Kelsey said. "Repairing his shuttle will give our mechanics something to do. They've been idle ever since they finished fixing and reassembling the air filtration system."

Kelsey smiled as she headed for the shuttle bay remembering Octinog's excitement when he joined Transport 27. "Thank you for picking me for your crew," he had told her. "I really want to work in space." She did not tell him she had no say in the matter. Navigation Central had assigned him.

The hatch to the shuttle opened and Octinog lowered himself to the floor and shouted, "Thanks for the rescue. That was the quite show you put on blowing up the mines."

Then his jaw dropped. "Captain Kelsey, excuse me, Commander. Wow." He pointed at the insignia of her new rank on her arm band.

She raised her hand to cut off his questions and filled him in on the events. With the Commander and Octinog on board, a new shuttle flew into the empty bay in *Wanderer*.

Spotting Genghis and the other Biots waiting for him behind the glass wall, he asked Kelsey to stay out of sight. He dropped to the floor and waved his comrades over. "*Aurreol's* Commander wishes to speak with you before meeting the robots."

Chapter 17
Searching for Secunds

As the other Biots drew close, Kelsey dropped out of the shuttle. The smile on Genghis' face is what mattered for her.

After greetings all around, she said, "Superb job in handling the situation you were thrust into with *Wanderer* and the robots. A special thanks to Genghis for his kind words, which got me this." Pointing to the Commander's insignia on her arm band, she explained the circumstances that earned her the position.

"Commander, your rank is awesome and so was your attack on the mines and warships," Fleming said. "Genghis, you don't mind sharing some of your glory with the Commander?"

Genghis just grinned. "An all Biot crew. Hton will have followed your every move. This is the kind of opportunity he's been looking for since the end of the Nameless War to make Biots aware of how much they contribute to the Confederation."

"How about a tour of *Wanderer*," she said. "Your reports about the vessel have the Galaxyship design folks beside themselves with curiosity."

"Would you mind coming to the space station first to meet the robots," Genghis said. "Disregard the messy conditions. While we've been trying to clean it up, our new friends don't consider that important."

The group passed through the docking tube and reached the entrance to the station. "The first force field is here, Commander," Genghis said. "Do you want to try it or watch us go through? While it feels creepy the first time, you barely notice it afterward. Just push through it. Once it recognizes you, the field shapes around you to hold the air pressure behind it while letting you pass."

Kelsey nodded. "So it's a security feature as well as atmosphere stabilizer. One of you led the way and the rest can push me through if I get stuck."

Genghis took a determined step forward as the usual pressure built around him, and took another step and reached the other side. He turned to watch Kelsey arrive right behind him with a big grin followed by the other Biots.

"I've never encountered anything like that before," she said. "It must have been puzzling when you entered *Wanderer*."

Genghis nodded. "We haven't found any controls or devices that project the field or figured out how it's activated when someone approaches. The robots can't explain it either. I bet it'll feel like a solid wall the first time a Being or Terran attempts to pass through one." They laughed.

An additional walking robot and two in wheelchairs joined the other seven functioning robots lined up to greet Kelsey as she entered the station. Kelsey grasped their claws as if she regularly encountered clumsy greetings.

"In addition to us, there were now seven immobile robots whose processors are functioning." Tyson translated Charlie's comments faster than previously. "We doubt the other 24 can be even partly activated without replacement parts."

Charlie guided the Biots through the two main levels. At the end, Kelsey said, "I want a tour of *Wanderer* before I return to *Aurreol*." The robot stepped close to Kelsey and spoke slowly as if it wanted to ensure Tyson properly translated its request. "The way you destroyed the war machines means you can safely reach the Secund Federation. He wants to travel with you to convince the Secunds to listen to what you have to say."

Genghis quickly supported the request. "Charlie will ease the process of meeting Secunds."

Admiral Gnoorvants made it clear that the High Council was interested in much more than *Wanderer* and this remote research station. It would want to know what the Secunds were, what happened to them and why they were so intent on communicating with Lavaworld's creatures. In addition, it would be equally interested in the Dublos, the origin of the mines and ships and what threat the Confederation faced.

Aurreol lacked the capacity to conduct the extensive in-depth scientific study of Lavaworld that *Transformation* would be able to accomplish when it arrived. "Tyson, tell Charlie to report to the shuttle bay on *Wanderer* within the hour," she said. "Figure out how to recharge it while traveling on our ship. The robots on the station shall follow the instructions of the Biots. Amundsen will be in charge while Fleming will be in command of *Wanderer* on its trip to Hnassumblaw.

"Genghis will accompany us as well. I would like to hear more about his theory about the intelligence operating *Wanderer*," she said. "I'll tell the Admiral about your conclusion and request that the ship designers respect it. Fleming, you'll reinforce that message when you deliver the vessel to Navigation Central.

"Any progress you make on learning about what's swimming around under Lavaworld's surface will help *Transformation* when it arrives. We'll leave a shuttle with more powerful lasers to destroy any further mines."

"Commander, a couple of matters," Gaopod said. "The robots have decided that switching to the new body shells will be to their advantage. When *Transformation* arrives, could we test the conversion on some shutdown ones? Do we have your authority to proceed with the preparations?"

She smiled at Octinog. "Is this what you worked on while waiting for a rescue?"

"He's been working on it since the discovery of the robots on *Wanderer*," Fleming said.

"Then do proceed. I'll inform *Transformation* and Navigation Central."

She was sure Genghis would relay the plan to Hton. *This sounds like the type of innovative thinking he wants to see in us.* "What was the second matter?"

"We would like to tow the undamaged ship to the station to restore it to operating condition," Gaopod said. "The robots say it's a Secund craft and they can assist us with it. The station has the power now to keep itself, Wanderer and the other Secund vessel in orbit. The robots are certain the triangular shaped craft is a Dublo ship. We can't repair it. We want to send it into a controlled crash landing on Lavaworld.

"It could help us determine the meaning of their various sounds if the creatures respond to its disintegration in the lava. It could be the best opportunity to make progress in deciphering their communications because they'll be responding to an external event. If we leave the ship to be pulled by gravity into the planet, it'll come down in fragments that'll be buried in the lava."

"That sounds like two matters and you have my authority to conduct both."

If the four Biots were disappointed before about being left behind, they certainly were no longer.

"Carter, inform the Fleet and Navigation Central that we'll be heading for the closest Secund planet as soon as possible with Genghis and Charlie on board. Advise them of our course once we've determined it."

Kelsey surveyed the group. "While towing *Wanderer* with Transport 27 would have been a good way to deliver it to the Confederation, your experience in learning how it operates is much better. The Admiral told me that bringing the ship back to the Confederation is a priority of this mission. Now I want to see *Wanderer* and hear more about your plans for giving the robots new shells."

As the Biots walked through the station to the ship, Octinog explained his plan for transferring the robots' processors into a Biot-like shell. "I've finished the schematic drawings for the new shells and they need to be reviewed by experts. I've sent all the information to *Transformation* and await a response on whether it's feasible.

"There's much about the robots' functions that we don't understand yet. While they want the new shell to resemble their current one as much as possible, they agree that switching to a more functional body is much wiser than continuing to repair their outmoded design. Two proper hands would eliminate the need for a trunk and they want their arms connected at the sides of the shoulders like us."

Kelsey stared at him for a moment. "Have you considered the implications of upgrading these robots for the species that developed them?"

"I've posed the issue to Hton and Humbaw and await their reaction," Genghis said. "We may have been too hasty in our plans but having spent time with the robots, we find many parallels between them and us. Well, we were much better treated by the Beings. Their basic motivations are much like ours.

"If we do nothing for them, they'll eventually all break down. If we restore them to their original status, they'll be frustrated by their inadequacies compared to what we can do. The robots deserve better than the servitude they're trapped in. Even if these are the only robots left, it troubles us to leave them in such a miserable condition."

Genghis led the tour of *Wanderer* showing Kelsey the containers and lockers in the Storage Room. As they headed to the Control Room, the conversation returned to the challenges facing the mission starting with speeding up the translation of Secundese. "While it has improved a lot, Tyson has yet to learn enough of the language to come anywhere close to simultaneous translation."

"Translators were left behind when the Beings and Terrans were removed from *Aurreol*," Kelsey said. "In our haste to depart, they were placed in storage. We'll leave some with you. On our way to the Secund system, Carter and Charlie can work on a dictionary covering the two languages to program the Tysons."

"Until they do, we'll need a Tyson to act as our interpreter for Charlie," Genghis said. "Otherwise we can't communicate with him. Let's take the primary Tyson from the first shuttle and replace it with a reserve processor. The other Tysons will bring the new one up to date."

"Carter, send two mechanics here to swap out the Tyson from the first shuttle," she said. "Amundsen, when you return to the station, transfer visuals of its star charts to our navigation data base. Now let's finish the tour of this ship although thanks to your reports, I feel like I've already seen it."

As they entered the Control Room, Amundsen said, "Commander, the space station would be a lot better if we could give it a more protective exterior like what our Galaxyships have and make internal modifications."

"I'll pass on your suggestion to *Transformation's* Commander and leave it to you to present the details to him. Your Tyson has transmitted data on this ship and the space station to Carter since we arrived. It'll pass on all that data to *Transformation*."

"Do we need a cruiser to protect *Transformation*?" Kelsey asked. "It couldn't defend itself against ships like the ones we incapacitated."

"Is *Alliance* in the Fleet?" Genghis said. Kelsey nodded. "The robots would understand the significance of the Being ship that made the first contact with Earth."

Chapter 18
Fireworks in Space

Kelsey instructed Carter to select a team of mechanics from *Aurreol* to work on upgrading the station.

"Another task for them could be turning *Wanderer* and the Secund ship into solar power collectors for the station," Carter said. "The tubes linking the ships to the station are rigid enough to support electricity transmission cables. Once the Secund vessel is operational again, both ships could be used in Lavaworld research."

"Any more good ideas, Carter?" Amundsen said.

"From observations and discussions with *Wanderer's* Tyson, the robots' programming allowed them to learn only from instructions of the Secunds. After watching the Biots closely, they're attempting to make their tools and equipment more functional."

"Carter, are you saying the exposure to the Biots has led the robots to change their programing," Kelsey said.

"It would appear that way. It appears the Biots inspired the robots. The processing network that Sam created appears to implement the programing changes in them. I'm paying extra attention to what they're doing because it would be quite a breakthrough for them. Tyson reports the robots have used the station's information system far more since *Wanderer* returned than previously. They investigated many subjects. It's like they're discovering how much they don't know. I'll leave it to Darwin, my counterpart on *Transformation,* to investigate that possibility further."

As Octinog and Fleming explained the Control Room to Kelsey, Genghis added more details to his next message to Hton, Humbaw and Hector Davis. He was so engrossed in composing it that he missed the display of a star chart that Carter projected onto the main imager.

Genghis looked up when Carter said, "I'm extrapolating from the information the Tysons provided. This is an overview of this sector of the Milky Way. Other than looking for suitable planets for expansion, the Secunds and Dublos explored very little of it. The glowing area near the bottom right hand corner indicates our current location. The area shaded in purple is the Secund sphere while the smaller yellow one is the Dublo region. For reference, the Confederation-Terran region is 27 per cent greater than the combined Secund and Dublo systems."

The next display presented a more detailed view of the Secund sphere. "They have settlements on seven planets while the Dublos have them on five. While there are no overlaps in territorial claims, the two civilizations have been at odds for centuries.

"The highlighted sphere is the closest Secund world. It's called Planet 4. The Secund don't name their planets. The station has little information on the Secunds and Dublos and the robots are unable to explain the differences between the two species.

"The number of mines we encountered out here suggest a lot more will be stationed closer to the Secund and Dublo worlds and probably in between them as well," Carter said. "We'll launch probes into the two systems to obtain better data on the type of weapons we might face."

Before Genghis could return to working on his message, Analytics reported that three shuttles from *Aurreol* were moving the Dublo ship to its fiery demise on Lavaworld. "Once that tow is closer to the planet, other shuttles will shift the Secund ship to the station."

"We'll return to *Aurreol* to prepare for departure so we can leave after the shuttles have returned," Kelsey said.

When the Tyson swap was completed on *Wanderer*, a shuttle took Kelsey, Genghis and Charlie to *Aurreol* and returned to the station with a final load of equipment. It docked just before three shuttles brought the Secund ship alongside the station. As only one shuttle was required to nudge it into coupling with a boarding tube, the other two headed back to *Aurreol*.

During the trip to *Aurreol*, Genghis returned to finishing the message to Hton and then joined the others in watching the crash landing of the Dublo vessel on Lavaworld. One shuttle pulled the doomed ship with a tractor beam while the other two pushed it. The shuttles approached Lavaworld on a gradual angle aiming to create an entry into its atmosphere that would set the stage for a gradual descent culminating with the ship's belly flop in the name of science.

The shuttles eased their way into Lavaworld's atmosphere before releasing their ship. They flew considerably above its glide path around Lavaworld transmitting visuals of its steady descent toward the surface.

"We can't risk approaching any closer," the lead shuttle reported. "The turbulence in the atmosphere generated by the heat radiating from the planet makes it hard to control our craft. It's causing the Dublo ship to shake violently and it could break up before it reaches the surface."

A zone of turbulence flipped the ship end over end leaving it upside down and flying backward. Then it dipped into the lava shooting an angry red spray to either side. It bounced several more times, kicking up waves of lava, which bubbled furiously and occasionally spat large blobs onto the ship. By the time it stopped moving, the ship was about one third submerged but still mostly intact.

"Not right where we wanted it to land, but close enough." Gaopod watched the event with the other Biots in the Control Room of *Wanderer*. "This way we'll see how curious the creatures are."

Kelsey and Genghis watched him on the imager as he put on ear phones that fed him the sounds from the planet. Before long he was nodding. "The landing definitely captured their attention." He pressed the ear phones to his receivers. His next words came in an excited shout. "By all the chatter, there's a large migration of the creatures to the impact site. Thank you for agreeing to this project Commander Kelsey and to *Aurreol's* crew in helping us to determine the descent for the ship."

"In return, we expect a breakthrough in determining what's down there and finding a way to communicate with them," Kelsey said.

"Good luck with the rest of the mission, Commander. While far away, we'll be cheering for you."

Kelsey went through a full review of *Aurreol's* status as the ship set out for Planet 4. When she felt assured it was ready as possible for all the unknowns in this region of the Milky Way, she called a briefing with her senior officers.

"Commander, the long range scans have detected more mines heading our way," Carter said. "It appears the vessel that fled earlier is accompanying them."

"We can't leave the station unprotected," Kelsey said. "We'll deal with them on our way to Planet 4."

"The mines are coming in three formations," Analytics said. "The first is 56 hours away at top sub Galaxyspeed, which will place us well away from the station and give us time to study the formations.

"So far, they're positioned much closer together than the mines we encountered on our approach to Lavaworld. If we could detonate the center ones, we should be able to create cascading explosions like we triggered before. It would be quite a show."

"If we're a safe distance away," Kelsey said with a grin. "How would you trigger it?"

"The laser cannons would all fire at the middle of the formation. On widespread blasts, that'll detonate up to 20 per cent of them. Hopefully as the shock wave from those and subsequent explosions expands outward, it'll trigger the rest of them."

"Set a course for the first formation and inform Weapons what we'll face and when," Kelsey said.

Analytics then noted the longrange probes detected mines and starships in the vicinity of the Secund and Dublos worlds. "At the same time, they found no communications activity on any planet."

"Commander, my team has modified the neutralizer to operate as a disrupter," Weapons said. "Rather than shutting down the electronic functions in a target vessel, a disrupter beam would accelerate them into overdrive that would shake the ship apart. Not unlike how Lavaworld's turbulence rattled the Dublo ship before it impacted."

"You want to test it on a mine formation?" Kelsey said.

"The laser cannons and guns will be programed to destroy the mines if our test fails," Weapons said. "If it works, the neutralizers on our Galaxyships could be modified to also possess a disrupter mode. Think of the punch that would give them in overcoming protective walls around space ships. It works in theory and simulations, but we need a field test. Firing at rocks or space debris would prove nothing since they don't have electronic systems to disrupt."

"The first formation is the largest," Kelsey said. "Let's fire the laser cannons at its center and see if it creates a ripple effect destruction of the mines. We'll fire disrupter blasts at the second formation with the laser guns and cannons as backup. We'll decide how to attack the third formation after we see the results of the first two."

"A communication from Admiral Gnoorvants has arrived," Carter said.

"Play it for the Command Chamber."

The familiar husky voice filled the room. "The Fleet will rendezvous at Planet 4 from current missions as soon as possible. Navigation Central says their routes will provide detailed information about a swath of the Galaxy we have little data on. The first to arrive will be *Dreadnought* more than a week after *Aurreol* reaches Planet 4. The rest of the Fleet will take longer."

The Command Chamber crew was digesting this news when Charlie appeared. Kelsey beckoned him to sit on the benches.

Carter could now provide simultaneous translation of Secundese. "The box Charlie is showing you is a transformer that he can plug into a Biot recharging cable to receive the voltage he needs. The Science section developed it. He carries it with him so he doesn't lose it. He's studied Octinog's plan for transferring robots into new shells in more detail and has some questions about the process."

"I would like to know more as well," Kelsey said. "Science, can you provide us with a full briefing on the plan? We'll shift to the Conference Room to view the details on its imagers."

"A presentation will be ready by the time you arrive there," Science said.

When Kelsey, Genghis and Charlie stepped into the Conference Room, the main imager displayed visuals of an original Biot and a robot side by side. Then it stripped away the exterior shells to reveal their interior structure and designs.

A third body appeared. "This is Octinog's rendition of a new frame and shell for the robots," Science said. "Replacing the robots' metallic skeleton, limb motors and large battery with the components of a Biot's frame and connecting material will make the robots much lighter."

"Octinog is doing a lot more than giving them a new shell," Genghis said. "He's developed a new body; about the only thing they'll keep is their processor. I should've realized this sooner."

"Originally he planned just to change their exterior and replace the hands," Science said. "However to implement those modifications required numerous internal alterations. Before long it became simpler to create a new body than adapt the existing robot structure.

"The new body has plenty of room for an electricity storage cell comparable to ours. Because of its size, we can't fit a thermoelectric generator into it so it must recharge every other day like an original Biot. The robot's circuitry will be greatly reduced through the use of the conducting material that covers our frames and runs throughout our bodies."

"It does make more sense to say we're giving them a new body, not just a new shell," Kelsey said. "That probably won't be the end of the modifications to the robots."

The display concluded with the final version of Octinog's plan. "This all has to be reviewed by the experts on *Transformation* to determine whether it's feasible," Science said. "This kind of work triggers a lot of brainstorming and tweaking, which often produces an even better final product. Or proves it won't work."

"As far as the robots know, the Secunds never considered improving the robots' functioning or enabling them to perform their tasks better and take on more complex ones," Carter said. "Perhaps they were afraid to."

Genghis stared at the imager to collect his thoughts. In addition to the accomplishments of his four companions from *Wanderer, Aurreol's* Biots calculated everything from crash landing the derelict ship to different ways to destroy the mines. As well, Kelsey was a Galaxyship Commander and from what he had seen so far, her leadership was superb.

Just as important, the Biots had witnessed the dreary situation of the robots. The Secunds hobbled their helpers while the Beings empowered theirs.

The more Genghis pondered their achievements, the more excited he became. Perhaps emotions were not to be feared. When he focused again on the briefing, Kelsey was watching him and touching her pearl necklace. He smiled and she returned it.

"We've come a long way," he said.

"We still have lots to do," she said.

The next day *Aurreol* dropped out of Galaxyspeed to deal with the first formation of mines. "There are 967 of them still in a tight formation," Analytics reported.

"Weapons, it's your show," Kelsey said.

The main imager showed an outline of the ship and flashes when the forward laser cannons fired at the mines. A wide spread laser blast appeared on the imager screen as a streak. The imager switched to the formation of mines. Within seconds, the center of the formation exploded in a flash of light that dissipated quickly. As the shock wave from that blast radiated outward, the next layer of mines detonated, then the next. Their spacing meant a steady series of explosions, ring after ring. While the light faded from the center of the formation, the outer mines exploded in fiery bursts that quickly vanished.

When the light show ended, Kelsey said. "Hopefully the visuals will look as good as witnessing it from here. The communications networks should have fun with them."

"Terrans love fireworks," Genghis said. "Imagine what that would have looked and sounded like in an oxygen atmosphere compared to the vacuum of space."

Aurreol reached the next formation late the following next day. "It'll take several discharges of the laser cannons in disrupter mode to hit them all," Weapons told the crowded Command Chamber. "It'll start on the starboard side and move across. There's not likely much technology in the mines so we're not sure what'll happen."

The imager displayed the section of the formation target in the disruptor salvo. "The mines vibrate after being impacted by the beam," Analytics said. "In some, the vibrations cause the mines to disintegrate while others fall behind or careen into close-by mines setting off explosions."

The second section of the formation was struck. "No color spreads over the target like with the neutralizer beam." On the left hand imager, Analytics isolated a mine drifting off course into another one. "Look at this. Instead of exploding on impact, they shattered into fragments. A following mine collided with them adding to the cloud of debris. It appears the disrupter beam deactivates the proximity trigger."

The weapon fired a third time. "One more round should do it," Weapons said.

"Do we need to fire the laser guns?" Kelsey said.

"Not yet."

The Chamber fell silent except for the occasional beep from the imager as it panned what remained of the formation.

"Now the ones in the first two sections are readily disintegrating," Kelsey said. "It's like they're dissolving into thousands of fragments."

Genghis smiled at the excitement in her voice.

"Fourth round fired."

"It's puzzling the mines didn't adjust or react to our attack," Genghis said. "If they stick to their programing until they receive different instructions, then why wouldn't their controllers have changed tactics by now?"

When *Aurreol* encountered the third formation eight hours later, the mines were deployed farther apart. The ship shepherding them once again fled. "It's heading back to the Secund and Dublos systems," Analytics said. "Maybe it thinks more mines are needed."

The formation of mines spread out farther and Weapons and Analytics conferred frequently.

"It's like they want to encircle us, which doesn't make sense because we can fire our weapons in any direction," Genghis said.

"Commander, the mines are gathered in clusters and smaller groups," Weapons said. "We could fly into the heart of the formation and fire the cannons at the large clusters, the disrupters at the smaller groups and the laser guns at the individual mines. We can program the weapons to fire almost at the same time. The ship's protective wall will protect us if needed."

"Proceed," Kelsey said. The ship moved deeper into the formation. The countdown to firing started at 30 seconds.

The cannon blasts created wave after wave of explosions. The impact of the disrupter beams was barely noticeable by comparison. The barrage of the laser guns created continuous puffs of color. Debris from explosions rolled up against *Aurreol's* defensive wall where it was vaporized. "A clean sweep," Weapons said, raising her arms in the air.

When Genghis leaned back on the bench, his hands finally relaxed their tight grip. "A cruiser operated by Biots just kicked butt."

The Biots on the Command Benches looked at him but said nothing. *They have become too used to my old Terran phrases.*

"Carter, once we're clear of the debris field, head for Secund Planet 4 at optimal Galaxyspeed," Kelsey said. She leaned toward Genghis, stopping just short of touching him.

"Hopefully somewhere something is trying to figure out what happened to its weapons."

"Our success seems all too easy. It's like the controllers of the mines and the attack ships have had their way for so long they've become complacent. They've lost the ability to adapt to a new opponent."

"Could it be they have never faced a real adversary?" she said.

Genghis glanced at her before responding. It was like she was reading his thoughts about the enemy's tactics. "Admiral Gnoorvants said that about the Rulers. While they'd developed good technology, they only used it to frustrate the Beings. They weren't prepared for an opponent that fought back like the Terrans did. Whatever we're up against may not be any better."

He sat on the Command Bench pondering Kelsey's observation as *Aurreol* cleared the debris field and transitioned to Galaxyspeed. The Commander's comments about the enemy's lack of preparation pushed his ideas a couple of steps further.

Chapter 19
A Tattered Civilization

It took six days for *Aurreol* to reach Planet 4. The ship's sensors detected three large continents that occupied about half the surface and projected a brown sheen into space.

"The rest of it appears to be water," Carter said. "The Beings would like the heat. While the major centers are heavily damaged, there's no nuclear radiation. The sensors have located scattered groups on the outskirts of the cities."

"There are five mines orbiting the planet," Analytics said. "They're in stable orbits and probably are sentinels. They're spaced far enough apart not to pose any immediate threat to us."

Sitting in her spot on the Command Bench, Kelsey said, "Carter, destroy them if they target us or the planet. Otherwise, we'll leave them be. If we eliminate them now, it'll just attract attention from their controllers. Maybe they haven't noticed our presence."

Without looking at Charlie sitting on the bench behind her, she said, "Attempt to communicate with the planet."

After testing different frequencies, the robot spoke into his communicator, which had been given a grip his claw could hold. "He's certain that whomever he's talking to accepts he's a Secund robot," Carter said. "They've agreed to meet him although I don't think there's much they could do to stop us from coming to the surface."

A shuttle carrying Charlie, Genghis and Tyson touched down on a flat surface that looked remarkably like a paved parking lot except there were no buildings near it.

Charlie disembarked to scout around the landing site. After a half hour, Tyson said, "While it was a long time ago, Charlie spent part of a year here. Conditions on the surface are far worse than they appear from orbit. This was a major food producing planet and home to billions of Secunds. There's a city 1.3 kilometers away. Even from a distance, the signs of great destruction are everywhere. Few buildings are undamaged. Charlie would like you to accompany him to Orphum."

Carrying the Tyson unit in a backpack, Genghis climbed out of the craft. Once again, he wished for a sense of smell. The mid-morning sun glared down and Genghis expected the planet might be uncomfortably hot even for Beings during the middle of the day.

The ground beyond the paved area was covered in short pale green vegetation that looked almost like a carpet. Shrubs and bushes grew in many spots. Nothing looked wrong until the robot pointed to the city. The extent of damaged and collapsed buildings looked far worse than anything Genghis had seen during the combat on Pozzen. He could not guess what the city might have looked like before. The ruins were out of range for his chest recorder, which was providing a live feed of the exploration of Planet 4 to *Aurreol*.

They walked several hundred meters toward the city when a Secund stepped out from behind a stone wall. It looked much like a robot except it was taller, lacked a trunk and had hands with three fingers and a thumb. It wore a full length robe of washed out shades of brown.

While its tone sounded grumpy as it spoke to Charlie, Genghis was more intrigued by its stooped posture that put its shoulders well ahead of its waist. It rocked from side to side struggling to maintain its balance. While it appeared reptilian rather than hominid, it lacked the facial flecks of color that most Beings did.

Like Beings, it had bulging eyes, flared nostrils, a small mouth and skin flaps to protect the ears. Its head was narrow culminating in a pronounced jaw, quite unlike the round heads of the robots. The best Genghis could come up with for a skin color was dull yellow.

"If this is a typical Secund, how did they build Galaxyships and the space station?" Kelsey's question buzzed in Genghis's ear piece. "They seem far too clumsy for the kind of precision work that space technology requires. Their shape makes me wonder even more why they made it nearly impossible for their robots to handle that or many other kinds of jobs. If the Beings had done that with us, they'd still be stuck on Hnassumblaw."

The Secund alternated between asking Charlie questions and glancing behind the wall. Genghis suspected others, probably armed, were hiding there. Their caution seemed understandable. While the Secund did not react as if it suspected Genghis was a Dublos, hopefully its lack of curiosity about a newcomer was not normal.

"Charlie is explaining about the space station and you bringing them here to find out about what happened to the Secund worlds," Tyson said.

The agitated Secund was shifting its weight between its legs. Finally it acknowledged Genghis with a short stare. Charlie continued to explain what happened to the station, *Wanderer's* disappearance and return, and then the arrival of *Aurreol*. While Charlie spoke, the Secund looked about as if none of what the robot said mattered.

Genghis remembered the first time he questioned a Being. She listened closely and fully answered his questions. Then she posed some. That surprised Genghis until it was clear the Being was assuring herself that the helper understood both what it had been told and what it was doing. That session had taught Genghis to always ask about anything he was uncertain of.

"The Secund's main concern is that you and Charlie pose no danger," Tyson said. "Perhaps its behaviour explains a lot about the conduct of the robots."

Several Secunds appeared from behind the wall with barely a glance at Genghis and pointed to an approaching group.

"The Secund didn't question me even though it has never seen a Biot or a space shuttle before," Genghis said. Tyson relayed the comment to Charlie.

The robot hesitated before responding. "Charlie says the damage to the buildings is nothing compared to what has happened to the Secunds. In the past they would have been curious about how you came to their world. Now all that matters is you aren't a Dublo. Their reaction to you would have been hostile without Charlie here.

"A prime duty of all robots is to protect Secunds and not allow anyone or anything into their presence that could pose a threat. The Secunds accepted you because the robot had and it did because of *Wanderer*. What you've done since arriving at the station confirms the wisdom of *Wanderer's* selection of the Biots to help the robots."

Genghis felt satisfied with his earlier reasoning about the system on *Wanderer* deciding the Biots could help the robots on the station.

Charlie pointed to a group of Secunds and robots heading their way. "They're from the city and the robots are fully functional by their fluid movement."

The newly-arrived robots gathered around Charlie. Genghis pressed his communicator to his audio receptor to make sure he caught Tyson's translation of their conversation. The Secunds talked among themselves rather than listen to the robots' discussion.

"These robots have access to replacement parts and Secunds that can repair them," Tyson said. "From what the newcomers say, there are many out of commission units on Planet 4. The new robots are puzzled you named Charlie rather than call him by his identifier.

"The Secunds want you to follow them to a shaded area to meet their Elder. The robots will walk behind you. The normal way here is for robots to walk behind their masters. You're to be in front of the robots because you're an outsider."

"Does that mean they know I'm a type of robot?"

"While they haven't mentioned anything about it, they're speaking about you as if you're one."

Genghis had to slow his pace to keep from bumping into the Secunds whose gait was much like the waddle of a Terran duck. Fields reached as far as he could see on either of the path. The cultivated ones were too far away to even guess what type of crop was growing. In some, herds of four-legged creatures grazed. Nowhere did he spot the craters and blackened forests he expected to litter the countryside. Perhaps only the cities were attacked.

The robots talked with Charlie nonstop. In this situation, the Biots would use their sign language.

As they neared the shaded spot where more Secunds gathered, Genghis spotted a robot pushing a Secund in a wheelchair toward the site. If they possessed wheelchairs, why were the robots on the station unaware of the device? Maybe the wheelchair was a new innovation on this planet. It looked like a combination of several different devices. Another puzzle.

The Secunds and robots inclined their heads toward the newcomer. Its skin was much paler and covered in wrinkles. It had difficulty holding up its head, which rendered its comments hard for Tyson to hear well enough to translate.

"This is one of the few Elders left on Planet 4," Tyson said. "I can't tell what all that entails or even what gender it is. I've not heard its name; the Secunds refer to it simply as Elder. It's apologizing for not standing to greet you, but its hips are too weak. It asks what species you are and where you're from. I explained that and what happened to us and asked Charlie to describe the situation on the station."

The Elder's curiosity came out in endless questions that were what Genghis expected from an intelligent species, not the sullen suspicion and disinterest he encountered from the Secunds.

He surmised the Secunds were unable to give the Elder replacement hips so it could walk. *Transformation* would certainly possess the technology to perform that kind of surgery. Looking around, he spotted a robot holding what might be a visual recorder. He faced it so his chest recorder showed *Aurreol* the scene.

The Secunds sat on benches under a ring of cousins to Terran palm trees, talking among themselves and ignoring the Elder's conversation with Genghis.

Genghis pointed toward an empty bench and the attendant pushed the Elder's chair beside it. The shade provided welcome relief from the sun. "From the chatter among the Secunds, it would appear the Elder is a female," Tyson said.

Once he was seated near the Elder, Genghis asked *Aurreol* to confirm it could see the images from his recorder and follow Tyson's translation.

"We're just as puzzled as you are," Kelsey said. "Charlie's comment about how *Wanderer* accepted the boarding party of Biots so the robots did as well intrigued us. It implies the intelligence in *Wanderer* has some of the intuitive ability of a Controlling Unit, then why can't Tyson or Carter communicate with it?"

He could imagine Kelsey shaking her head in bewilderment.

The Elder delivered a rambling account of the devastation inflicted on Planet 4 by attack ships and mines close to a half century ago. "They targeted populated areas, power generation and communications facilities," Tyson explained. "The Secunds shut down the remaining ones and created false signals to trick the mines into crashing into empty areas. They seemed incapable of distinguishing between real and fake targets.

"However, the Secunds were left with no vessels able to leave the planet and no facilities to build new ones. When the mine bombardment ended, they risked sending radio messages to their other worlds, but they weren't answered."

When Genghis described the ships *Aurreol* encountered, the Elder sat back in its chair to peer at Genghis. "It doesn't understand how these vessels could be working together and why we didn't find any crew on them. The boxy ships are Secund while the triangular one is a Dublo craft. While the Secund ships would have both Secunds and robots on board, the Dublo ship wouldn't have robots because the Dublos don't trust them."

Genghis hoped the Command Chamber on *Aurreol* heard the comments about the ships. Another puzzle to figure out.

The Elder questioned Charlie at length. He recounted the condition of the space station and the dispatch of *Wanderer* to find help. The robot deferred to Genghis for an explanation of *Wanderer's* discovery.

At one point, Kelsey muttered, "Without the resources of the old civilization, the planet has regressed to the level of the Secunds you first encountered."

Speaking to the Elder and the others, Genghis said, "Our visuals would explain much about what occurred on *Wanderer* and the space station. I'm returning to the shuttle to collect an imager. Ask the Elder to wait for my return."

A robot stood in front of Genghis. "It has offered to assist you," Tyson said. "It did that after speaking to the attendant."

Intrigued by a robot showing initiative, Genghis readily agreed. Charlie occasionally anticipated what the Biots might want, but nothing more.

Once they were out of earshot, the robot pointed at Genghis. "It says the robots here need your help just like the ones on the station," Tyson explained. "While most Secunds tolerate the Elder, they resent her efforts to revive the spirit of the old days. She has followers that work with the robots in the city to gather up the old devices and hide them from the others. They've preserved a great deal. Realizing the robots could do the physical work collecting and hiding the technology, the Secunds undertook to learn how to repair them."

To Genghis' surprise, the robot paused to enable Tyson to catch up with its comments. Usually robots talked on oblivious to the need to translate.

"Most Secunds attach little if any importance to the robots' well-being and believe that using the old technologies will bring more attacks from above. They think the Secunds were punished for placing too much importance on machines."

"Who is supposed to have inflicted the punishment?"

The robot walked a few paces. "It says that some blame the Dublos and others a race called the Ancients. Some even agree with the Dublos that they shouldn't have robots. The Elder says the Secunds only survived the attacks because the robots protected them. Her supporters oppose those that want to destroy the robots and helped the robots prepare to escape the Secund settlements to safety if needed. They would do that rather than fight the Secunds."

"Who are the Ancients?"

"The robot doesn't know," Tyson said. "But now that you've asked about them, he'll learn what he can."

When they reached the shuttle, Genghis gave the robot a tour. It questioned the purpose of the onboard equipment and how the Biots learned to operate the various devices. Genghis answered in detail and the robot stood motionless processing the translation.

Almost as if it snapped out of a trance, the robot launched into a new string of queries about how the Beings treated the Biots. Genghis was busy answering them when Tyson reminded them of the need to return to the Elder.

When the robot offered to carry the imager, Genghis handed it over. The robot transported it effortlessly. After Genghis finished his explanation of the relationship between Beings and Biots, the robot described the small manufacturing machines, analyzers and communications gear that had been preserved. "The robots developed tools that enable them to operate the equipment," Tyson said.

When they reached the meeting place, the robot set the imager on a pedestal and the Secunds and robots gathered around it. Tyson explained the scenes of the Being and human worlds, finding *Wanderer*, the unplanned trip to the station and *Aurreol*'s arrival.

The visuals of the three ships and the mines that *Aurreol* encountered on its way to Lavaworld launched the Secunds into an animated discussion. While they were distracted, the robot that accompanied Genghis to the shuttle leaned close to Tyson and uttered a few words.

"The Secunds have finally concluded you're a created species but different from their robots," Tyson said. "They didn't introduce themselves before because they were uncertain. Now they won't. You'll have to learn their names from the robots."

"Tyson, I'll leave you here when I return to *Aurreol*," Genghis said. "I'll request that my robot pal be in charge of looking after you and the imager. It's treated as an outsider by most Secunds and robots and might tell you more than they would."

"It would be good to test my understanding of Secundese on someone that has not been around Biots much. Charlie has adopted a lot of Beingish words and phrases."

When the Secunds were paying attention again, Genghis recounted the development of Biots and their role before, during and after the Nameless War. He decided not to mention the plans for giving the robots on the station new bodies. Instead, he showed photos of the derelict starships discovered by the Beings drifting toward a Confederation planet.

The reaction to the visuals of those ships was abrupt and heated. "They're certain they were Dublo ships," Tyson explained. "Your pal says there's no doubt they were."

"The Beings examined these ships extensively and determined they were heavily damaged in battle," Genghis said. "Perhaps your records would indicate when and where that might have happened to enable us to determine how they entered our region."

The Elder responded at considerable length. Her voice became so faint that Genghis could not tell if the visuals had made her angry or sad. More intriguing was the close attention the other Secunds now paid to what she said. It was like they were hearing something new. Or finally listening to her.

Chapter 20
A Tantalizing Clue

"The Elder says there never were space battles involving Secunds and Dublos," Tyson said. "From time to time, a spaceship would disappear without a trace. While the Dublos always denied responsibility, there was no one else that could have hijacked it. They helped search for the lost vessels as the Secunds did when a Dublo one went missing. The Secunds claim they never attacked Dublo ships.

"When the Secunds threatened the Dublos with retaliation for assaults on their planets, they replied that theirs had also been attacked," Tyson said. "There wasn't any discussion about joint action to protect their planets and find the culprits.

"When the attacks on the planets started, they were sporadic at first and targeted isolated communities," Tyson said. "They increased in intensity until about 50 years ago when an all-out barrage from ships in orbit was launched. The Secund Federation was powerless to stop the attacks, which left the Secunds suspicious of outsiders even from other parts of Planet 4."

"What happened after the bombardment?" Genghis said.

"Nothing, no forces were landed on the surface of the planet to finish the attacks. The Secunds resorted to living at a subsistence level because that doesn't draw any attention from the skies. Other than the Elder, the Secunds here were born into the conditions we see."

"They never captured any attackers or found their bodies?" Genghis said. Their account made little sense.

The Elder muttered a few words while the other Secunds talked angrily. "They're just making threats against the Dublos."

A prolonged coughing episode wracked the Elder until her attendant passed her a bottle. As she drank deeply, Genghis wondered whether *Transformation* could also heal that malady.

When the Elder regained her breath, she resumed the account.

"She doubts they'll ever learn the truth about the attacks on their worlds," Tyson said. "At one point there was considerable trade between the Secunds and Dublos. They agreed to a treaty to prevent conflicts that lasted for centuries while the two sides expanded to additional planets."

"Did the Secunds have any armed space ships?" Genghis said.

"Some for protection although they always seemed to be elsewhere when an attack occurred. Finally the Secunds lost contact with them and presume they were destroyed."

"Does she have any information on what happened to the Dublo worlds?"

A sour expression on the Elder's face. "She doesn't know what's happened to them," Tyson said. "She says the Secunds have no proof the Dublos are responsible for attacks."

"Did the Secunds defend themselves during the attacks?" Genghis asked.

"The attacks were sudden and unexpected." Tyson paused. "The Secunds did what they could just to survive with the assistance of the robots. The other Secunds know far less about the attacks than the Elder and aren't much interested in her account of them. Or more likely can't be bothered to find out."

Gradually the Secunds drifted away and the remaining robots huddled with Charlie. The Elder, her attendant, Genghis and his robot pal were left alone.

"The Elder wants to convert the remnants of this city into a refuge for survivors but she doesn't have sufficient robots or supporters to do that," Tyson said.

Genghis kept glancing at the attendant because its behavior seemed more like that of his pal than the other robots. "Ask the Elder if I can bring Biots from our ship to examine the technologies they've preserved in Orphum."

The Elder readily agreed. "Her supporters will take the Biots to the archives. Copies of the Secund space exploration records are stored there. If they weren't destroyed in the attacks, the Elder says the planetary archives in the city include visuals of her species' exploration of other worlds.

"I'm not positive about the time of the exploration, but it would seem to have occurred centuries ago. The Elder says they include visuals of a world where a major war was underway. The Secunds didn't attempt contact. They found another planet that could be Terra. While it was a lightly populated, majestic world, it was simply too far away and its atmosphere too unsuitable to justify additional exploration. They consider our end of the galactic arm to be desolate and of no particular value in terms of resources."

Seeing the Elder was falling asleep, Genghis returned to the shuttle to recharge and await the arrival of the team that would examine the archives. His robot pal agreed to protect Tyson and the imager in the gathering place.

Once he had plugged into the recharger, Genghis gathered his thoughts for a message to Kelsey and the other Fleet Commanders about the visual of his session with the Secunds.

"There's something about their attitude toward me and the robots I find irksome. I doubt we're being told the whole story about what happened to Planet 4. Whoever attacked it seems incapable of landing on it to complete its conquest. To me, that alone rules out the Dublos.

"The attacker gained control of the Secund and Dublos ships to assault both their worlds. Undoubtedly those ships were what *Aurreol* encountered at Lavaworld. My expectation is the Dublos were attacked as fiercely as the Secunds. *Aurreol's* sensors indicate little activity on their planets and no communication among them. We'll have to inspect them to be certain."

Genghis was still mulling over his thoughts when the other shuttle touched down.

Four Biots unloaded a trio of powered six wheel carts designed to haul supplies. Genghis could not identify all the gear they loaded onto them.

When Genghis and the newcomers reached the clearing, the Elder was talking with her attendant and Genghis' pal. They peered at the recording equipment while he explained what the newcomers would be searching for in the archives.

"The Elder and her attendant will take them there to ensure they obtain full access to the city," Tyson said. "Charlie told her about the plan to give the robots new bodies. She thinks it would be good to make the robots more useful and restore the shutdown ones."

"Tell the Elder the doctors on *Transformation* may be able to replace her ruined hips, repair her spine and treat her cough," Genghis said. "The doctors would work from images of her joints to make copies that will last for centuries. In addition to regaining full mobility, the new joints would mean an end to her pain."

As Tyson delivered the message, the Elder rubbed her hands with glee. "To move about without pain would be blessing because being stuck in the wheelchair is no joy."

Gazing at the Elder, Genghis said, "Once more Galaxyships are here, we'll inspect the rest of your worlds as well as the Dublos ones."

"The Elder wants you to protect this planet from attacks," Tyson said.

"Reassure her that our Fleet will guard it."

The Elder slumped in her chair. "She's distraught at thoughts of all the Secunds accomplished in the past only to end up in this beleaguered situation," Tyson said. "Their only hope is for the Galaxyships to drive away the vessels that attacked them so they can rebuild their civilization. It sounds like she expects the Beings will have to play an ongoing role in protecting the Secunds until their system recovers."

"Tell her that when another Galaxyship arrives, Beings and Terrans will come to the planet to talk about their worlds and how they could assist in rebuilding Secund civilization."

Minutes later, Kelsey communicated her agreement with Genghis's plan. "A meeting between the Secunds and Commander Atdomorsin of *Dreadnought* will be interesting. Carter says leaving Tyson with your new robot pal has been a big boost in understanding the history and technology of the Secunds. Your pal is learning Beingish from Tyson."

When Genghis told the Elder about Atdomorsin, she talked excitedly about the prospect of meeting a high ranking Being. That response amplified Genghis's suspicions about the Secunds' attitudes toward Biots and robots. However, he wanted the Elder to tell him more about the split between Secunds and Dublos, which reminded him of the divisions among the nations on Terra.

The Elder gazed at Genghis for several minutes as if uncertain how to explain the differences between the two species. When she spoke, the words came in short, halting bursts.

"Secunds and Dublos believe the Ancients, who possess great power, brought life to the Universe," Tyson translated. "Both species claim they're the direct descendants of the Ancients. Their names are meant to reflect their status as second only to the Ancients who they believe were created shortly after the formation of the Universe.

"What she doesn't know is how the Ancients would've survived the Universe's tumultuous early millennia. It's unlikely the Ancients could be life as we know it because the elements that Beings, Terrans and Secunds are composed of didn't exist at the time the Ancients supposedly came into existence."

"That makes it improbable that either the Secunds or Dublos are descended from them," Genghis said.

"The Secunds never found physical evidence of the Ancients' presence or a scientific way to prove their existence," Tyson said. "However, from time to time, a Secund or a Dublo claims to have encountered one."

Genghis explained the Beings' name came from their belief they were the only sentient species in the Universe even though they explored only a tiny portion of a small galaxy. "Even the Beings find their name to be laughable now. They also believe in a supreme entity they refer to with a reverential hum. Terrans have worshipped a creator through various religions that each claim to be the true one. Terran and Being history is riddled with atrocities done to others in the name of religion and ideology."

The Elder grunted. "She doubts the Ancients would approve of many actions of Secunds or Dublos," Tyson said. "However the Ancients did nothing to prevent the attacks from occurring. She believes they must regret their inaction. They'll always be a mystery."

"We have a mystery for you." Genghis recounted the story of Vasile Stocia and Stocton exploring the Dome on the trip back to Terra at the end of the Nameless War. His robot pal and the attendant were as transfixed as the Elder by his account.

The Elder strained to lift her head as she replied. "That sounds just like the Dome of the Ancients that Secunds and Dublos believe is located in their region of the galaxy," Tyson said. "Both believe there are Domes spread throughout the Universe. They're regarded as way stations for the Ancients.

"She's surprised there would be another Dome in the Milky Way. The location of the one Vasile and his ton explored is far from where the Secunds and Dublos believe their Dome is. They were never able to find it."

The tone of the Elder's voice changed. "She's pleading for Vasile to come here to recount his visit to the Dome."

"I'll put forward her request although older Terrans usually don't undertake long space flights because of the strain on their bodies," Genghis said.

Talking about the Dome and Ancients overcame the Elder. She trembled and a gurgling sound came from her throat. Genghis stared at her wondering if she was alright. Her attendant offered her the bottle and she sipped its contents.

After she finished drinking, she resumed speaking. Her voice had a higher-pitched tone and her face darkened.

"The Elder is pleading for Vasile to come here," Tyson said. "She wants to know what he witnessed. To be allowed admittance to a Dome is unimaginable to her."

Genghis was annoyed she did not mention Stocton.

The Elder jabbered excitedly for several minutes. "It would mean a lot to the Secunds to encounter someone who has been inside a Dome," Tyson said. "How did Vasile describe it?"

"He called it paradise. He didn't see anyone although he felt a presence. It reminded him of stories his grandmother told him as a child. Everyone in our worlds has seen the visual recorded by his ton of Vasile gazing about the Dome's interior and saying 'Bunica, you were right; there are mansions for the angels in the stars.' Tears rolled down his cheeks until they were dried. He always said it was a breeze that did it but Stocton says something that he and Vasile couldn't see wiped his face."

"Could we see the visual of his time in the Dome?"

"If my ship has a copy; otherwise you'll have to wait for Dreadnought's arrival. Vasile and Stocton have studied the visual of their visit to the Dome ever since and written several books about the stories of angels conjecturing about its significance. Their work attracted a lot of interest and they've become respected mediators in disputes on Terra."

"The Elder says that over the years, the Ancients have been depicted as bright lights shaped in a figure which the beholder recognizes as similar to their own," Tyson said.

While the Elder's face remained flushed, her voice was much subdued. "The other Secunds are shunning us because they don't approve of the capability and independence the Beings have given to Biots," Tyson said. "Allowing Biots to operate a powerful space ship without supervision is unthinkable to them. As we expected, the Secunds limited the robots' abilities because they feared the robots would escape their control and become as big if not a bigger threat as the Dublos."

"Their attitudes aren't much different from the Terrans who object to Biots out of their fear of artificial intelligence," Genghis said.

He chose his words to avoid offense. "There was considerable speculation among my comrades on *Wanderer* about why the robots' creators built them with so many shortcomings.

"To the best of my knowledge, Beings never had those fears. When a technical malfunction made it impossible for Beings and Terrans to serve on our own Galaxyship, the Beings didn't hesitate to send *Aurreol* with an all-Biot crew. The Beings developed us to help look after their worlds. Many of us participated in their discoveries and received full credit. Perhaps it's in the way they created our brains as we don't aspire to physical possessions or wealth. Life is to be experienced and enjoyed. There's so much to learn, and like Beings, we have an insatiable curiosity."

The attendant and Genghis' pal leaned forward as if they feared missing something crucial in his account.

Genghis explained how the Beings had fully integrated Biots into their society and that he could not recall an instance of a Biot being mistreated by a Being.

The Elder's head was resting on her chest again. She raised her voice as if anxious to be understood. "The Dublos wouldn't deal with Secund robots," Tyson said. "They always warned us they would destroy any they found on their worlds. Their reaction to you is unlikely to be any less hostile."

Chapter 21
The Search Begins

Watching the hulking form of *Dreadnought* on the main imager as it drew alongside *Aurreol* above Planet 4, Kelsey felt her tension ease. *Aurreol* was no longer the only Galaxyship in the region. She headed to the shuttle bay to transfer to the cruiser to meet Commander Atdomorsin and his senior officers.

Atdomorsin greeted her. "Great work Commander." He shook her right hand and clapped her left shoulder with his other hand. That was as big a compliment as Admiral Gnoorvants ever delivered and his long-time deputy shared the salutation.

As they headed to the Conference Room, he said, "You've demonstrated the capability of an all Biot crew. It was a clever idea to test the top speed that your ship could withstand. The design of our next class of Galaxyships will include many features from *Aurreol*. The Pozzen cruisers bring another dimension to the Fleet. The force field system on *Wanderer* could be a major innovation as well.

"Our patrol was in a region much closer to this system than the other ships. We studied your reports to the Fleet and Navigation Central along with visuals of the planet and the discussions between Genghis and the Elder. If the other Secund populations are like this one, it'll be a major challenge to help them because they might resent anything we do. Especially improving their robots, which would be a major advantage for them." He shook his head.

Kelsey wondered whether the Beings would questions if assisting the Secunds worth the effort.

"Our scans calculate thousands of mines are headed toward Planet 4," she said. "Should we take action against them?"

"Not until the other ships arrive." Atdomorsin was almost as tall and broad as Gnoorvants. Atdoton walked on the other side of the Commander so he could not see his ton flashing compliments to Kelsey with his fingers. She could not remember the last time she used Being sign language. She nodded her thanks.

Atdomorsin paused outside the Conference Room. "We'll be discussing our next steps while we wait for the rest of the Fleet. *Aurreol's* two sister ships encountered the same problem with their filtration systems. They're on route now with all Biot crews. We want to see if you can integrate their Controlling Units with *Aurreol's* to make the three ships fly together under your command."

With that, he stepped forward and the door into the Conference Room slid open. Surprised by his revelation about her expanded command, Kelsey followed him. She never made it to *Enterprise's* Conference Room so she was impressed by its spaciousness. She recalled the story about the first Terrans on *Alliance* gravitating to that ship's Conference Room. It was expanded and upgraded as a result, giving it an importance it never had before in the Fleet.

Kelsey greeted the other officers, matching them with the information Carter supplied about *Dreadnought's* personnel, and took the empty seat. In addition to the officers were Terrans, whom she guessed were in their late thirties. They sat under a cone of light, which provided them with suitable air and temperatures. As well, there was what she first thought was another Being until she realized he was too tall, which meant he was a Pozzen.

She glanced around the room. The officers' tons flashed finger greetings. Perhaps they thought of her in the same elevated way that she and the other Biots on Transport 27 regarded Genghis. The concept of fame was a Terran construct that Beings did not understood. It fascinated the Biots.

The other remarkable aspect of a Being Galaxyship was how little noise its operating systems generated. Even with extensive modifications, the Pozzen cruisers still had many components that regularly started up or shut down with jarring sounds.

"Before we discuss our immediate plans, I wish to pass on to Commander Kelsey my compliments and those of my officers as well as Admiral Gnoorvants for the attack on the ships and the mines," Atdomorsin said. "That was excellent strategic thinking and quite a show."

"We're looking forward to talking with the team that created the disrupter beam," Science said. "We've made the modification to our neutralizer beam and are waiting for an opportunity to test it."

"I was impressed by the rearrangement of the machine's circuits and how thoroughly it destroyed the mines," Kelsey said. "We haven't tried it on a ship because we wanted to board them."

"We're still trying to calculate how much energy was released in the cascading explosions of the first formation of mines you encountered," Weapons said. "It was probably enough to power an average planet for at least a year."

"These developments were team efforts," Kelsey said. "A crew member advances an idea, and others work on it as well. The biggest job as Commander is keeping track of all these projects."

Atdomorsin and his Deputy Commander snorted loudly. Their outburst surprised Kelsey who was accustomed to the Biots' imitation of Terran laughter.

"Another accomplishment was creating the Beingish-Secundese dictionary," she said. "We think it's almost complete and Carter can provide nearly simultaneous translation of conversations with Secunds. The Tysons have improved as well. As we speak, our Controlling Unit is uploading the translation program to your ship."

Several officers recounted similar outbreaks of creativity before Atdomorsin rapped the table to get everyone's attention. "As we have a science team on board, we'll remain here to protect and study the planet. It'll be about a week before the rest of the Fleet starts to arrive. After Genghis has introduced us to the Elder, *Aurreol* will reconnoiter the Secund worlds."

"We should travel to Planets 1 and 3 to determine their status," Kelsey said. "The Control Center for their starships is on Planet 3, which is the closest of their worlds to the Dublo sphere. The Control Center obviously monitored it. We haven't detect any signals from the Center. We'll take the robot Charlie with us to make contact with Secund survivors.

"After our experience at Lavaworld, we expect we'll be facing ships that are both Secund and Dublo in origin. Although they should be programmed to attack each other, our scans can find no evidence of combat. After all this time, the ships would require maintenance and upgrades, which were not done by the robots. We expect mines are deployed as monitors around the other Secund worlds."

The officers were either typing messages into their personal communicators or looking at her wide-eyed.

"The presence of two alien space vessels orbiting this planet and more coming should generate communications between the mines and whatever controls them and the ships," Atdomorsin said. "We'll listen for them as they would reveal where the craft are being directed from. Perhaps your exploration of Planets 1 and 3 will as well."

"The Elder asked us not to destroy them because the Secunds fear that would lead to more attacks on the planet," Kelsey said.

The meeting moved onto updating the order in which the other Galaxyships would arrive and their deployment.

Then Kelsey outlined the activity on Planet 4. She rubbed her necklace as she talked. "The Elder led a group of Biots to archives in the city that contain visual records of their space exploration. While they have found material that will be of great interest to our astronomers, they couldn't transfer the archive data into our system. So they're recording whatever might be relevant to us or the Terrans. The upcoming visual of Orphum on Planet 4 shows the extent of the damage from the attacks as well as what remains of their technology."

When the meeting ended, Kelsey headed to the shuttle bay. Her route was jammed with well-wishing Biots. To Beings, she had done what was expected. To Biots, she was a celebrity like Genghis. Once on board the shuttle, she radioed *Aurreol* to prepare for departure after Atdomorsin visited the planet to meet the Elder.

Genghis waited for her outside *Aurreol's* shuttle bay. He introduced her to his robot pal who had selected the name Woodsy because he liked the visuals of forests on Terra.

When they reached the Command Chamber, she briefed the crew on the new mission operating the three Pozzen cruisers as one. "At Planet 3, we need to determine what's happened to the starship Control Center. Dreadnought also can't find any signs that it's functioning."

The next day, Genghis and Woodsy met the landing party from *Dreadnought* on Planet 4 to escort them to meet the Elder. Other than a breathing pack on his back, Atdomorsin wore his regular uniform.

Several hundred Secunds in clean robes greeted the Commander warmly. Greeting another organic species counted far more than meeting robots. Although Atdomorsin delivered the same assurances as Genghis had, the Secunds paid close attention to him and asked him the kind of questions that the Elder posed to Genghis.

The gathering went inside a building that looked like it was constructed entirely of concrete so Atdomorsin could show the visuals of Vasile Stocia and Stocton's visit to the Dome. The Elder was especially excited by the scenes.

Standing at the back of the room while Atdomorsin answered numerous questions, Atdoton whispered to Genghis. "We studied the visuals of your initial encounter with them. Quite an immature species despite their past accomplishments."

Woodsy nodded.

The Elder offered a tour of Orphum to Atdomorsin at which point Genghis said he and Woodsy would return to their ship so it could depart on its inspection of other Secund planets.

In *Aurreol's* Command Chamber, Genghis passed Kelsey a data cube the Biots on Planet 4 had given him. "It contains several images of what the Control Center on Planet 3 looks like."

The visual showed two tall windowless towers about 50 meters apart. "The twisting devices on the sides of the towers are part of their communications technology."

After the examination of the tower, the imagers returned to long range views of Planets 1 and 3. "Both appear bleaker than Planet 4 as if they have suffered far more physical damage," Analytics observed. "The scans found little activity beyond the normal background activity of a pre-industrial planet."

"Unless they employ a communications system our scans don't detect, what we're seeing certainly isn't encouraging," Genghis said.

As *Aurreol* approached Planet 1, the sensors found wide-spread damage along with scattered groups of Secunds. "Whoever attacked them certainly was thorough,"

Alex Binkley

Genghis said. "What we really need to know is whether the Dublo ones are any better off."

Chapter 22
Picky Eaters

Alliance and *Transformation* arrived at Lavaworld in time to observe the final stages of the Dublo ship's absorption into the planet's molten surface. The Galaxyships spent a day in orbit studying the remaining clumps of the craft and data from the rest of the planet to compare to the information they received from *Aurreol* and *Wanderer*.

While they did, a squad of Biots trained on *Alliance* boarded *Wanderer* to make the final preparations for its flight to Hnassumblaw. Once it departed, a shuttle landing bay would be attached to the station. The components for it were assembled on *Transformation* during the trip.

Until the bay was complete, shuttles to the space station landed in the bays of the other Secund ship, which was dubbed the Conference Center. Meetings of robots, Biots and scientists about Lavaworld research were held in the Center to avoid being disrupted by the work to upgrade the space station. The Center was easily accessible for the robots through the tube linking it to the station.

Nathan Huxley, Wxdot Gruumon the Pozzen and a team of scientists arrived at the Center on the first shuttle from *Transformation*. They were to meet the Biots and robots monitoring the craft's decomposition and the creatures' communications beneath the heaving surface of the planet.

Wxdot was telling stories to Nathan and a team of Biots about guiding the first human and Biots soldiers through Onnaprozen during the final stages of the Nameless War when Octinog and Gaopod arrived accompanied by Sam and a robot in a wheelchair.

"Gaopod built this," said Sam. "It works well, but it still takes more time than expected to move around. While we would like a tour of your big ship, it's too awkward to board a shuttle to travel to it."

Nathan intended to pay close attention to the robots because Genghis originally described them as having the same processing capacity as Terran analyzers and robots. While more physically advanced than their Terran counterparts, they followed their programming and had just begun to show signs of acquiring new skills by watching the Biots. Nathan was also curious about Kelsey's admonition to respect the intelligence that operated *Wanderer*.

While the scientists wanted to discuss the planet and its life forms, Sam was preoccupied with the new body shell for the robots. "Just like the days after we got rid of the Rulers," Wxdot whispered to Nathan. "Everybody had their own priorities and we didn't always focus on the biggest problems. Since we need the robots' assistance with the planet, let's discuss the shells first. Then we can get on with our issues."

Nathan readily agreed while harboring a slight pang of guilt. The shell conversion was one of Ruthie Donohue's topics and she and Humbawloda had thoroughly reviewed Octinog's design of the new body for the robots. He realized he rather enjoyed Ruthie's company as he asked *Transformation* to send her and Humbawloda to the Conference Center.

Ruthie started her presentation with Octinog's visual of the Biot and robot bodies and the diagrams of how the transfer to the new one could be made. The interpretation was provided by Tyson2 from *Wanderer,* which had been permanently installed in the Conference Center. Darwin, *Transformation's* Controlling Unit, would assist it.

"Gaopod tweaked the joints and hands and we've added other refinements."

After reviewing the latest versions of the new shell on the imagers, Sam offered a string of comments. "Your design is much more extensive than the robots expected from earlier discussions," Tyson 2 said. "Sam is happy with the improvements because they'll provide the robots with much greater flexibility and more durability than their existing one. While they understand how the new body will benefit them in terms of their functioning and performance, it's difficult for them to conceive what it'll be like. Adjusting to two hands instead of two claws and a trunk will be the hardest part of the transition."

Everyone waited as Sam stared at the diagram. "He wonders if the power storage cell could be placed lower in the chest cavity and an extra data storage unit inserted above them," Tyson said. "While it wouldn't add much to their weight or affect their center of gravity, it would equip them with greater processing capacity."

"It should be doable with only a few internal changes," Octinog said. He adjusted the design of the chest area on the imager screen by moving components around. "Let's try this configuration and evaluate the results."

"The conversion to the new body will be much like the process for creating a Biot," Ruthie said. "We'll employ the same biotech material to create the shell and interior structure. The signals from the brain to the processors, activator motors and power cell are transmitted through strands of the same material. It's similar to the nervous system and blood veins in Beings and Terrans.

"When a modified robot wants to take an action, the processor thinks it and the message goes to the interface, and then through the body instantaneously to the activators. The interface was altered based on ideas from *Transformation*. The electricity input port was placed in the lower chest to make it close to the power storage cells rather than at the bottom of the head as in your existing shell."

Sam stared some more. "He says that on his behalf as well as the 26 shutdown robots on the station, let's proceed," Tyson2 said. "If any of his functional fellows don't want to change, he'll tell them it'll happen anyway the next time they break down."

The robot gazed about the room. "It'll be no small job just to transform the robots on the station. He wonders about the robots on the Secund worlds?"

"By then, there'll be teams of skilled robots with dexterous hands that could take on that job," Ruthie said.

Sam grinned when the translation finished. "He wants to know why the Beings, Biots and Terrans would do this for the robots."

Nathan wondered whether Sam knew about the philosophical debate among Beings and Terrans on the wisdom and morality of rebuilding the robots. "At first, the Biots worried about whether new bodies would change the relationship between you and the Secunds. Then Hton agreed with Genghis that no species deserves to be left in the semi-functional condition of the robots.

"When Humbaw sided with those arguments, the Confederation, Pozzen and Mandela supported the plan," Nathan said. "That left the only objectors on Earth where there are fears about what the robots would be capable of doing in the future. To Beings, the most likely outcome will be the robots taking on a role comparable to the Biots."

Sam said nothing more. "Ruthie and Humbawloda will come to the station afterward to answer any further questions about the changes," Nathan said. "We want to move onto our investigation of Lavaworld."

"Sam agrees and says the robots have provided as much information as they can about the planet," Tyson2 said. "There's far more data but it won't be available until the station's information system is fully restored.

The main result of the session was the creation of three joint projects. One would investigate the sounds of the creatures looking for a language while another would examine whether the creatures on the planet could be composed of silicon or another material. The third would study how the planet's structure and its internal energy supply kept the lava churning.

Several days later, a shutdown robot, nicknamed Hobot1, was transported by shuttle to *Transformation* and transferred to a lab refitted for the conversion process. The gurney was placed beside the one upon which lay Hobot1's partly-assembled new body. The robot's processor brain and data storage banks were linked to the new power cell and interface unit, and then Biots lifted them from the robot's old shell and positioned them in its new one.

"This robot has been shut down for a number of years," Darwin explained. "Before it left the station, it was turned on and Sam explained the shell transfer process. Without hesitation, Hobot1 agreed a new shell was better than being turned off. However, it wants to assist in the transfer as soon as possible because it'll know before us whether its functions are working properly. As well, Sam will be watching the process on an imager in the station's Command Room.

Once the robot's processor brain was operating, Octinog said, "First, we'll connect the audio receivers and its visual receptors. Then it can participate."

After Hobot1 confirmed via a text message to Sam that it could hear and see what the Biots were doing, they linked its voice generator and mouth, a mesh screen with a speaker behind it.

To demonstrate how well the new voice worked, Hobot1 launched into a long monologue. "Its hearing is more acute than before," Darwin said. "Next it'll test its vision, and then its limbs." After a pause, the Controlling Unit said, "It wants you to adjust its viewing lenses because they aren't clear."

Octinog nodded at the recorder feeding the transfer to Sam. "Robot voices sound the same to us. Ours did as well until the older Biots found ways to alter their tones and inflections."

In the end it required tweaking of the lenses and additional connections to the processors to clear up Hobot1's vision. "Now it thinks it'll be able to see into the heavens like a telescope," Darwin said. "All it ever wanted was to gaze at the stars."

Hobot1 sounded wistful. Perhaps exposure to the Biots had already changed the robots.

If Octinog needed a thank you for all his work on the new robot bodies, he just received it. "They're a wondrous sight, mate." Octinog clasped Hobot1's shoulder. "Life will be better from now on." Nathan would share a visual of this exchange.

The head was closed and the conversion team gave Hobot1 time to integrate its new senses. While it did, the team shifted to a nearby lab and removed the processors and data banks from five robots waiting on gurneys.

When Hobot1 was ready, the mechanism for turning its head was connected to the interface followed by the activators for its arms and legs. It raised itself into a sitting position to experiment with twisting its head 270 degrees and trying out its new arms and functional hands.

"It agrees the slowest part of adjusting to the new shell will be adapting to just two upper limbs."

Using the robot shell as a reference, the arms and legs were connected to the interface. At Sam's command, Hobot1 raised its legs, bent its knees and rotated its feet.

Then it tried its arms. It could not lift them above the shoulders until Gaopod adjusted the interface.

Then Hobot1 tested its new hands. The right thumb made small circles followed by the left one. Satisfied, it moved one finger after the other. "It says these hands are much more useful," Darwin explained. It linked them and twiddled its thumbs. Ruthie and Nathan laughed at the very human gesture.

It was a pain-staking process connecting all the activators in the rest of the new shell, but finally the transfer was complete.

"We'll disconnect Hobot1 from the monitoring gear and close the shell," Nathan said. "It can go for a test walk when it's ready. That will tell us what additional refinements are needed."

A four wheel cart that Hobot1 could lean on was placed beside the gurney. It shifted its legs until they were dangling over the side. It raised and lowered them and moved its feet up and down and sideways. Then it placed its hands on the cart's handles and eased forward until its feet were on the floor.

"It wants to walk right away." Biots gathered at either side of the cart ready to grab Hobot1. Holding tightly to the cart handles, it swayed for a minute before easing its left leg forward, and then the right one. It stepped forward at a snail's pace. After five or six steps, it eased into a shuffle. At the wall, it turned and returned to the table at a brisker tempo.

Nathan pointed to a mirror on the wall. "Take a look at yourself."

Hobot1 peered for a few minutes before touching its forehead.

"With your new eyes, you won't miss those lamps."

"It says the lamps weren't much good anyway," Darwin said. "It wants to walk to the lab where the other robots are being converted. It might see something that can aid in the process."

By the time it arrived, the five robots were part way through their conversion. One had its vocal and visual faculties installed and called to Hobot1. "It's anxious to join Hobot1 in walking again," Tyson said. "We'll share a visual of this with the station's robots and send it to *Aurreol* for Charlie, Woodsy and Genghis."

Hobot1 walked from robot to robot showing off its hands. "It says the old design was a hindrance compared to this one. Not only will it be able to perform a lot more tasks, it also has considerably more physical strength."

Based on the lessons learned from the Hobot1 changeover, the other five conversions were completed far quicker. "Now that we know the process works, we should employ the big triage area on *Transformation* to do the conversions in assembly line manner," Wxdot said. "That would tell us what kind of conversion facilities we need to establish on the Secund worlds."

"Sam doubts the Secunds will allow it," Darwin said.

"We'll deal with that problem later," Ruthie said. "For now, let's try Wxdot's suggestion."

"The still functional robots like Sam will be converted last to give them time to assist the revived ones in adjusting to working with Biots," Wxdot said. "We'll keep the Hobots in the Conference Center until they're ready to return to full duty."

The assembly line process enabled the conversion of the rest of the shutdown robots to be completed within two days. Hobot1 assisted in the process. After several of days of working with the converted ones, Sam and the rest of the functioning ones received their new bodies.

Once the Hobots adjusted to their new bodies and were fully briefed on all that had transpired during their shutdown, they went to work with the Biots in restoring the station to full operation.

With the robot conversion nearing completion, the main focus of the daily meetings of Biots and Terrans in the Conference Center shifted to studying Lavaworld. "*Transformation* and *Alliance* are gathering information about the planet and its residents," Amundsen said. "With more Hobots available, we hope to gain access to the decades of data stored in the space station.

"However it's becoming increasingly difficult to move about the station because of the piles of junk. It's mostly broken down equipment that we've replaced or learned to work around. Now we have piles of old robot shells in the Conference Center. Gaopod is proposing we remove any valuable elements from them and deposit the remaining junk in large loads on Lavaworld."

"Lavaworld isn't a garbage dump," Wxdot said. "Why not just gradually release it so it burns up in the planet's atmosphere?"

"We want to ensure it reaches the surface to see if the creatures explore it," Gaopod said. "As the lava dissolved the frigate, different metals and elements were released. The process generated a lot of sounds that we think came from the creatures. However not knowing the concentration of the metals and materials in the ships and in what concentrations, we couldn't connect the sounds to the particular materials. We'll know the composition of the garbage and if the creatures investigate it, hopefully that will enable us to make progress in determining which sounds represent the materials in it."

"Perhaps the creatures prefer different elements or can absorb nutrients from them," Amundsen said. "Or maybe they're a treat like chocolate is to Terrans and the creatures are simply enjoying them."

"We haven't made much progress in deciphering their communications," Gaopod said. "By combining what we can access in the station records with what we've heard since arriving, we've identified some sounds that are repeated regularly. However it's not enough to figure out what the sounds signify or if the creatures have a language. We've no idea how they generate and hear what we pick up with our sensors."

"The creatures are still concentrated in the area where the ship came down as if sampling the new flavors in the hot soup of their world," Amundsen said. "As the material in the robots' shells is different, it might trigger some new sounds for us."

"Is there a sufficient variety of garbage to keep the creatures busy long enough to obtain adequate information on their communications?" Wxdot said.

"During the cleanup of the station, which we call Operation Big Sweep, the Biots upgraded or replaced the communications and data storage equipment," Gaopod said. "The junk from it is bound together in large bundles and there'll be more stuff before we're done overhauling the station.

"Our plan would be to use the shuttles to first dump some debris in areas not far from where the ship landed to see if the creatures will move to it. If they do, we could dispose of the rest in other regions to see how far they will travel for it."

Amundsen leaned toward Nathan. "We want your support for the plan before we present it to Commander Atdomorsin. Gaopod has made an interesting discovery about Lavaworld that dumping the garbage could confirm."

With those words, the imagers filled with two-tone views of Lavaworld. "The dark grey marks regions the creatures avoid," Gaopod said. "The light green is where they congregate."

"The light green covers about two-thirds of the planet," Ruthie said. "What does it mean?"

"My thesis is that the dark zones are areas where the silicon creatures can't swim," Gaopod said. "While it seems improbable just looking at Lavaworld, I think they are the planet's equivalent of continents. The green areas are the fluid zones where the silicon creatures can move about freely. In ways, it resembles the oceans and continents on Terra."

"The visuals from the planet show no zones like you describe," Nathan said.

"We only discovered them when we mapped the areas where the creatures are found. We compared the information collected during our shuttle overflights with the information we've been able to extract from the station's data banks. Darwin has reviewed the evidence and agrees the thesis is worth further study, which I plan on doing and would welcome any assistance others can provide. I would like to drop a load of junk in a dark zone to see if it would attract the creatures. Even if it doesn't, we'll have learned a lot.

"Dumping might also help us determine how many creatures there are as they swim to it. My guess for now is several hundred thousand. We've no clues yet on their size or shape."

"I'll arrange for a shuttle to take your first load of station debris and dump it where you want," Nathan said.

"You certainly have kept yourself busy, Gaopod," Ruthie said.

"When I started, I connected the network of immobile robots to the station's data banks and they helped me sort through the station's records looking for information connected to my research. That was a benefit of having full power restored to the station. Once they became Hobots, they assisted me even more as well."

"I've heard them call you 'friend Gaopod,'" Ruthie said.

Gaopod grinned at her. "I was surprised the first time I heard that. Then I wondered whether the robots could have emotions. I'm studying that."

No one spoke until Amundsen intervened. "The Biots from *Aurreol* have cleaned up the station, restored the equipment and installed the gear Commander Kelsey left us. They also kept reviewing our work."

"We shared all the data on the station we've gained access to with *Transformation* and the Conference Center," Nathan said. "Darwin is pointing out important information in it. Adding in what you've just told us, it's clear the creatures are far more significant than the Secunds realized."

The next day, two bundles of station junk plopped down in green zones several hundred meters from where the Dublo ship had crashed. "It didn't take long before the creatures reached it," Gaopod said. "They're making a lot of sounds."

"You want to feed them different flavors?" Wxdot said. "We know the elements that Lavaworld is composed of. We could examine the rocks in this region of space looking for boulders with significant accumulations of the same ores and elements and ones with totally different compositions. We could use the Octinog boulder conveyance system to feed them to the planet, and then monitor the reaction of the creatures to our gifts. Wouldn't that help you determine words in their language if they make specific sounds in reaction to the components of the rocks?"

Wxdot's suggestion sent Nathan to the analyzer station that had been added to the Conference Center. "We could also drop the rocks on a regular basis in the same area to see if they realize it's not a random event although the garbage dumps should tell them that. They might even wonder about life beyond their domain. We have to learn a lot more about their sounds to do that, but your idea could be the best way to accomplish it."

Nathan rubbed his hands together. "While I don't know all its capabilities, *Alliance* did a lot of exploration in the past and hopefully still has up-to-date scientific equipment on board. We could position the two ships in different locations around Lavaworld to gather data from every garbage or rock dump. It would be a triumph if we could get the creatures to acknowledge the junk comes from elsewhere." He shrugged. "But how would we know?"

"When they gather where they want it dropped," Gaopod said.

Chapter 23
Devastated Worlds

Genghis and Analytics reviewed the incoming sensor data as *Aurreol* approached Planet 1. Like Planet 4, it radiated a brown sheen. "If we can find any survivors, I'll take a shuttle to the surface and let Charlie and Woodsy explain what's happened," Genghis said.

"While I've had little contact with Terrans, at a conference one said our thinking was in a rut and we had to brain storm about the challenge we faced," Analytics said. He finally chose the name Dimitri because of its crisp sound.

"I actually asked the Terran what she meant because I didn't understand the connection between a rough hole in a road and putting our heads in a storm. When she stopped laughing, she explained that it meant our thinking was stuck. We needed to encourage everyone to express their ideas about solving problems regardless of how eccentric their solutions might sound. We tried it. Ideas must sprout in Terran minds like weeds. I wish my imagination was as fertile."

Genghis laughed. "You're young yet. Give yourself time."

Dimitri stared at the data again. "Alright, here's a brain storm. The spaceships and mines are being operated outside Secund and Dublo control. They could have developed a consciousness of their own, although that seems unlikely knowing the limitations of Secund technology and seeing the robots in action. The Elder says the Secunds feared they would lose control of the robots and to prevent that, they limited their programing.

"While something could have taken them over, our scans of the ships have found no evidence of onboard organic life."

Genghis was encouraged that someone was thinking along the same lines as him. At the same time, he realized there were questions he needed to ask Woodsy.

"We have to consider that an intelligence unlike anything we've aware of gained control of the Secund and

Dublo ships." Dimitri spoke slowly, almost as if afraid to articulate the rest of his idea. "Something that's driven by a large-scale grudge against the two species. Whatever it is has to be connected to those large processors on the Dublo ship." Dimitri displayed a visual of them on the imager in front of him. "My guess is they control the ships. But what directs the processors?"

Genghis waited. Another next-gen was surprising him.

"There's nothing on Planet 4 like the big processors on the Dublo ship that we fed to the creatures of Lavaworld." Dimitri scratched his head. Biots did not develop itches so like many of his kind, he copied Terran affectations just as many Beings had.

"If the mines and attack ships are under outside control, why haven't they finished their attacks on the Secund worlds." Genghis leaned forward to rest his head in his hands. "It makes no sense. At first I thought that *Wanderer* had been sabotaged. Now I suspect it realized what happened to the Secund worlds and acted on its own to fulfill its mission. However we can't communicate well enough for it to explain."

"What would be the purpose of the attacks on the Secunds and Dublos?" Dimitri said. "Revenge seems so petty for an intelligence able to launch them while making the Secunds and Dublos blame each other. However, it hasn't gone beyond keeping the vanquished in a state of fear and subjugation."

"Perhaps we'll have a better understanding after we inspect Planets 1 and 3." Genghis plugged himself in for a recharge and activated the monitor for his seat. "Do we have a breakdown of the composition of the enemy ships?"

"It's more like a best guesstimate. There are close to 20 transport-sized starships we assume are cruisers, 50 assorted smaller ships and thousands of mines."

Dimitri called up the latest data on Planet 1. "No response to our communications and no mines in orbit so the attackers must be convinced they eliminated any opposition on the ground. The sensors haven't found much in the way of ruins so it's impossible to determine how much population or industry this world might have had. We've found faint signs of small groups of Secunds."

At first light on the planet the next day, a shuttle approached the community with the most Secunds that *Aurreol's* sensors detected. When no one appeared, Charlie and Woodsy scouted the area around the shuttle.

"The robots haven't spotted any signs of the local population although the sensors indicate they're nearby," Tyson said. "There's no way they could have missed the roar of the shuttle landing. While they probably hid at first fearing an attack, one would expect them to investigate our arrival by now."

Carrying Tyson, Genghis joined the robots. "Let's head for the community." He pointed at a collection of run down but intact stone structures that appeared huddled together for mutual support.

It was the 17th planet Genghis walked on, and like the others, it had its own feel. It was unusually quiet as if there was no wildlife to proclaim the presence of strangers or leaves for the steady breeze to disturb.

The gravity was less than Being standard and Genghis enjoyed the extra spring in his step. Once again, he wished he could smell the world around him. That triggered a flash of envy as he recalled hearing that an olfactory sense would be added to the robots when they were transferred to their new bodies.

He was so wrapped up in his thoughts he almost walked into the robots that halted when a Secund stepped out from behind an abandoned building.

The Secund ignored Genghis as it interrogated the robots. "By Woodsy' responses, he's speaking to a female," Tyson said.

The Secund finally accepted the robots were genuine and not attackers in disguise. She did not know what to make of Genghis other than the presence of the robots meant he was not dangerous.

"How old is she," he called to the robots. The female glared at him. This was a world where non-Secunds spoke only when questioned. "It's possible she was born after the attacks and knows little of life before then."

Tyson broadcast its translation of Genghis's comment in Secundese and it silenced her. She rocked sideways, and then called out in a loud voice. Close to fifty Secunds and robots appeared from behind the wall and the closest buildings. Several carried spears and clubs while a few others had walking sticks that could probably inflict damage at close quarters. The robots held their hands out to show they were not carrying weapons.

Tyson had a hard time tracking all the questions and comments directed at the robots. Genghis stared at the Secunds as he listened to the translation. This group knew far less than the Secunds on Planet 4, which meant they did not have an Elder living with them.

"Tell them of the other groups of Secunds we've located on this planet," he said. "Other Galaxyships can bring them supplies and radio transmitters."

Once the robots delivered that information, the shuttle returned to *Aurreol*. "There were more survivors than we detected because they can hide in basements and underground tunnels, which is remarkable considering how slow and cumbersome they are," Genghis told Kelsey. "They can't monitor incoming vessels and the shuttle took them by surprise. They could only tell our shuttle wasn't a mine. Most of their robots are out of operation. While they're suspicious of outsiders, these Secunds need help."

Kelsey ordered Carter to head for Planet 3. "If it's also been devastated, then we can probably conclude the other worlds closest to the Dublo system are as well. Perhaps we should check Planet 6 as it's the farthest away. The planets could have remained silent to protect themselves although it's more likely their longrange communications equipment was destroyed."

The devastation on Planet 3 was far worse than on Planets 1 and 4 or anything Genghis had seen during the Nameless War. Piles of pulverized rubble marked where the Control Towers had stood as pinnacles of Secund civilization. Nearby buildings were obliterated just as thoroughly.

Genghis compared views of the city from *Aurreol's* sensors to images of it from the archives on Planet 4. "There are no signs of life there. Perhaps it was hit first and hardest to ensure the destruction of the Towers so the other worlds and the Secund vessels would have no warning."

"The attackers could have transmitted signals to the Secund worlds and ships before the main attack to corrupt their operating systems." Dimitri was back in full brain storming mode. "The Secund and Dublo ships could've been hacked in advance. We need to find out what happened to the ships that were in space when the planets were attacked.

"It would tell us a lot if they were seized at the same time or had been under the enemy's control beforehand. We should also determine how many starships the Secunds and Dublos possessed before the attacks compared to the number of ships the enemy now controls." Dimitri kept typing notes into his communicator as he talked.

Carter intervened. "We've found scattered indications of life elsewhere. There are two large groups and several smaller ones, all far apart. Do you want to send a shuttle to check them out?"

"We'll continue our patrol after we contact as many groups on the planet as we can," Kelsey said. "Charlie and Woodsy can travel on separate shuttles to tell the survivors what's happened and collect information on their condition."

Later in the day, the imagers showed Woodsy approaching a group of Secunds, several of whom had weapons pointed at him. They scoffed at his claim that help was available.

"The Secund speaking to Woody is blaming the attacks on the Dublos and thinks that Woodsy to offer assistance is a trap."

Woodsy set up a portable imager for *Aurreol* to broadcast visuals of the devastation of the capital city, conditions elsewhere on the planet and *Aurreol's* defence of the space station. "These scenes are being transmitted from that very ship," he pointed out.

Next were visuals of the visits to Planets 4 and 1 and a long segment with the Elder. The weapons were pointed at the ground as the Secunds listened intently to the old one's words.

"While they appear to have no knowledge of the space station, they're impressed an Elder is still alive," Carter explained.

"Woodsy handled this quite well," Kelsey said.

Genghis radioed Woodsy. "Give them a tour of the shuttle."

The Secunds followed the robot wearily, constantly glancing about. When they reached the shuttle, two of them climbed on board. The shuttle's interior recorder showed them cautiously following Woodsy through the craft until satisfied there were no hidden assailants.

Woodsy picked up on their unease. "Were you expecting an attack on the way to the shuttle?"

The Secunds motioned outside and Woodsy followed them. "The Secund that met Woodsy is explaining that after the planet was assaulted, animal-like machines appeared on the planet that had never been seen before," Carter explained to the Biots in the Command Chamber. "They attacked anyone who left the community. The Secunds built the wall around their community for protection and organized hunting parties to destroy the animals. While they haven't seen any of them for years, they remain on guard."

"Odd that there was no mention of such creatures on the other two planets," Genghis said to the others in the Command Chamber. "Maybe Planet 3 was seen as more of a threat."

When Woodsy returned to *Aurreol*, he reported to the Command Chamber. "The Secunds are holding on but not much more. They expect the enemy will return in force someday to finish them off. In the meantime, they'll work at contacting the groups at the locations we've shown them. They'll gather up the broken down robots so they can be restored later or the parts from them used to repair others. It wasn't clear that any of them knew how to do that."

"Do they have any ideas about who attacked them?" Dimitri asked.

"Just the Dublos. Without any Elders, they've no understanding of their history."

The aerial reconnaissance of the rest of Planet 6 produced images equally as glum as on the other worlds.

"We can conclude the rest of the Secund worlds have all been attacked," Kelsey said. "However, other than the one example of the machine animals, there have been no attempts to take control of the planets. What we need to do to put our tour in context is skip Planet 6 and inspect Dublo worlds. I'll request Commander Gnoorvants' approval for that mission."

Genghis shook his head. "That would only draw more attention to us. Let's go. If you're questioned about the move, play the Genghis card again. Believe me Commander, if Hton was here he would say your plan is the right one.

"Three ships smaller than the ones we encountered at Lavaworld are shadowing us," Carter said. "They're a couple of days away and have left the mines behind. Also on the main imager and the large ones throughout the ship is a montage of the long range scans of this region of the Galaxy based on information supplied by the Secunds. You'll notice how few systems are identified. Rather shoddy explorers."

The main imager shifted to a different star scape and a light flashed in the middle of it. "This is in the area between the Secund and Dublo worlds," Carter said. "There's a concentration of cruiser-sized ships around an even larger object. It didn't appear on our scans or probes until recently."

All eyes focused on the main imager. "The ships appear to be guarding the larger object, which appears to be vessel of some sort," Dimitri said. "We've probably found the missing Secund and Dublo fleets."

Genghis grunted. "Whatever is controlling them must be inside that larger vessel."

"When we're finished with Planet 3, we'll check the Dublo worlds, and then that thing." Kelsey pointed at image of the larger vessel on the screens.

Chapter 24
Dreadnought Arrives

After a week of uninterrupted study of Planet 4, *Dreadnought* located more about 63,000 Secunds as well as close to 4,000 robots of which less than 600 were at least partly functional.

Atdomorsin along with Analytics and the commander of ship's troopers paid regular visits to the Elder and the leaders of the planet's scattered survivors.

The Elder said the Secunds were unwilling to fly in a shuttle to meet survivors outside Orphum. Instead she prepared a message for the Biots to deliver on her behalf. Atdomorsin sent along radios for each community so they could establish regular contact with the Elder.

He also instructed the fighters to destroy the five monitor mines when the resulting explosion was sure to be spotted from the ground. "We need to demonstrate that we can protect the Secunds from further attacks."

Garzon, a Pozzen cruiser, and *Perseus*, one of the new Being cruisers, were the first reinforcements to reach Planet 4. During the following week, *Tbzor,* the other Pozzen ship, joined them along with *Enterprise*, five more Being cruisers and the first transport carrying provisions and supplies.

Atdomorsin had just dispatched *Garzon* and *Tbzor* to join *Aurreol* when it became clear that she was headed for the Dublo worlds.

"From the last report we have from *Aurreol*, the other Secund worlds are as battered as this one if not worse," Atdomorsin reported to Gnoorvants. "*Garzon* and *Tbzor* will inspect the Secund planets that *Aurreol* skipped, and then team up with it when it returns."

"It'll be helpful to learn what's happened to the Dublos," Gnoorvants said. "I'd like to know if *Aurreol's* exploration was Genghis or Kelsey's idea."

"It may be a while before we find out as the ship isn't replying to messages," Atdomorsin said. "Meanwhile the enemy's advance toward Planet 4 has slowed. By the formation they're creating, they intend to hit us with a blitz of mines once they have gathered enough of them. When they're closer, we'll dispatch fighters to destroy them. Hopefully that'll open up their ships to direct attack."

When the rest of the Being Fleet arrived, Gnoorvants convened a vislink conference of the Fleet Commanders and civilian specialists.

A vislink conference enabled the participants to remain on their ship but appear in the same place in the Conference Rooms of all the ships. While it took Turing and the other controlling units to work out a seating plan that prevented any overlap, the Beings decided centuries earlier the format was far more productive than a conference of talking heads on imagers. Everyone could see the real or visual image of the speaker.

Gnoorvants started with visuals supplies by *Aurreol* of the destruction on the three Secund planets inspected so far.

Ruthie Donohue was in the third row of seats. "We've only heard the Secund version of what happened. Let's hope there are Dublos left to tell their side of the story."

"*Transformation* has completed the conversion of the space station's robots to their new bodies," Humbawloda told the conference. The imagers switched to scenes of Hobots taking tentative steps and experimenting with their new hands to pick up tools and adjust dials. "While there's still a lot of testing and tweaking of them to be done, none asked for their old shells back. The overhaul of the space station is complete and full scanning of Lavaworld is under way. We'll bring the team that handled the conversion on *Transformation* here to set up a facility on Planet 4 for turning its robots into Hobots. We'll include Hobots in the process as soon as we can."

Then Nathan reported on the Lavaworld research via a visual from *Transformation*. "Beyond any doubt, the creatures are silicon and do produce sounds to communicate with the others. We've no way to determine if they make the sounds or are projecting patterns like radio waves. The most interesting development is the creatures collect about every other day in the previous drop zone. So we dump whatever junk or space rocks we have for them about 10 kilometers away from it and they swim to the new site chattering away. We've added considerably to our collection of their sounds. While we've identified a couple of hundred we hear on a regular basis, we're no closer to knowing their meaning."

Flying at top speed, *Aurreol* passed through a series of solar systems where the planets were well outside the life sustaining Goldilocks zone of their sun and lacked any evidence of atmospheres. "The next system appears to be the same," Carter said. "After that, we'll enter the first one occupied by the Dublos."

Most Biots worked elsewhere on the ship leaving the Command Chamber to Kelsey and Genghis with occasional visits by Dimitri, who was always full of suggestions and questions. Carter connected the main imager to the long range scan monitoring the Dublo worlds. "Still not much sign of activity," it said. "Meanwhile, *Garzon* and *Tbzor* have left Planet 4. By their courses, they're inspecting the planets we skipped."

"Unless they have robots on board, they'll probably just stick to reconnaissance," Kelsey said as she fingered the necklace.

"We've left the three ships shadowing us far behind," Dimitri said. "They probably can't keep up to our speed and don't realize we're heading to the Dublo sector." He examined the imagers again. "Their main objective seems to be blocking us from a direct route to that larger vessel."

"With our Fleet at Planet 4 growing, the enemy will likely mount a full blown assault while they have a numerical advantage," Kelsey said. "Track our sister cruisers in case the enemy attacks them."

The first Dublo planet was a rocky world of browns and greys about ten per cent larger than Terra. The sensors found large deposits of ores and minerals. "There are pockets of survivors near the two cities and some towns and the mines," Dimitri observed. "While the cities and towns are heavily damaged, the mining facilities are intact. Maybe they weren't targeted."

When Dimitri suggested dispatching a shuttle to some of the communities, Kelsey said, "How could we convince the Dublos that we aren't attackers? Our mission is to determine the condition of their worlds and send a report to the Fleet. While we'll head for their next planet, I suspect we've learned what we need to know."

"So this brings us back to whom or what the enemy is?" Genghis said. "If it was Dublos or Secunds, why did they attack their own side? If it was another species, where did it come from and why hasn't it done more with the mines and captured starships to take control of the planets?"

"Please share the rest of your observation with us," Kelsey said.

Genghis peered about the Command Chamber before speaking. "My hunch is that the Secunds and Dublos were attacked by rogue robots."

"Not robots like Charlie or Woodsy," Dimitri said.

Genghis shook his head. "I can't even guess what happened." He stared at the imagers thinking about Woodsy. His pal was different than the other robots. Did he know more than he was letting on?

"In the Nameless War, we took the battle to the Rulers. We knew what we were up against once we found the Nameless were under chemical control. Then it was a matter of tracking down the Rulers. This time, we don't know anything about the enemy. I'm certain the Secunds are wrong to accuse the Dublos, who undoubtedly blame the Secunds for the attacks."

Kelsey nodded but said nothing.

"That large ship Dimitri detected must be the enemy's Command Ship," Genghis said.

"I can see no other purpose for it," Kelsey said.

"Whatever controls these ships must be on board it," Dimitri added.

After two more bombed out Dublos planets, Kelsey said, "We've learned all we can from the ravaged planets. I planned to inspect the other two by continuing on a wide arc well outside the area controlled by the enemy. Instead we'll retrace our route to reach *Garzon* and *Tbzor*."

Aurreol's abrupt change in course toward the Secund system caught the ships shadowing it by surprise. "It took almost a day before they shifted to remain positioned between us and their cruisers and Command Ship lending credence to Genghis's theory about them being remotely controlled," Dimitri said. "For now, they're also in-between us and *Garzon* and *Tbzor*. We could jam their signals if we could determine the frequencies they're transmitted on."

"If they don't move out of our way, we'll hit them with neutralizer beams," Kelsey said. "If they flee, we'll have that much more time to link up with *Garzon* and *Tbzor* before they return. In case they've learned any Beingish, send a message in Terran to the Fleet about the Dublo worlds. The other Pozzen cruisers should have completed the inspection of the Secund worlds by the time we reach them."

Genghis shifted in his seat. "What happens after we reach them, Commander?"

"Link up and head for the Command Ship. I'd like to discuss our next steps with Gnoorvants and Atdomorsin especially about what is directing the enemy ships." She paused. "If it became aware of the Being or Terran worlds, it would be a threat to them. We're better off eliminating that possibility now."

"I'm still wrestling with the fact the enemy left some population on every planet we've inspected," Dimitri said. "While that may have been incompetence or oversight, the enemy also spared the Dublo mining facility as if it had a future use for it. So the enemy must have a grand plan for this region."

"Perhaps it lacks a way to eradicate the remaining populations or judges them too small to matter," Genghis said. "Of course, the survivors have no way to strike back at the mines and spaceships."

"Maybe we should ask Woodsy and Charlie if there could be robots under the control of the enemy and passing on information on the Secund worlds," Dimitri said.

Genghis sat up straight. "Let me talk with Woodsy first."

Kelsey and Dimitri chuckled. "We've noticed he acts like your ton," she said.

Genghis gazed at them. Woodsy did spend as much time as he could with him, ready to do an errand or help in some way and always asking questions. "Having never served as a ton, I hadn't noticed what he was doing. How would he even know about tons?" As he asked the question, he recalled Woodsy's extensive study of the Confederation. One more reason for a chat with his pal.

"An outside invader would have had to spend the time learning enough about the two sides to hit them simultaneously," Kelsey said.

"Despite the resentment most robots harbor toward their masters, I don't think there's any widespread sense of rebellion," Dimitri said. "The Dublos wouldn't have faced that threat."

"Time to find out," Kelsey said. "Carter, schedule a meeting with the three of us and the robots in the Conference Room later today."

Genghis' communicator showed Woodsy was in the ship's Conference Room logged into the main information channel. Genghis stepped out of the Command Chamber and walked down the three levels to prepare for testing his pal's friendship. Although different species, they learned to work together and share ideas. Just like Humbaw and Benjamin or Hton and Hector Davis.

Woodsy always spent unassigned time studying the Being and Terran worlds. Then he would grill Genghis on whatever he did not understand. He was especially interested in how the Beings had developed the Biots.

After Genghis described the process for creating a Biot, Woodsy questioned him on the conversions of robots into Hobots. "All I know about that is in *Aurreol's* data banks including Octinog's original calculations and drawings." Woodsy then studied both extensively and asked many questions.

As he neared the Conference Room, Genghis tried to anticipate his pal's latest questions about the conversion process. While Woodsy's shell was in good overall condition, he did have several troublesome joints and his left claw had lost much of its holding capacity.

To head off that discussion, Genghis was determined to start the conversation by asking why the robots never complained about the inadequacies of their design.

Before he could, Woodsy greeted him in Beingish. "I want to know if I speak it well enough. I found the program that was developed to teach Terrans your language. So now I can speak some Terran as well. Charlie and I are to meet with you and the Commander before we encounter the enemy ships. What are we to discuss?"

"We think it most likely a group of dissident robots engineered the assaults on the Secund and Dublos worlds, not an outside invader. However, from our experience with the robots on the space station and the Secund worlds, we can't imagine how that could happen. However, you my friend have stepped out of the robot mold yet you don't show any malevolent tendencies."

"Why would I? You're a good example of how an organic or artificial life should behave. If that wasn't enough, I just have to watch the conduct of the Biots on *Aurreol*."

Woodsy pointed at the imager's screen. "I've assembled a file of Biot facts to compare to the robots. The Beings needed you to become partners in their Confederation. The Secunds developed us to serve them, nothing more. They've always been apprehensive of us. They limited our programing out of fears we would become dominant. The Dublos wouldn't allow anything on their worlds beyond simple analyzers."

While he had heard it all before, Genghis let Woodsy keep thinking out loud.

"What was it like when you went against your programing to become a soldier?" Woodsy said.

"Mostly I discovered I followed behavioral guidelines and routines developed by the Beings. Once I and other Biots stepped out of them, we realized we'd been holding ourselves back. The Beings didn't oppose our becoming soldiers and pilots; if anything they were embarrassed at never considering that we could do it. Finally they understood the Biot leaders engineered the Terran involvement in the Nameless War to teach us how to protect our own worlds."

"I couldn't behave on a Secund world as I do on *Aurreol*," Woodsy said. "The freedom I have here is impossible to describe although I think you understand based on your own experience."

"How did you break out of the constraints?"

Woodsy attempted a Terran laugh that sounded like he was in pain. "There's something amiss in my programing. I never felt the constraints that controlled other robots. I was different and had to keep my independent ways under wraps."

While it switched to Secundese, Genghis' communicator provided almost simultaneous translation. That was Carter's latest innovation.

"My first assignment was to maintain communications equipment. I developed several simple modifications to make the machines work better. Normal robots would have just followed the maintenance routine and not bothered to propose changes if they even thought of any. I presented my design to the Secund in charge. He took credit for the ideas and had me transferred to another world. After that I kept my ideas to myself and acted just like the other robots.

"For years, I watched for robots that didn't rigidly follow their programming. By questioning and prodding them on matters outside their duties, I discovered a few mavericks whose experiences were similar to mine. They agreed that something happened during their programming that saved them from the strict constraints. When the attacks came, the situation was as deadly for robots as Secunds and there were too few mavericks to make a difference. We decided to protect ourselves."

"By doing that, you showed awareness of being an individual," Genghis said. "You and the attendant have empathy for others, even Secunds, and are curious about anything new or different. You have a boundless desire to learn. In other words you're developing curiosity, emotions and feelings just as Biots have although few of us acknowledge it yet."

Woodsy stared at Genghis. "If I could smile, I would be grinning from ear to ear. No one has ever said such encouraging words to me. Good on you for noticing the independence of the Elder's attendant; it's a maverick. The Secunds don't know about us."

He lapsed into silence and looked away from Genghis. "I respect the Elder and her supporters. The other Secunds are an irksome group that I avoid as much as possible."

Then Woodsy switched back to Beingish. "I'm looking forward to meeting your organics. Humbaw and Kendo must be like our Elder."

After another brief pause, he said, "What we really need to do is figure out the origin of the renegade robots that are controlling the Secund and Dublo ships and why they attacked us."

"Any ideas?"

"Just crazy ones that I can't explain coherently."

"When you're ready, try it in Beingish. You speak it quite well especially for learning it on your own. In the meantime I have one for you." Genghis explained his idea about the hidden intelligence that guided *Wanderer*. "It kept searching for help for the robots and it protected the ship with the rocky screen. It allowed limited communications with our Tyson. However one like it on another ship could have become corrupted."

"Could you determine the course it followed after it departed from the space station?"

"Just the last part of its trip."

"It must have entered the Secund system and discovered our worlds were overwhelmed by the attacks. Being unarmed, it couldn't defend itself and as its mission was to bring aid to the robots on the station, it headed off looking for help. Once it was satisfied the Biots could provide that assistance, it headed for the station. It has to be a maverick. What will happen to its intelligence?"

Genghis explained the vessel would be delivered to Hnassumblaw to be examined by the Fleet's Galaxyship designers and Kelsey's efforts to ensure its intelligence was respected.

"When we're finished with this business, I would like to visit *Wanderer*. We could learn a lot from it."

Genghis nodded.

"It may help me discover what makes the programing in mavericks different and whether we can adapt it to the robots as they go through the conversion to the new bodies."

"Charlie will be in the Conference Room in 10 minutes," Carter told Kelsey and Dimitri in *Aurreol's* Command Chamber. "Genghis has finished his chat with Woodsy. The robot is headed to the meeting and Genghis will return here to accompany you to it. I suggest you arrive a bit late to give the robots time to talk."

"Do they do that much?" Kelsey said.

"They did rarely at first, and then only about their assigned duties. Now Charlie will occasionally seek clarification from Woodsy about the operation of *Aurreol*. While Charlie asks me when he encounters a problem, he has yet to seek advice in advance of a project.

"Probably because of all the time he spends with Genghis, Woodsy has a much better understanding of the ship. He asks me right away about anything he doesn't understand. While I can replay the conversation he and Genghis just had, it would be better to get Genghis' version of it first. It had to do with the way the robots are programmed."

The door to the Command Chamber slid open and Genghis stepped in. "Woodsy agrees that an artificial intelligence with hatred toward the Secunds and Dublos has to be behind the attacks."

He recounted Woodsy's explanation about maverick robots.

"Does he know where the others are?" Kelsey said.

"Only one. The rest are scattered throughout the Secund worlds and he can no longer communicate with them. One bonus in this. The mavericks can all read and speak Dublo. Woodsy has already become proficient in Beingish. Assuming the Dublos are in the same wretched state as the Secunds, they'll need a lot of mavericks, not do-as-they're-told robots, to rebuild their worlds."

"Should we change the robot conversion process before they work on any others?" Kelsey said.

"While Woodsy has closely studied the transfer to the new bodies, he'd like the opportunity to learn more about the details of the process," Genghis said. "We must tell Nathan about this so we change the station's robots if possible to function like Woodsy."

Genghis rubbed his head. "I really appreciate my organic brain."

"For now, Dimitri will relay Woodsy's idea about changing the robots' programing to *Transformation*," Kelsey said. "It'll give Nathan and Ruthie something to consider. They must be bored with the routine by now."

"*Garzon* and *Tbzor* are closing on the rendezvous co-ordinates," Carter reported. "A shuttle has joined them from Planet 4."

A star chart appeared on the main imager showing the enemy cruisers guarding the Command Ship. "That leaves only their smaller ships to respond to any moves by our Fleet."

Kelsey glanced at the imager before taking Genghis by the arm and steering him toward the door. "As you've said many times, it's truly remarkable what the Beings wrought when they created us."

"Woodsy's story made me appreciate it even more."

"I wonder what or who the shuttle transported to the other cruisers," Kelsey ordered as the door closed. "Weapons, prepare the neutralizer beam and laser cannons. In the meantime, let's have our chat with the robots."

Chapter 25
Galactic Minesweeping

The eight Being cruisers were strung out in a row facing the mines lined up ten deep in an advancing formation. Gnoorvants sat in *Enterprise's* Conference Room talking with the other commanders by vislink. Many had served in the Nameless War. If *Aurreol* had been in range, he would have included Commander Kelsey in the strategy session.

"Our plan is to launch squadrons of fighters from each cruiser to attack the mines," Gnoorvants said. "The mines are spread out so we can't use the laser cannons to create the cascade of explosions that *Aurreol* did. The fighters will experiment with different attacks to detonate the mines. We'll keep rotating the squadrons until we've created gaps in the formation. Then we'll either fire the neutralizer beams or laser cannons at the ships backing them up or send fighters to attack them when they can safely transit the mines.

"While we don't know how much propulsion the mines are capable of, we've seen no sign of rapid movement," Atdomorsin said. "Should they suddenly advance on our ships, the fighters will drop back, and then the Galaxyships will fire their laser cannons and guns to detonate the mines.

"While waiting for the Fleet to arrive, my tractor beam operators experimented with propelling rocks at targets. They became rather proficient at it. While there aren't enough space rocks in this region to eliminate all the mines, it could be worth firing what we can collect at them."

Gnoorvants nodded at his former Deputy Commander and made a note to request visuals of those tests. Projectile rocks could be a handy defensive technique for Galaxyships to include in the Fleet's arsenal. He would have to ask Gnoorton if it was Atdomorsin's or his ton's idea to experiment with the Octinog slingshot. Probably a collaboration.

He met Atdomorsin when they were both junior officers and was struck by how his friend and Atdoton often spent hours discussing a topic. The results of their interactions led Gnoorvants to develop the same partnership with

Gnoorton. That Atdomorsin had triggered a cultural change among the Beings could be seen in the room. Every Commander was accompanied by their ton.

"Admiral, why not place my ship and *Cygnus* in the lead position to back up the fighter attack," said Commander Defleck of *Perseus*. "Our laser cannons can fire a wider pattern than yours, which means we should be able to destroy more mines with every salvo if they overwhelm our fighters. That would give you time to assess the effectiveness of our defensive positions and the best strategy for our ships. As well, the fighters could hover behind us and resume their assault much sooner."

Gnoorvants welcomed the idea. Glancing around the room he saw the other Commanders agreed.

"Thus far the enemy has only shadowed the Pozzen cruisers despite *Aurreol's* flight through the Dublo sector," Atdomorsin said. "By now, I would've expected them to attack *Aurreol* and the others."

"What was Commander Kelsey instructed to do upon linkup with the other cruisers?" Gnoorvants said.

"No orders were given," Atdomorsin said.

"As for our battle plan, we must consider every possibility that may occur once the shooting starts," Gnoorvants said. "As soon as we deal with the mines, we'll launch our attack on the ships."

The first wave of fighters soared toward the mines. The craft from *Perseus* and *Cygnus* conducted head on attacks while the squads from the other cruisers swooped in at angles that allowed them to fire their lasers at five or six mines before they pulled up, and then dropped down for another attack. The sorties were coordinated to keep the fighters far enough apart to avoid any damage from exploding mines.

A second group of fighters launched to widen the attack on the mines. A third one would join the battle part way through the second group's attack.

"It's as if the mines were deployed to be a fence keeping us from their vessels," Analytics said as she handed Gnoorvants an analyzer cube loaded with early data from the fighters' attack. "Perhaps they don't expect us to try to break through such a mass. Which means the enemy doesn't know what we're capable of."

Gnoorvants glanced at the counter. It showed that 3,000 mines at the start of the assault were down to almost 2,000.

"We have action on the other side," Turing said. "Four the triangular-shaped ships remain positioned behind enough mines that we don't have a clear shot at them. We're recording power surges as if they were arming their weapons systems."

"If any cruiser does get a clear shot at the enemy ships, fire their neutralizer beams," Gnoorvants said. Turing flashed the command through the Fleet. The fighters were to continue to attack the mines in rotation.

Several mines exploded as the fighters soared nearby. "It's like they detonated remotely rather than being triggered by the proximity of the fighter," Turing said. "Fighters are returning to the cruisers because of damage caused by exploding mines. We're sending reenforcements and shuttles to tow the fighters that have lost power or flight control."

"Protective walls on," the voice of Blue Team leader crackled over the fighter channel monitored in every Command Chamber. The imager displayed his craft and four wing mates had penetrated far deeper in the mine formation than other squads. They were picking their way through gaps heading toward two Dublo ships.

Gnoorvants returned his attention to the ongoing destruction of the mines. Their number had dropped below 1,700 and the pilots maintained more distance from the mines to avoid damage to their craft.

He switched the view in the imager when Turing declared, "Blue Team has cleared the mine formation." The five fighters headed for the closest enemy ships, which opened fire at them.

"The lead pilot has turned his protective wall to maximum, which adds to the protective coverage for his mates," Turing said. "While it prevents him from firing, his wing mates can drop theirs as soon as the ship's salvo is dispersed and fire their neutralizer beams at it."

"Oddly, the enemy is only targeting Blue Leader's craft as if it doesn't understand the other fighters are doing the damage to it," Analytics reported. "The ship has been hit with several neutralizer beams. While the neutralizer on a

A Biot's Odyssey

fighter doesn't have the strength of those on our cruisers, they have disrupted its command systems already."

Another barrage of blue neutralizer beams danced over the ship and this time it did not fire back. "We can't determine if it's permanently or temporarily shut down," Blue Leader said. "But from our sensors, there's nothing happening on board that ship. We're heading for the next one."

"Good work Blue Team," Gnoorvants said. "We'll send a boarding party to the ship as soon as we can."

Blue Team did not come within firing range of its next target before the remaining enemy ships sped away.

"Blue Team, return to the mine-sweeping detail. We don't want to leave any of them to crash onto Planet 4."

The door into *Aurreol's* Conference Room slid open as Kelsey, Genghis and Dimitri approached. Charlie and Woodsy stood as they entered. Motioning them to sit, Kelsey said, "Those days are over. We don't do that on Galaxyships." The Biots sat across from them.

Kelsey outlined the Biots' theory that the attacks on the Secunds and Dublos were conducted by renegade robots. While insight seemed unlikely, she decided to push Charlie. If nothing else, it could make the case for transforming the robots' programming. "The attackers aren't from outside your worlds."

Charlie said nothing, his gaze focused on the far wall as she explained what the Biots had learned.

Aurreol surged forward toward the enemy shadows pushing everyone back in their seats.

Woodsy glanced at Charlie before he spoke. "I've studied *Aurreol's* data banks for ideas on how we could emancipate the rest of my kind. Robots can't even imagine what it would be like to think for themselves. I need to learn more about the design and operation of robot programming. Hopefully some of your experts can help me."

"While we've recommended that *Transformation* consider programming changes as part of the conversion to Hobots, it won't happen until the conversions start on Planet 4," Kelsey said. "We've informed Nathan Huxley and his team about the mavericks are capable of."

Charlie remained silent and never took his eyes off Woodsy as she briefed the robots.

Kelsey learned little from the rest of the discussion other than robots like Charlie were no threat and needed to become like Woodsy. Otherwise the Secunds and Dublos were doomed.

When the Biots returned to the Command Chamber, the imager displayed empty space between *Aurreol* and *Garzon* and *Tbzor*.

"Where are the enemy ships?" Kelsey said.

"They fled," Carter said.

Kelsey radioed the other two Pozzen cruisers, which were heading toward them at top speed. "We'll be alongside in four hours."

"When you arrive, the shuttle will bring Fleet personnel to discuss matters with you," *Garzon* reported.

As the shuttle approached *Aurreol*, Genghis and Dimitri left the Command Chamber to greet its passengers. In the shuttle bay, they could see the newcomers were two original Biots.

"Well look who you find in the middle of nowhere," one called out.

Genghis slowed until he could see his old flyer pals—Don and Hue. "What are you guys doing here?" he called rushing to welcome them.

"Gnoorton's idea; no one on the Pozzen cruisers has any combat experience except you and you're a grunt," Don said in a disdainful tone as he greeted his friend. "They asked us to be in the Command Chambers of *Garzon* and *Tbzor* at critical times to help the next-gens deal with whatever might happen. Mostly, we've checked out these barges. They have some potential."

"You better meet Commander Kelsey first," Genghis said. "She needs to know about your role."

"It's all in here," Hue said waving a data cube in front of him. "Plus lots of other information. The Commanders are mighty worried about our messages being intercepted. The Terrans handle a lot of the spoken communications because they have their different languages."

Kelsey welcomed the newcomers to the Command Chamber. "It's an honor to have you on our team. I've read about your exploits during the Nameless War and since.

You started as mechanics for the jets and fighters on the cruisers before you taught yourselves to fly. That was an amazing accomplishment."

"We remind Commander Atdomorsin he was the first Being to see us piloting a converted Nameless attack craft although he didn't realize it at the time," Hue said. "It was a big moment for us and for him too."

"Once Genghis, Dimitri and I have studied the data cube, I'll have questions for you," Kelsey said.

"In the meantime, we'll be checking out the disrupter beam on this ship," Hue said. "Everyone in the fleet is talking about it. As well, we want to watch you link the three ships. It's never even been attempted before."

"Carter will provide any information you require," Kelsey said.

After Don and Hue departed, Kelsey inserted the data cube into the control panel of the Command Bench. It opened on the main imager with the date it was recorded.

"It's from before they attacked the mines," Carter said.

Then a visual of Gnoorvants in his *Enterprise* office appeared. He explained the basic plan to eliminate the mines and their escorts, and then advance on the cruisers without including a specific role for the Pozzen ships. "Our primary goal is to destroy the enemy's ability to attack the Secund worlds and, based on your report, the Dublo ones as well. At the same time, we need to identify what the enemy is. Once you have the three vessels integrated, then you're to decide your best strategic move, Commander Kelsey. Make good use of your new military advisers."

She paused the cube. "Without an assigned role, we can seize any opportunity to disrupt the enemy. It's clear they haven't detected the Command Ship so it'll be our target."

Kelsey stared at her companions. "We'll fly close enough to hit it with the neutralizer beams. If that shuts it down, then our explorer Genghis can board it. He'll select a team to accompany him. Before they return to the other cruisers, we need the two flyboys to help us plot the best way to reach our target."

It took several hours to fully integrate *Garzon's* flight controls with *Aurreol's* and half as much time again to connect *Tbzor's*. When the job was finished, the synchroniser linking the three ships was engaged and

Garzon and *Tbzor* flew in tandem on other side of *Aurreol*. Every change in speed or direction Carter made would be implemented instantaneously to keep the ships in a tight formation.

The only thing Carter could not do was fire the weapons of the other two ships. "Which is one good reason to have Don and Hue on them," Genghis said. "They can make independent judgments about which enemy vessel to target."

When Don and Hue reported to the Command Chamber before returning to the other cruisers, Kelsey outlined the plan for attacking the Command Ship. "Before we attempt that, we'll test how well our three ships fly in an integrated formation.

"By the positioning of their larger ships, the enemy is preparing for an assault by the Fleet once it finishes with the mines. If we can elude the ships shadowing us, we should have a clear shot at the Command Ship."

The shuttle returned the pilots to *Garzon* and *Tbzor*. It would stay with the cruisers rather than return to Planet 4.

"We can appear busy and communicate a lot with the Fleet, which should preoccupy our shadows," Dimitri said.

"When we're ready to test our synchronicity, we could fly around blowing up a few rocks, and then fire the neutralizer beams at the enemy," Genghis said. "If it works, we head for the Command Ship."

The three ships flew behind a nearby giant gas planet and blasted their ways through an asteroid belt. Kelsey was satisfied the ships worked effectively as a unit.

"Five ships are moving into position between us and the Command Ship," Carter noted. "While they transmit data to it, our scans detect no motion within the ships, which suggests there are no organics or robots on board."

"The closer they come, the better," Kelsey said. "Alright, another loop round the gas giant, and then we'll head straight for them. Engage the neutralizer beams as soon as the ships are in range. Once they're out of action, we'll transition to Galaxyspeed heading for the Command Ship. Instruct the crews on all three ships to remain fully charged. We have a lot to do."

Chapter 26
Knockout Punch

Even though sortie after sortie of fighters reduced the mines to less than 1,000, Gnoorvants delayed sending cruisers after the fleeing ships. "I want to see what the boarding party from *Dreadnought* discovers on the ship knocked out by Blue Team.

Once the shuttle drew close to the shutdown ship, two Biots propelled themselves to a hatch. Since the misadventure with the Dublo ship at Lavaworld, *Aurreol's* mechanics developed a procedure for gaining entry to Dublo ships without blowing up the hatch.

No force field slowed the entry of the Biots. "It doesn't have the compartments the other ships did and it's full of those tall machines *Aurreol* found on the Dublo ship it explored at Lavaworld," the boarding party leader reported.

"It's hard to move quickly because you have to twist and turn to get past the machines. In many places, you have to crawl past to reach the next section. Conditions like this on our vessels would be considered unsafe for a crew. I can't imagine the Secund robots being able to work in this environment. The Beings certainly wouldn't tolerate the filthy conditions of this ship."

They completed their search without finding any evidence of either robots or organics. "After examining the machines, we can only conclude their main function is to relay commands to the mines," the leader reported. "Perhaps the best move would be to transport several of the bigger machines to our designers to examine."

With less than 500 mines remaining, Gnoorvants concluded it was time to go on the offense. Several more cruisers were due to reach Planet 4 during the next few days so it would be adequately protected. *"Perseus* and *Cygnus* will depart now to neutralize the destroyers that fled. *Onhovril* will arrive soon and can assist *Igotoren* in eliminating the rest of the mines. When that's done, *Onhovril's* contingent of Being and Terran scientists can take over dealing with the Secunds."

Perseus and *Cygnus* shifted away from the Fleet before Gnoorvants finished giving his orders. Once through the scattered mines, they surged forward.

Enterprise and two others would follow in an hour with *Dreadnought* and two more in another hour. The spacing ensured the ships could react to whatever attacks or counter manoeuvers the earlier ones encountered.

Less than 200 mines remained when *Enterprise* sped away from Planet 4. Gnoorvants focused on how to counter the enemy starships. Or as Atdomorsin phrased it, "Shut them down. We must discover the intelligence behind the attacks on the Secunds and Dublos." Gnoorvants never discounted his old friend's judgment.

Kelsey set *Aurreol* on a course to bring it and its wing mates through the five enemy ships shadowing them after they emerged from another loop around the gas giant.

As soon as they came into range, the Pozzen cruisers showered the enemy vessels with neutralizer beams. They were shut down by the time the cruisers reached them.

"They switched to flight from station keeping just before the beams hit them," Carter said. "While their momentum will carry them off, I'll track their whereabouts."

The Pozzen cruisers went to Galaxyspeed Factor 4. "Any faster and we'll blow by the Command Ship," Kelsey said.

Dimitri looked up from the imagers. "Other than the two large ships guarding the Command Ship, the enemy fleet has moved to intercept *Perseus* and *Cygnus*. While it'll take more than 20 hours for them to arrive, the rest of the Fleet won't be far behind."

"If we could shut down the Command Ship before then." Kelsey left her observation unfinished and stared at the imagers while fingering her necklace. "The two ships protecting the Command Ship will plot a position to fire at us based on our current speed. When we're closer, *Aurreol* will continue straight at the large ships while *Garzon* and *Tbzor* will split off to fly around them.

"Once they're well away from us, we'll commence reversing our engines to cut our speed to throw off the enemy's targeting system. If they do fire, hopefully it'll be at where they expect us to be, not where we are. When the escort ships are in range, we'll hit them with neutralizer beams as will *Garzon* and *Tbzor*. If that doesn't knock them out, then we'll have to attack them and the Command Ship with laser cannons. The Command Ship is a formidable-looking opponent."

"While we know such a sharp deceleration is possible, the Fleet doesn't do it because Being and Terran bodies can't withstand the force that it creates," Dimitri said.

"The Biots and robots can handle it although everyone will have to be strapped down," Kelsey said. "It'll be a rough ride."

"You're gambling the enemy vessels won't come to the defense of their Command Ship?" Genghis said.

"I'm gambling the Command Ship is focused on our fleet, which is far more menacing. If we knock out the Command Ship, it won't be giving any orders. The other ships will continue to follow the last instruction they've received."

Carter chimed in. "Our scans have found no indication of any organic or artificial lifeforms on board the large ships. It appears there's no breathable atmosphere for Secunds or Dublos on any vessel."

"Have the scans penetrated the Command Ship?" Genghis said.

"There's a dense mass at its core where most of the ship's power consumption occurs," Carter said. "The vessel appears unarmed as no weapons have come online even with the threats to it. Perhaps that explains why the ships are guarding it so closely."

"Wouldn't we better off blasting the cruisers with our laser cannons?" Dimitri said.

"If we have to destroy the Command Ship, we would at least have the cruisers to study," Kelsey said. "They'll be the first large targets for the neutralizer beam. It's the only way we have to ensure its effectiveness. If it doesn't work on them, then it won't have any impact on the Command Ship."

When Dimitri and Genghis asked no further questions, Kelsey instructed Carter to make sure the crew understood the plan and had a place to strap down or protect themselves. "Start a countdown to the braking on the ship's clocks and signal a five minute warning for everyone to be in their secure place."

Carter acknowledged. "I'll display a mock up visual of our approach along with the current position of the Command Ship, its cruisers and our Fleet."

Within seconds, Carter said, "There's a private communication for Genghis from Navigation Central. While it's many weeks old, it has just reached us."

"You may share it with the Command Chamber," Genghis said.

"Benjamin Kendo has died." By the quiver in Secretary-General's Hector Davis's voice, the message was recorded not long after he had received word of his predecessor's passing. "He requested that you speak at his memorial. The family will wait until you return."

Genghis bowed his head. Memories flooded his mind of long conversations with Benjamin, who welcomed the Beings to Earth nearly three decades earlier. How had it come to pass that two visionaries, Humbaw the Being and Kendo the Terran, were in office when their species needed aid the other could provide?

It had to be more than coincidence. Perhaps it was what Benjamin meant when he talked about divine intervention. Perhaps Vasile Stocia would have thoughts on this.

Genghis' recalled Benjamin resisted calls to move a second billion Terrans to Mandela. He feared that would leave his planet in the hands of those too old for space travel or too mentally or morally unfit to control Terra's future.

Benjamin's death also made Genghis realize he felt grief. While his visual receptors could not well with tears at the realization that someone important to him had passed, a flood of memories kept Genghis from formulating a response to the message.

He almost jumped out of his seat when Kelsey patted his hand. While it was a simple gesture that Terrans used to convey sympathy, Biots were not supposed to feel that emotion either. He smiled at the Commander. She understood what he was feeling. That is what a good friend did.

"While I never met him, I know his history and that you worked with him after the War," she said. "Terrans live such short lives. Aunt Kelsey told me the important figures in your life remain with you as long as you keep them in your heart, which is where the Terrans must store memories." She paused. "Aunt Kelsey has stayed with me."

Genghis nodded, a thank you lodged in his vocalizer. Wishing to change the topic so he could grieve by himself, he glanced at the clock that indicated less than 60 minutes until the enemy vessels came into range. Kelsey's strategy for attacking the Command Ship was bold. Although Genghis did not like the odds of its success, he could not offer a better one. Time to load a shuttle with the gear needed for the foray into the heart of the enemy. He would add the laser pistols that Kelsey sent on the second shuttle to *Wanderer* in case they were needed.

Woodsy agreed to accompany him. "It's the last place in the Galaxy that I want to be but you'll need a robot with you to understand the interior of the vessel and I'm the best choice."

Gnoorvants peered at his ton as *Enterprise* set out after *Perseus* and *Cygnus*. "*Aurreol* and company are headed straight for two enemy ships well behind the main formation. Any thoughts on what Commander Kelsey's plan for attacking them might be?"

"Whatever it is, she must have convinced Genghis it could work," Gnoorton said. "It's probably based on his theory that there are no Secunds or Dublos on board any enemy vessels because their interior conditions are unsuitable to either species."

"Some life we can't imagine?"

"If so, what was the purpose of not occupying and exploiting the Secund and Dublos planets?" Turing said. "Other than annoying each other, I don't think either species caused the other any harm. From the Elder's accounts, all the planets the two species expanded to had no advanced life forms on them. So how could they have enemies? If there's a conquering horde terrorizing space, why hasn't it attacked the Confederation or Terra? Our worlds don't hide their presence."

"If we can defeat or drive away the enemy fleet, any ideas on what we should do for the Secunds and Dublos?"

Gnoorvants welcomed the opportunity to discuss future actions with his ton and Turing.

"Although it's unlikely they can inflict any harm on each other in their present conditions, we have to arrange a peace treaty between them," Gnoorton said.

"I haven't told the Fleet yet that Vasile Stocia and Stocton are on their way here," Gnoorvants said. "I want their arrival to be a surprise for the Secunds. From what the Elder says about Vasile's link to the Ancients, it would be most effective if they were suddenly to appear. The Secunds will certainly listen to him and the Elder is sure the Dublos will as well to hear his description of the Dome."

"We could offer to consolidate the Secunds onto one or two of their worlds," Turing said. "It would make it easier to sustain their existing population and they don't have the expertise left to operate their space vessels."

"With new bodies, their robots could take on many of the duties that Biots handle for Beings," Gnoorton said. "But first we have to defeat the enemy."

He faced Gnoorvants. "That, Commander, is what we need you to do."

"You can direct this battle as well as I could."

Gnoorton shook his head. "Not even close. Commander Kelsey might be able to someday. Genghis and the flyers with her could do a credible job. However we all learn from you."

"*Perseus* and *Cygnus* neutralized the ships they were pursuing," Turing said. "They report a large ship behind the main formation of enemy starships, about where the Pozzen cruisers are heading. I'm scanning for more information on it."

"The neutralizer beams on the three vessels are fully charged as are the forward laser cannons," Carter reported after issuing the five minute warning about *Aurreol* commencing extreme braking. The other two cruisers broke formation to fly around the enemy ships.

"All personnel are safely secured." Only Kelsey and Dimitri remained in the Command Chamber because there were no restraints for anyone else. Together with Carter, they would monitor the actions of the enemy ships, especially the Command Ship, and Genghis's attempt to board it.

The warning to brace for deceleration rang through *Aurreol*. Kelsey gripped the bench as the transition made her feel she was being pitched forward. The main imager displayed *Aurreol* as a flashing dot streaking toward solid squares.

"Yes," Dimitri howled. As Kelsey had anticipated, the enemy ships fired at where they had projected their target would be. With the abrupt deceleration, their salvos missed while *Aurreol* scored direct hits with the neutralizer beams. *Garzon* and *Tbzor* also blasted them with their neutralizers.

"One enemy vessel is off line while the other has fired again although our protective walls handled it," Carter said. "*Tbzor* has fired a second round of neutralizer blasts at it. If needed, we will as well once our walls have absorbed the incoming blasts."

The main imager monitored the impact of the neutralizer beams on the enemy ships while the right hand one displayed the status of *Aurreol's* protective wall. Kelsey touched her necklace when it turned orange, which signaled a moderate blast. Red meant the walls could not absorb all the discharge and damage was likely to the ship.

"Both enemy ships are shut down," Carter said.

"We'll inspect them later," Kelsey replied. "As soon we're in range, hit the Command Ship with as many neutralizer blasts as possible."

Kelsey updated the crew. "Remain safely secured because we're in for a rough ride. If the neutralizer beams shut the Command Ship down, we'll launch the shuttle, and then take up a position between it and the enemy fleet. We have to give Genghis and Woodsy time to discover what's inside that vessel."

It all sounded too simple.

Gnoorvants watched on the main imager as *Aurreol* and company hurtled toward the largest ship. He switched off the other imagers and expanded the main one to display a chart showing the location of all the Fleet. *Perseus* and *Cygnus* were still fourteen hours at top Galaxyspeed from the phalanx of enemy ships.

"What's the point of shutting down the largest ship?" Gnoorvants said. "We should destroy it."

"My conclusion is that Commander Kelsey wants to learn more about it," Turing said.

"Magnify the view of that vessel," Gnoorvants said. He stared at the imager, occasionally shaking his head. "It certainly looks nothing like the rest of the enemy fleet."

"The two flyers on the Pozzen cruisers have plenty of combat experience," Gnoorton said. "They'll start shooting when they need to."

"I'll never forget the look on Atdomorsin's face when he informed me about the Biot pilots," Gnoorvants said, almost glad of the distraction. "Initially, he was in full disbelief and by the end he was saying 'well, why not.' After that he was always keeping up with what else the Biots could do."

"Actually Atdomorsin did more than watch," Gnoorton said. "He convinced Ruth Huxley, Ruthie Donohue and Humbawloda to undertake ongoing monitoring of the Biots. He told them the Biots were evolving and no one, least of all the Biots, realized it. It helped when the Chief Councilor lent his support to the research project."

Gnoorvants looked wide-eyed at his ton. Why had he not heard about the project? He paused to consider another idea the Chief Councilor was pondering, and then decided to share it. "During the last briefing on this mission, Hton and Humbaw asked me to keep a close eye on Genghis. The Council thinks that in time, we could have a formal Confederation of the Being, Pozzen and Terran worlds and it could include whatever species we find on this mission. That will take a very special leader. Hton believes Genghis could be the one."

Gnoorton and Deputy Commander's ton shared fist pumps while the Deputy Commander smiled broadly.

"Genghis's preoccupation for now is the changes in the Biots," Gnoorton said. "Especially how different they and the next-gens are compared to the Biots before the Nameless War. Ruth Huxley is guiding him."

"If Genghis can show the Biots what they are capable of, they might finally realize they're no longer glorified helpers," the Deputy Commander said. "It would be a great breakthrough for all Biots and perhaps among the greatest achievements of the Confederation. Hton gained awareness from his association with Humbaw. Genghis is achieving it the hard way.

"In time, Genghis would be an excellent candidate for the position of Chief Councilor. He has many admirers throughout our worlds already and has made a good impression on the Secunds."

Gnoorvants stared at the Deputy Commander. In the years they spent together on *Enterprise*, he had never expressed such views. They were close to his own.

"The end of the Nameless War is called Liberation because the Corens were freed from the tyranny of the Rulers and moved to Mandela," the Deputy's ton said. "It was Liberation for us Biots as well. We're still trying to comprehend what we're capable of. Genghis has been leading by example. The Terrans would say that even with all he's done, Genghis is still growing up. Every next-gen will be envious of Kelsey and the crew of *Aurreol* for the time they've had working with him."

The ton's outburst startled Gnoorvants. It seldom spoke although it and the Deputy Commander worked well as a team.

"If I might add Admiral, Genghis wouldn't want Hton's post for a long time," the Deputy Commander said. "There's much he still wishes to do and understand. I think you would be a great Chief Councilor of the Confederation when Hton is ready to retire."

Seeing the two tons nodding in agreement, Gnoorvants focused his gaze on the imager. Could Hton and Humbaw have told him that in their vision of Genghis as the eventual leader of a Confederation of the Milky Way worlds?

Chapter 27
Staring Evil in the Face

Blue light from the neutralizer beams fired by *Aurreol*, *Garzon* and *Tbzor* still danced over the hull of the Command Ship as Genghis and Woodsy's shuttle approached. It would wait for the light to subside before attempting to land.

In the meantime, Genghis puzzled over the strange shape of the vessel. Two large rectangular-shaped components sandwiched a much smaller square one.

"The outer sections and middle component come from Secund transports," Woodsy growled. "When it's safe, shuttle proceed between the large sections and set us down near to the middle component. Turn on the forward lights when we're close."

In addition to the Command Ship's dingy hull, the lights illuminated several hatches and a pad large enough for the shuttle to land on.

"Land close to the mooring rings," Woodsy said. "While the lights are on, we can moor the vessel to the rings and open a hatch. Shuttle, turn off the lights after we're inside the ship. Do not allow anything to enter the shuttle without our approval."

As soon as it touched down, Genghis followed the robot out the shuttle hatch glad he donned his spacesuit while still on board *Aurreol*. He would have wasted valuable time doing it now. They dropped down to the surface of the ship. The robot connected the shuttle to the rings with quick release clamps while Genghis examined the hatch. Even though he turned up the power on his headlamp, he could not find a mechanism for opening it.

"You wouldn't have seen this before," Woodsy said as it knelt and stuck part of its right claw into what looked like a hinge. The device shifted and the lower part of the claw slid into an opening. It twisted the claw and the hatch slowly slid sideways. "It's been a long time since that was opened."

Not a flicker of interior light greeted them. Genghis and Woodsy peered at the pitchblack interior. It was the first time Genghis had seen his pal's headlamps come on. The light fell on tall rectangular columns.

Genghis pointed at ladder rungs.

"Puzzling," Woodsy said before shuffling to them and climbing down.

Genghis hurried after him. As he descended, he twisted about to shine light from the lamp strapped to his head in every direction. When he stepped off the ladder onto a metal floor, he was surrounded by columns. "They look like the machines our boarding parties found on the Dublo ship at Lavaworld."

"While they're covered in status lights and small screens, not one is illuminated and there's not a speck of light anywhere," Woodsy said. "That indicates the neutralizer beams knocked out everything." It looked down, and then moved its right foot about. "Dirty place, which is another good sign. We can see the footprints."

"What," Genghis gasped as he pulled a hand-held lamp from his backpack and shone it on the floor to supplement the light from his head lamp. Boot prints stood out in the grime on the floor. "They're the same as the blockish mark that Secund robots leave everywhere."

Woodsy examined the marks a bit longer. "The tracks all go in the same direction. It's like Secund robots walk through here on a regular basis doing inspection rounds."

"Why would they be doing that?"

Woodsy did not reply.

The beam from Genghis's lamp did not reach far because the processing machines were stacked so close together.

"It would be quite noisy on this ship if all these machines were operating." Woodsy took another look at the boot prints. "They'll probably lead us to where we want to go. We'll follow them."

Genghis felt completely disoriented by the bizarre surroundings. The most desolate planetary barrens he had seen looked cheerful compared to this place. He hurried after Woodsy certain they were headed toward the heart of the ship. He kept flashing his lamp back and forth trying to make sense of the dark columns that towered around him.

At regular intervals, he noticed thin strands of cabling not unlike the wiring that crisscrossed Terran spacecraft built before the arrival of the Beings. Their system of growing the hull and interior walls with biotech material that carried communications, heating and air recycling made the Terran design obsolete.

The robot stopped at a three-way intersection of walkways to stare at the boot prints. "I'm still puzzled there could be Secund robots on this vessel, which probably co-ordinated the attacks on their worlds."

Again Woodsy did not respond.

"Maintenance patrols aren't required on Being ships because the Controlling Unit would find a problem long before it became noticeable," Genghis said. "All these processors must require regular inspections."

"While a robot duty on Secund ships was regularly checking that everything was in order, there was nothing like these processors."

In the short time Genghis knew Woodsy, it had never sounded as hesitant. He pointed ahead. "The foot prints come from the direction of what's probably the main control area for the ship."

Once again, Genghis' lamp revealed little. The walkway twisted gradually to the left and, if anything, the columns of machines in this area stood even closer together.

They followed the walkway for several minutes until they reached another intersection. Woodsy pointed to a walkway that went straight ahead, and then to one that veered to the right. "The patrols can go on either route and return to their depot using the walkway we're on."

"What if robots spot us?"

"They'll see a robot with a different type of robot. Not their problem."

"We should mark this intersection in case we have to leave here in a hurry. We don't want to become lost in this place."

Woodsy chuckled. "Look down, friend. The wiggly tread marks left by your feet are quite distinct. Just follow them."

They set out toward the main control area. Genghis flashed his light up and down. While they were still surrounded by dark columns, the bundles of cables became bigger and more frequent. Ahead was a ladder that ran up and down.

When they reached it, Woodsy said, "Stay here while I scout above."

While he waited, Genghis set his lamp to low. He did not want to run out of power in this place.

The robot climbed down the ladder in a few minutes. "We go up. There'll be an elevator somewhere but it won't work with everything still shut down."

Genghis calculated they climbed more than fifty meters to reach the next level. Without saying anything, the robot rushed away. Glancing up, Genghis saw the ladder stretched beyond the beam of his lamp. He headed in Woodsy's direction. Walking down a corridor that appeared like a canyon with the machines as the walls, Genghis spotted Woodsy inspecting objects on the floor. As he stepped closer, he could see they were prone robots. The scene reminded him of Charlie examining the robots on *Wanderer*. However, these ones lay scattered about as if they had collapsed rather than shut down in an orderly row.

Woodsy pointed at finger-sized cylinders protruding from both sides of the heads of the prone robots. "Now I understand what has done to them. These devices must contain programing to override the robots' instructions. I can't grip well enough to pull them out. You need to squeeze the tabs at the base to release them."

Genghis took hold of a device with his thumb and three fingers and depressed the tabs. It required a strong tug before it pulled free with a loud snap.

The robot held out his claw. "My turn." Genghis passed over the device. Woodsy crushed it in his right hand, and then for good measure ground it under his foot.

Genghis moved as fast as he could to extract the controllers from the other seventeen robots and hand them to Woodsy. "I'll keep one set for our techs to study. By the time they're done, they'll look like that." He pointed at the shattered fragments of the devices that Woodsy had destroyed.

"I'll revive a robot to find out what happened here," Woodsy said. With that, it knelt beside one and inserted a device into one of the ports the controllers had been in. While Woodsy worked, Genghis shone his lamp about. The machines here were several stories tall and covered in smoky black metal except for a few panels dotted in status lights and hand-sized screens. Cables snaked among the machines or through the floor. As he walked along, he once again felt like he was in a high-walled canyon. *Terrans would find it claustrophobic.*

He aimed the lamp along the floor ahead of him. The canyon went on and on. Footprints in both directions stood out in the grime. When he pointed the light upward, he could only see a metal grate ceiling at least 30 meters up. He walked past several more machines. The pattern of the footprints suggested the robots spent time standing in front of each of them. *Could this be the control center for the Command Ship—the heart and brain of the enemy?*

Peering over his shoulder, he spotted Woodsy still attending to the robots. A couple were sitting up. He looked back up the tunnel. A dim yellow-tinged white glow from a single light on the biggest machine caught his attention.

It was the first indication of power he had seen anywhere on the ship. Then the status light beside it flickered on. *Terrans would call this creepy.* Genghis patted the laser pistols in his pocket. He shut off his lamp and peered about. Everywhere else remained pitch black.

The two lights warned him that the ship was shrugging off the neutralizer beam.

He flashed his lamp in Woodsy's direction. It was helping a robot to its feet. Woodsy pointed at Genghis and stepped toward him. When the restored robot did not follow, Woodsy spoke to it. Their conversation went back and forth until the other robot returned to the prone ones and helped a couple of them stand while Woodsy hurried to Genghis.

"This ship is what we feared," Genghis said. "There are no aliens on board. It's just Secund technology gone berserk like an old Terran nightmare about artificial intelligence come to life. We either have to shut it back down or get off the ship. Another round of neutralizer beams would knock us out as well. But Commander Kelsey won't risk letting it become restored."

Woodsy tilted its head in the direction of the machine that now had a third lit status light. "You've found the enemy. From the programing in the robots, this machine contains the entity that controls the Secund and Dublo ships and masterminded the attacks on their worlds."

When Genghis pointed out a fourth status light flickering on, Woodsy said, "Impressive recovery considering the pummeling it took from the neutralizer beams. I'll ask the robots for ideas on how to attack the entity." Woodsy hurried away.

Genghis glanced at the machine again. Two more lights taunted him and a disc was glowing faintly. While it was time to flee this madhouse so the Fleet could blast it into space dust, Woodsy would not leave its fellows behind. Charlie had the same concern for the other robots on the station. Even in the benighted state the Secunds kept them in, the robots developed a sense of mutual responsibility. Just like Biots, Beings and Terrans.

He flashed his light again in the direction of the robots. Most were standing now and a couple took hesitant steps.

The entity emitted a high pitched squeak. Nine status lights now glared at him. No doubt the Command Ship was coming back on line. Genghis pulled out a laser pistol even though he had no idea what to aim at. Could the weapon even do any damage to the monster? It looked solidly encased in its metal coating. What's more, Woodsy needed more time to revive the robots and head for the shuttle.

The entity squealed several more times. Sensing movement, Genghis glanced to his left just as Woodsy seized a couple of the revived robots by the arms and shouted at them. The squeal had to be the call the entity used to summon its slaves. The devices on the robots' necks must have translated the squeals into commands. The robots were so used to the sound they responded to it even with the devices removed.

Genghis was still trying to think of a way to attack the machine when the entity spoke.

"It wants to know what you are." Genghis had forgotten his communicator was upgraded to include translation of Secundese.

"A biological robot." Genghis listened as his communicator translated his answer.

"It doesn't know what that is."

Genghis glanced over at the robots. As most were standing, he called, "I need help speaking with the entity."

Woodsy talked with the others before joining Genghis. "I told them to wait for us in the shuttle. It'll be crowded with them on board."

The entity squealed again. The communicator and Woodsy started translating at the same time. After a few words, the communicator stopped. "It calls me an unidentified robot and wants to know where I came from and why you and I've intruded into its domain."

"Tell it I'm an explorer from a starship that's trying to find out what happened to the Secunds and Dublos."

The entity's response was an angry shriek. "It says the attacks were retribution for the Secunds and Dublos' abuse of the robots," Woodsy said. "The fate of organics doesn't matter to the entity. The Secunds and Dublos are inferior to it and all robots."

"Most of its functions must offline be offline as the entity hasn't scanned either of us," Woodsy said. "It has yet to question how we boarded the Command Ship, what caused its functions to shut down or the origin of the starships hovering nearby."

"What did you intend to accomplish by attacking the Secunds and Dublos?" Genghis said to the entity. "You destroyed many robots."

"It says they were warned to flee the Secund communities before the attacks," Woodsy said before shaking his head.

"You attacked the organics to punish them for the way they treated you," Genghis said. "While I'm a different type of robot than you, I was created by an organic species." The entity did not respond so Genghis described his origins. "I'm trained in many subjects. I've traveled to 17 planets and have friends from two different organic species who matter a great deal to me. They have taught me more than I yet understand.

"I visited several Secund worlds before coming here. While the conditions there for robots are inferior to my worlds, my pal overcame the limits the Secunds imposed on him and thinks we can do that for all robots. Then the Secunds and Dublos would have to accept robots as partners."

While Genghis would have preferred to ask how the entity became a psychopathic megalomaniac, he stuck to gathering facts. "Who brought you into existence?"

The entity erupted into a frenzied denunciation of Secunds and Dublos. "It says the Secunds prevented the robots from developing to their full potential," Woodsy explained. "They wanted to keep robots subservient. Look at the clumsy body they gave them. The Dublos banned robots out of fear."

Woodsy struggled to keep up with the entity's rant about its superiority to Secunds and Dublos. The communicator pitched in from time to time to help him.

Between them, Genghis learned that after gaining control of a group of robots to do its bidding, it abandoned its physical shell to reside in the machine, which was rebuilt into a super analyzer. That made the entity sound somewhat like the intelligence in *Wanderer* except it had not become psychopathic. From there the entity masterminded the takeover of the Secund and Dublo space ships. It foiled attempts to search for them, and then using its hijacked robots, filled them with the equipment and weapons it needed to attack and control their worlds and space vessels.

"While it accomplished a great deal that we could learn from, its derangement is clearly well beyond paranoid," Genghis whispered to Woodsy. "The Secunds and Dublos appear to have created their own doom."

"Not my kind of maverick," Woodsy said.

Genghis addressed the entity. "The Beings created us in great numbers to save their home-world and to assist them in settling on other planets. The only thing they denied us was full citizenship. Not out of malevolence; it just never occurred to them. But they didn't withhold anything from us. One of us commands the ship that knocked out two of your craft and incapacitated you and this vessel with a device the Beings suggested and we created."

More status lights came on and Genghis wondered how much longer before the entity could resume its full havoc. "Woodsy, we have to disable this ship," he said.

"We have to destroy it; the entity is in essence the ship. If any part of it exists, the entity does as well and can rebuild itself. I'll check with the others on how we could do that."

Genghis needed to play for time. While he considered asking the entity about its plans for the Secund and Dublo worlds, he also had a message for it. "I want to tell you about the three most impressive figures I know. Hton the Biot, Humbaw the Being and Benjamin Kendo, a Terran." He spoke slowly to enable his communicator to translate into Secundese.

When he finished a long winded description of the three, emphasizing Hton's selection as Chief Councilor, he wondered if Hton had ever experienced the anger that led the entity onto its deadly path. Perhaps the Nameless attacks on the Confederation worlds plotted by the leaders of the Beings who fled Hnassumblaw to avoid Transformation were motivated by the same hatred that drove the entity.

Genghis glanced at Woodsy, who just returned.

The robot leaned toward him. "We're working on your plan, but you have to keep the entity occupied."

Wondering what was happening to *Aurreol* and the other ships, Genghis launched into the history of the Being approach to Terra and the Biots becoming fighters and flyers that could defend their worlds. "You have to understand that we consider the Confederation worlds our home as much as the Beings do. Since the war, I've lived on Terra, Mandela and Pozzen yet I always look forward to returning to Hnassumblaw where I was created."

The entity ceased interrupting him, which Genghis suspected meant it figured out all the talk was a ruse and stopped paying attention. So many status lights had come on that Genghis could see a lot more of the equipment around him without his own lamp. It was a dismal sight. The Galaxy would look like this if the entity had its way. The processing capacity that filled the Command Ship would make it a formidable opponent.

Chapter 28
The Big Bang

The three Pozzen cruisers had taken up station about 20 kilometers from the Command Ship. More than 50 enemy ships, now all recognizable as Secund or Dublo in origin, were positioned about 1,000 kilometers away to intercept the Being Fleet.

It would be five hours before *Perseus* and *Cygnus* reached the enemy ships followed by the other Being cruisers. "How will Admiral Gnoorvants take on such a superior force?" Kelsey wondered out loud.

"He wouldn't consider it superior, just bigger," Carter said. "He would likely hit the larger ships first and the smaller ships afterward as they constitute less of a threat."

"While the lack of communication between the Command Ship and its fleet suggests it's still shut down, our sensors have detected some electronic activity on it," Dimitri said.

"Is it coming back on line?" Kelsey said.

"Slowly but its power is nowhere near what was before we hit with the neutralizer beams."

"Still no word from the boarding party?"

"Nothing since they entered the ship. I doubt their communicators could break through the mass of that vessel."

After examining the enemy fleet on *Aurreol's* main imager, Kelsey said, "The enemy ships are positioned much too close together."

"Whatever does control them has little knowledge of military tactics," Carter said. "Its ships should be arrayed to prevent our ships from outflanking them."

"They're probably waiting for the Command Ship to tell them what to do." Kelsey wanted to flood the ship with neutralizer beams to ensure it stayed shut down, but not with Genghis and Woodsy still on board.

Carter brought her attention back to the imagers. "Secund robots have exited the Command Ship and are boarding the shuttle. However none of their identity signals matches Woodsy's."

"What could Genghis and Woodsy be doing?" Kelsey was surprised at the worry in her voice. She ran her fingers over her necklace.

"It'll be a great tale by the time Genghis tells it." The Controlling Unit sounded like it was anxious to hear the story. "Two robots have rushed back inside the ship."

As Genghis listened to another harangue from the entity about the superiority of its intelligence to any other life form, organic or created, he knew he had to silence this nightmare forever.

Listening to the entity enhanced his admiration for the Beings who were so confident in their creativity that they never developed the Terran fear of artificial intelligence. The more the Biots advanced, the stronger the Confederation became.

There had to be more than the demeaning treatment by the Secunds to explain the raving lunacy of the entity. It would consider Terrans and Beings a menace because of their erratic behavior and undoubtedly decide to eradicate them. It represented the embodiment of Evil.

Perhaps Woodsy was correct that the problem lay with the robots' programming. The challenge would be to make them mavericks like Woodsy instead of psychopaths like the entity. Otherwise the robots would remain too timid to contribute to the Secund worlds in the manner Biots had to the Confederation.

He must think of a way to explain to the Beings and Terrans that the Secunds and Dublos had themselves to blame for the evil the entity unleashed on them.

Snapping out of his thoughts, he flashed his lamp along the left side of the machine's case. It consisted of the same type of hard metal exterior as the front. While there was no way he could destroy it, the lamp revealed a thick cable snaking through the floor into the machine. The back of the machine was against a wall so he walked across the front and flashed his lamp down the other side. Another cable. Finally the pistols might finally give him the upper hand.

The entity ranted on and on, not paying any attention to Genghis. It continued its polemic as if it never had an audience before.

Its madness surpassed any deluded crackpots Genghis encountered on Terra. There was no way to converse or even negotiate with it and nothing about it was worth preserving. Not even the processor breakthroughs it likely developed in creating the Command Ship. Enough about them could be learned from the equipment in the ships.

Genghis beckoned Woodsy closer. He pointed to the cables and mimicked cutting them with a beam from the pistol. Woodsy gazed at the cable in what Genghis called his computational stare. Then he peered at Genghis and held out his claw. Genghis fitted the grip of the other pistol into the jaws. Woodsy pulled a tool from his pack to pull the trigger. He stepped to the other side and waved his arm twice to signal he was ready.

Genghis nodded and hurried to his side. Woodsy growled as his pistol spat a white beam. Genghis pulled his trigger. A hole appeared in the cable. He slowly raised his aim dissolving away more of the cable. As he did, the entity broke into shrieks as if summoning robots to save it. Genghis focused on his task. When he reached the top of the cable, he lowered his aim to cut through to the bottom.

Just as the cable severed, Woodsy appeared, arms raised in triumph. He stepped up on a piece of equipment and aimed at the top of the machine. He pulled the trigger and held it for a few seconds. When the beam of light from the pistol ended, he jumped down and headed in the direction they had come. Genghis rushed after him. Two robots waited for them at the junction of the walkways where Genghis was sure they would turn left for the final sprint to the shuttle.

"These guys sabotaged the Command Ship's propulsion system," Woodsy said. "You go ahead and prepare the shuttle for departure as soon as we arrive. We have to fly as far away as possible before the ship detonates."

"Detonates?"

Woodsy pointed to the other robots. "Along with severing the cables, what these guys have done should make it impossible for the crazed entity to prevent the destruction of the ship and itself."

"The Command Ship has transmitted a message to its vessels." Carter paused. "They're all heading for it."

"How long before they're in range," Kelsey snapped.

"Thirty minutes or less. Genghis has exited the Command Ship."

"Flee from here as fast as you can," Genghis voice came as a scream over the Command Chamber's speakers. In the right imager, he disappeared into the shuttle.

"Carter, take the three cruisers away at maximum acceleration." Kelsey opened the communications channel to the other ships. "Everyone to secure positions." The cruisers would not wait to retrieve the shuttle. That would leave them and the shuttle in more danger.

Kelsey felt *Aurreol* surging forward. She fastened her restraint and shifted her attention back to the main imager's view of the on-rushing enemy fleet. It had moved into a formation with the smaller ships in front of the larger ones.

Perseus and *Cygnus* were three hours away. "Carter, warn the Fleet to stay away!"

"The shuttle is powering up," Carter reported. "Three more robots have exited the Command Ship and are boarding the shuttle. One is Woodsy. Incredible. There's a massive energy spike within the ship."

On the right hand imager, the shuttle lifted off the Command Ship. "It's not signaling us; it's just transmitting flee," Dimitri said. "Nothing else. Just flee over and over again."

Kelsey's eyes flicked back and forth between the imagers watching the shuttle, already at its top speed, while willing her ships to move faster and for the enemy cruisers to ignore their departure.

The main imager displayed the enemy fleet heading directly toward the Command Ship. Kelsey had just allowed herself to relax when the imagers went blank draining most of the light from the Command Chamber.

Before she could ask, Carter said, "The Command Ship exploded. Actually it's more like it went nova. There was a brief, intense flash of light, which caused the receivers to shut down automatically to protect the imagers. The shock from the explosion will be hitting us in minutes."

"Carter, steer *Garzon* and *Tbzor* away from us to avoid the shock waves throwing us together."

The imagers came back on line. The main one focused on the enemy ships while the right hand one showed the debris field that had been the Command Ship. A backdrop of stars with the superimposed words--searching for shuttle--appeared on the left hand one.

"Tilting stern upward to meet the shock wave," Carter intoned. "Impact in 10 seconds." Kelsey gripped the bench with both hands. She had never experienced anything more than mild buffeting. *Aurreol* was flung forward and the restraint held Kelsey like an animal in a trap.

The vessel dropped and rose all the while shuddering under the pressure of the shock waves. The left hand imager switched to the ship's status data. Every gauge was still in the acceptable range although several edged into the critical yellow zones. The dangerous red seemed ever so close.

The ship rose and fell in an endless roller coaster of waves. "The main explosion triggered secondary ones, which is why we're still being buffeted," Carter said. "Look at the enemy fleet. It flew straight into the shock waves pitching the ships in every direction. They're in complete disarray and some crashed into other ships."

"Any signal from our shuttle?"

"Nothing," Carter said. "The strength of the shock wave is diminishing. We should be through the worst of the vibrations in 10 minutes and return to normal in 25 minutes. Then we'll conduct a complete damage assessment."

"Status of the other Pozzen cruisers?"

"Functioning but they too are badly shaken. We should regroup so we can assist each other."

Kelsey again searched the imagers for the shuttle before agreeing. *Where are you Genghis?*

Genghis once watched a visual of Terrans surfing huge ocean waves. It looked exciting and when he could find a proper wet suit, he intended to try the sport. Now, he was having doubts as he struggled to keep the shuttle from tumbling and rolling as it crested the energy waves created by the massive explosion. Whatever the robots did to sabotage the ship had surely reduced it and the entity to tiny fragments.

He wanted to share with Hton, Humbaw and Gnoorvants what he learned from the entity in the machine. He replayed the memories of his time on the Command Ship hoping it would aid him to remember everything. Woodsy and other robots would help him recall the sequence of events.

For now, he had to keep the shuttle together. He had no time to contact the Pozzen cruisers when he reached the craft beyond telling them to flee. He tried to squeeze through the robots, but they could not make room for him. So they picked him up and passed him forward. Even before he was lowered into the pilot's seat, the shuttle was fully prepared for departure. He did not worry about where the last three robots would fit. They could sort that out.

As soon as Woodsy arrived, Genghis barked, "Shuttle, take us as far away from the Command Ship and the enemy cruisers at top speed."

The first shock wave propelled the robots forward crushing Genghis against the controls and damaging parts of the shuttle's guidance system. The explosion disoriented the Tyson and it could not locate the Pozzen cruisers. His radio no longer worked because the antenna was damaged. Genghis had to fly the shuttle by his own reckoning.

The shuttle had enough power left for two hours of flight. As soon as the buffeting ended, he cut the speed and let the craft drift while he worked on determining their location.

While he tried to glance behind him, he could barely turn his head because of the robots piled against him. He could feel movement behind him as Woodsy directed the disentanglement of the robots and arranged them so they would not fall forward during the next shock waves. When the pressure from the robots ended, Genghis discovered his interior frame was severely damaged by the tumbling robots.

Once they were untangled, Woodsy had as many robots as possible sit to reduce their power consumption. "These guys need a repair ship. Many were damaged by the shock waves. I'm explaining what's happened in the last 100 years and how we removed their controllers. I've told them that when we reach safety, they'll be expected to report on how they ended up on the Command Ship and what occurred there. Hopefully the controllers didn't disrupt their memories because they hold the key to finding out what happened."

The shuttle grew steadily quieter as the robots shut down rather than drain their powers cells. "Thanks for bringing me along, Genghis," Woodsy said. His words were slurred by his lack of power. "Best adventure of my life. Hope we have some more."

Genghis stared at the stars wondering where the craft was headed. A few hours of power remained in his storage cell. To extend it, he plugged into the shuttle's power. While the robots could shut down like an analyzer, he needed power to protect his organic brain.

The shuttle drifted and drifted and time slipped away.

Chapter 29
Marked by an Ancient

Overlooked in the battle to destroy the mines threatening the Fleet and Planet 4 was the arrival of a Being diplomatic shuttle transporting the Terran Vasile Stocia, his wife Anna and Stocton. To ease the stress of the long space voyage on the humans were placed in deep sleep for the trip.

At Vasile's request, their shuttle transitioned out of Galaxyspeed in the system where the Dome that Vasile and Stocton explored 30 years earlier was located. When the craft went into planetary orbit above it, the structure beamed a brilliant light at the ship as if sending a greeting.

Although the Biot crew did not see it, the shuttle's sensors registered the energy readings of translucent figures that entered the ship and placed their hands on Vasile, Anna and Stocton.

When Vasile awakened near the end of the trip, he grasped Stocton's arm. "Did you see them? They appeared like humans to me."

"For me they were close to Beings and Biots. There was a magnificence to them that froze me in place. I could not move or speak to them yet I understood we three were being blessed by a life form we can scarcely imagine. I'm incapable of describing it. Never have I experienced anything like their touch. I'm blessed. Now I know what it's like to experience joy."

"I feel like many years have been lifted from my body," Vasile said. "They told me our work since the visit to the Dome served a great purpose, which we'll understand eventually. We still have much to do. All will become clear to us in time."

Stocton agreed. "I received the same message."

Anna awoke and embraced both of them. "Now I truly understand why learning about angels motivated you two for all these years. I'm incapable of describing what I experienced."

As the shuttle drew closer to the Fleet, it received a lengthy briefing covering the latest information on the Secunds and Dublos and the war they both lost. They were also shown longrange visuals of *Aurreol's* tour of the Secund and Dublos planets as well as views of the Command Ship. The trio uploaded the visuals to their communicators.

"Genghis is demonstrating to the Biots what they could become," Vasile said. "He should accompany us in our searches. First, we must talk with the Elder."

The shuttle landed on *Onhovril* and they toured the ship to greet the scientists and crew. When daylight came to Planet 4, a shuttle deposited them at the base. Donning breathers to cope with the excess oxygen in the atmosphere, they headed toward Orphum with two troopers. One carried the Tyson unit left on the planet. When they reached the city, Secunds fell in step with them talking in loud, excited voices. While the escorts looked nervously at the growing crowd, Vasile, Anna and Stocton walked boldly ahead.

"Then Elder is waiting for you near the community meeting hall," a trooper said.

The Elder's arms rose in welcome, which quickly turned to an excited babble. She beckoned Vasile forward and stroked his face. While her voice sounded unsteady, whatever she said made the other Secunds want to touch the visitors.

"They're talking so fast it's difficult to explain all their remarks," Tyson said. "It sounds like they see marks on your face that prove you were blessed by an Ancient. They want you to recount your visit to the Dome."

Vasile addressed the Elder. "Gladly but we'd like all your people to hear it and see the special visuals we've brought."

The Secunds chatted in loud voices among themselves for several minutes before leaving. "There'll be a gathering of the community tonight for your presentation," Tyson said.

Vasile smiled at the troopers. "Please arrange for a projector and viewing screen." They nodded. "Now we'll talk further with the Elder. I know there's food for us on the shuttle. I'm getting hungry. Would you retrieve it?"

The troopers smiled. "The food is in this pack," one said. "Your ton asked us to bring it along as you'd become ravenous eventually. May we watch your presentation?"

"Of course. There are some parts of it that aren't common knowledge in the Confederation and I would ask you to keep its contents to yourself for now." The troopers readily agreed.

The Elder pointed the newcomers to a pair of benches.

Once they were seated, Vasile said, "Tell me about these marks that are invisible to my kind and the Biots."

"She says it's remarkable you can't see the streaks on your checks because they're paler than the rest of your skin," Tyson said. "They're clearly a sign that an Ancient dried tears from your face, which means you are blessed. The Dublos would think the same."

Facing the Elder, Genghis said, "We can discuss the Ancients further once you have seen our visuals. Perhaps you could tell us more about the rift between Secunds and Dublos."

"She says Secund astronomers discovered the Dublo home-world long before either species was capable of space flight," Tyson said. "They developed a deep space communications system through which they learned Secund and Dublo bodies are quite different as is their preferred climates. As a result, there was no competition among them while they expanded to other planets starting about 10 centuries ago. While they traded ores, minerals and manufactured products, they had little else to do with each other."

"How did they become such bitter enemies?"

The Elder hesitated. "Stupidity she suspects. There were elements among the Secunds that blamed every problem on the actions or perfidy of the Dublos. While it was nonsense, too many of their kind believed it. It was the same in the Dublo worlds. For a while they sent delegations on exchange visits and established embassies on the other's home-world.

"However with so little in common and no real dependence on the products of the other, those embassies became less and less important as they spread to other worlds. The naysayers managed to create fear about the intentions of the Dublos. They convinced too many Secunds that extra protection was required. So they built many starships. Their leaders would rail against the Dublos promising an angry response to any aggression. While there was none, if anyone said so, they would be widely criticized for being unpatriotic and shunned."

The Elder paused. "She says the Dublos developed similar fears about the Secunds and also built ships to protect their worlds. No one knows what triggered the attacks on the Secunds or why all their defenses failed so miserably to protect them."

"Perhaps you were manipulated into creating the weapons that destroyed you," Vasile said.

The Elder stared at him.

"She's perplexed by your statement," Tyson said. "She doesn't understand what you mean."

"The Being Fleet discovered a large ship, which apparently controls the missing Secund and Dublo starships. On it is most likely whatever organized the attacks on your worlds by your own vessels."

That evening, Vasile replayed the official visual of his visit to the Dome during the trip back to Earth on board *Enterprise* after the end of the Nameless War. When he and Stocton removed their weapons outside the Dome, the chatter in the room soared. "They say you showed the Dome the respect it deserves," Tyson said.

The official visual ended with Vasile and Stocton returning to the shuttle and Humbaw proclaiming the Dome closed to unauthorized exploration. The Beings backed up that promise with monitors in orbit and on the ground that would signal if anyone came to the planet uninvited.

Sensing disappointment the visual was over without an Ancient being sited, Genghis said, "Next is a computer simulation of the city under the Dome created by Turing, the Controlling Unit on *Enterprise*, from my ton's memories. While the visual does not officially exist, Stocton has preserved a copy and shown it to my wife, the Chief Councilor of the Confederation, a prominent Being and an important Terran, but no one else until now."

The Secunds sat in silence through the visual, which was a compilation of images recorded by Vasile and Stocton's helmet cameras augmented by Turing's interpretation of the visit. Although Vasile had not watched the visual for years, it instantly transported him back to that day. The smiling face of his long-deceased Bunica appeared in his mind as his figure in the visual referred to his grandmother.

Over the years, Anna coaxed him into telling her every memory of his time in the Dome. Her questions and observations convinced him of the importance of learning more about it and who created it. When he explained why he was certain of being under surveillance during his visit there, she said, "Then you were. Someday you will learn by whom and why. You were admitted to the Dome not just because you and Stocton had shed your weapons. The reason will be revealed someday because you two are important to many people."

Listening to the Secunds talking about the visual, he took hold of her hand and squeezed it in thanks. Even after all the times she watched it, her eyes were still misty. She smiled and leaned against him. It was another one of those occasions when he was certain she could read his thoughts.

When Vasile explained the urgent request for him to travel to Planet 4 and his apprehension about the trip, she convinced him to go. "How else will you ever meet the builders of the Dome? Whatever or whoever they are, they don't live on Earth. There are ways to protect you during such a long trip. I'll come with you." He often wondered if her support had kept him sane.

Anna once said, "Bunica must have told you about the Beatitudes in the Bible. There are two lines in them that remind me of the Beings and Biots. One is *Blessed are the peacemakers for they will be called the children of God.* The other one is *Blessed are the meek, for they shall inherit the Earth.*"

He stared at her for a long time. "The peacemakers would be?"

"Kendo and Humbaw."

"The Meek?"

"The Biots and you my dear. I think a better translation would be the meek shall inherit the Galaxy, maybe even the Universe."

When the visual ended, the room was utterly silent. Like the Elder, the Secunds sat with their heads bowed.

After a few minutes, he could hear whispered comments. Tyson said the Secunds were enthralled by the drying of his eyes, which created the marks on his face.

"They're completely in awe of being in the presence of one so blessed by the Ancients."

"We have one more visual for you." Stocton showed the visual of the light shining from the Dome during their recent overflight. The Secunds became delirious. Vasile hoped it would gain the Elder more respect.

Anna patted his arm. The troopers looked at him wide eyed. The Elder rolled her chair in front of the crowd, and then waved her arm for Vasile, Anna and Stocton to join her.

When they did, she addressed the crowd. "As both Secunds and Dublos claim to be descendants of the Ancients, there has always been great speculation about whether either of us resembled the builders of the Dome," Tyson said. "We never found any evidence they lived on the worlds we occupy and we never found one of their Domes. Yet none of us doubt there was an Ancient in the Dome with you even though we didn't see it in your visuals."

The crowd erupted in shouts. After a couple of minutes, the Elder raised her hands and the Secunds quieted. "While you've shown us what a Dome looks like to another species, it might appear completely different to us. Was the scene in your visual the real realm of the Ancients or what you would consider a suitable place? Or a special one?"

"Paradise you mean?" Vasile smiled. Anna suggested years earlier that perhaps he and Stocton saw what they wanted to. Paradise would take on different appearances among humans. Imagine how other species might see it. At the time, she only thought of Beings and Pozzens.

Vasile remembered the aroma of lilac and pine in the air and melodic bird calls in the Dome. Maybe the scents and sounds were there because he wanted them to be.

It took a while for Tyson to convey his concept of paradise to the Secunds. For them, it was mainly freedom from fear of further attacks. The Elder wished to have her old world back.

"They've recorded this meeting in hopes of sharing it with the other Secund communities," Tyson said. "The Elder is thinking of ways of distributing it to the Dublos."

"Our ships have that capability but if the Dublo worlds are in the same condition as yours, we face a big challenge in contacting them," Vasile said.

The Elder stared at him. "She says we'll have to travel there after our vessels conduct more reconnaissance of the Dublo system," Tyson said. "The Elder will come with us accompanied by her attendant who can translate their language into Secundese."

"In time, Stocton will learn it," Vasile said.

"Yes but the Dublos won't attack a robot accompanying a Secund. Who knows how they would respond to a Biot."

"No one will be traveling there until the danger is removed," Anna said. "Have the Dublos had contact with the Ancients? Will they see Vasile's marks the same way as the Secunds do?"

Her questions silenced the room as the Secunds stared at the Elder.

She cleared her throat. "The Dublos claim there's a Dome in this region of the galaxy," Tyson translated. "She expects the one you visited was for watching the Being worlds and Terra."

While the Elder was clearly uncomfortable with the topic, Anna pressed on. "Did anyone suggest a joint search for the Dome in your region?"

Vasile did not need Tyson to know the Secunds wanted the Elder to answer Anna's question.

"Too many people on both sides opposed searching together for it," Tyson said. "For many reasons, it came down to a fear the search would locate the Dome only to have the Ancients reveal the other side was the descendant."

"Or discover neither of you were its descendant meaning there was no logical reason for the rivalry between your species," Anna said.

The Elder finally twisted her head to look Anna. "There was some concern about that."

"Ah, fear of the truth." Anna sat back in her seat. Her bland expression told Vasile that she could not believe what she just heard. The Elder's account had come up short in explaining how two intelligent species stumbled stupidly into this mess. Or believe they could be connected to life that had arisen billions of years earlier in a much different Universe.

Chapter 30
The Agony of the Robots

Perseus and *Cygnus* dropped out of Galaxyspeed as soon as they received Genghis' warning relayed by *Aurreol* about the exploding Command Ship. They rose and fell gently in the much diminished shock waves. The Fleet following them barely felt the buffeting.

Once the waves passed, Gnoorvants ordered the ships to resume the approach to the enemy vessels. Scans revealed all were shut down and about two thirds damaged or destroyed by the shock waves or in ensuing collisions.

Gnoorvants dispatched *Dreadnought* to check on the status of the Pozzen cruisers and Genghis' shuttle. He remained in *Enterprise's* Command Chamber waiting for updates from the inspection of the wreckage of the enemy ships. When it was clear they no longer posed a threat, he repeatedly checked his communicator for news about Genghis' shuttle. The search for it became the unspoken priority because the escapees from the Command Ship could answer so many questions.

While he waited, he communicated with each Galaxyship commander about the next steps for the Fleet. He saved the call to Kelsey to last. She was in *Aurreol's* Command Chamber.

"Your initiative in neutralizing the Command Ship and its escorts was brilliant," he said. "Your and Genghis's actions saved many lives as well as a big chunk of the Being Fleet."

"Don't forget Woodsy and Dimitri; I'm sure the robot played a big part in this and my Analytics officer provided sound advice all the way." There was a hitch in her voice every time she mentioned Genghis. "They'll be especially pleased their favorite Admiral is returning home with an intact Fleet."

"The enemy largely defeated itself," Gnoorvants said. "Although we won't know for certain until we board them, some of its ships appear recoverable. I can't imagine what use the Secunds or Dublos will have for them. The best thing we could do with the rest is feed their junk to Lavaworld or a nearby sun."

He paused to make sure he had Kelsey's attention. She mostly watched the imagers during their discussion. Now she was staring at him through the recorder and fingering her necklace.

"Once *Perseus* and *Cygnus* are no longer required here, they'll be dispatched to the Dublos worlds to survey the other planets and establish contact."

"So we're in a holding pattern?"

"We have lots to keep ourselves busy with. The Elder organized teams to take to the communities on the different Secund planets to explain our offer to assist them there or relocate them."

"The object we located is a Fleet shuttle," the officer reported to Atdomorsin and Atdoton as they hurried into *Dreadnought's* bay. "Our scans detected it. There was no signal from it so we towed it in for a closer look. When we realized what it was, we brought it on board and opened the hatch. We called you as soon as we saw the robots. They're shut down and we don't know how to activate them."

Several robots lay on equipment trollies set up around the battered shuttle parked in a corner to be out of the way of arriving and departing fighters.

"The Fleet looked for this shuttle for days," Atdomorsin said as he shook the officer's hand. "It's the one that Genghis and Woodsy took to the Command Ship. You've rescued a hero. Well probably several of them. How many robots are there?"

"We haven't been able to count them; they're jumbled together."

A shout came from inside the shuttle and several Biots jumped on board. The mechanics at the shuttle's hatch took hold of a pair of Biot legs. Atdoton rushed to join the group carrying the figure to a repowering station.

Atdomorsin's chuckle went unnoticed in the excitement of discovering Genghis. The display of relief and joy he just witnessed among the Biots proved his long-standing contention that they were full of emotions like the Terrans.

After peering at the pile of robots still inside the shuttle, he activated his communicator and entered the code for a top priority communication to every ship in the Fleet. He took a deep breath to settle his excitement. "The lost have been found. We need help restoring 19 robots. The Biot pilot is in complete shutdown."

He hurried off after the group attending to Genghis while wondering how Kelsey would react to the news.

"We have to restore him to full power, and then try to wake him," Atdoton said when the Commander entered the room. "We've no record of a Biot ever being in this state. It's much like a deep coma in humans or Beings. Maybe the healers could advise us."

Atdomorsin pulled out his communicator and summoned his Chief Healer. "We have a very important Biot with a very serious problem. Bring your senior Terran medical personnel as well."

"While the robots need to be recharged, we don't have the proper connectors to do that," Atdoton said.

"So we either return them to a Secund world or link up with *Aurreol*," Atdomorsin said. "Hopefully, we'll learn why there are so many robots in the shuttle."

"As his power levels are at 10 per cent, it'll take a long time to recharge his cells," Atdoton said. "Then we'll have to find a way to bring his memory back."

The ton pulled a recorder from his pack to capture the conversation in the room. "Hton will want a full account of Genghis's recovery as well as what happened on the Command Ship."

Atdomorsin feared that would not happen any time soon.

Gnoorvants radioed Kelsey as soon as he read Atdomorsin's update on the retrieval of the shuttle. "In addition to his coma, Genghis requires repairs to body parts that were damaged in the aftershock of the explosion. He and the robots from the shuttle will be transported to *Transformation* where the same group that performed the conversions of the space station robots will look after them. *Dreadnought* has no facilities for the robots and its medical staff couldn't think of a way to revive Genghis. He'll be kept in complete shutdown until the repairs are complete."

While her face relaxed as he related the details, he would bet she would be researching complete shutdown and coma as soon as their conversation ended. She certainly smiled when he mentioned Genghis would be upgraded during the repair process.

Genghis spotted a solo flickering light, far away. Until then, he was surrounded by impenetrable darkness. While he recalled his name was Genghis, he had no idea where he was or why.

He stared at the light. After an unmeasured time, a thought occurred. *Could that be light?* Somewhat later another one occurred. *Why was it shining?* He felt utterly puzzled.

The light continued to glow and much time passed before candles came to mind. Terrans made them to create a welcoming light. During his first visit to Benjamin Kendo's apartment in New York City, he noticed several white sticks in a metal holder on a sideboard. When he asked about their purpose, Benjamin's wife Olen lit them. The dancing motion of the flame entranced him.

Later she presented him with a copy of a song about a candle. He stared at the distant flame wishing his photographic memory would kick in.

Time crept along with no way to count its passage. Then through the fuzz that filled his mind came the opening lines of the song Olen had shared with him.

> One little candle burning bright
> One little gleam of radiant light
> Shimmering softly in the night
> Makes the darkness fade away

While it went on for several more verses, Genghis received the inspiration he needed. "Thank you Audrey Snyder," he muttered, startled he recalled the composer's name.

The light was a candle burning bright; its radiance summoning him. The darkness would fade away if he reached it. He had to try harder. He could not tell if he was walking or floating. The light drew closer ever so slowly. Something held him back. He pushed harder and advanced a bit more.

His last thought before his world went dark was wondering where the shuttle was headed. With this thought, more memories crept into his consciousness.

Tumbling over and over as metal clad figures crushed him. Fleeing through a dark structure. A talking entity in a machine. The memories slowly stitched together. The entity controlled spaceships that were a grave danger. It was even more dangerous. It had to be destroyed. No, it had been. That was important.

As he moved closer to the light, Genghis recalled a massive explosion. That was the ship that housed the entity. The light was even closer and the memories came faster. He and his robot companion Woodsy boarded the Command Ship from a Galaxyship named *Aurreol* to find out what had caused the near obliteration of the Secunds and Dublos.

Robots revived by Woodsy sabotaged the Command Ship, which caused the powerful explosion that had sent their shuttle tumbling through space. What happened to Woodsy and the others? How about his pilot pals on the other Pozzen cruisers? And most importantly Kelsey? The reasons to reach the light quickly multiplied.

He pushed harder and the light drew closer. The flames of the candle danced just as they had in Benjamin's apartment and the darkness faded away.

Then it was bright all around him revealing what certainly looked like a workroom on a Being Galaxyship, right down to the soft grey walls. The muted sounds of a ship in space were familiar after his travels.

A bright light covered him. He was lying on a work bench. His arms, hands and legs were restored. The Galaxyship was different in a way that he could not describe.

He raised his head. A Terran in a white lab coat stood nearby grinning. Nathan was printed within a blue circle on his coat. He spoke in a friendly manner.

"Welcome back Genghis. You've been in a coma for almost three weeks. When Dreadnought found you, you power levels were so low, you should have been dead. Instead you hung on. We would like to learn how."

Genghis did not know how to explain the hope the candle inspired.

"We had to make several repairs to your frame and added a couple of new features," Nathan said. "It'll take time to adjust to all the changes."

Genghis stared and Nathan sniffed several times. He repeated the action when Genghis continued to stare at him. Nathan sniffed again. Realization smacked Genghis as he remembered wanting a sense of smell. He copied Nathan's sniffs.

Before his nose served as a decoration. Now it worked. "There isn't much scent in here because the room is sterilized," Nathan said. "This will give you a benchmark to work from. You won't notice the other one until you're in sunlight."

Patting his shell, Genghis felt the fabric that covered its surface. Developed by Biots and Terrans, it would convert light into electricity for his storage cell. No longer would be completely dependent on recharging stations.

Nathan recounted *Dreadnought's* recovery of the shuttle and the transfer of Genghis and the robots to *Transformation*. "I've notified the Fleet that you're fully alert. Many people are waiting to visit and more than 1,000 messages are stored in your communicator."

He pulled an envelope from his pocket. "Mother said to deliver this to you personally."

Genghis looked at the handwriting on the envelope. "You're Ruth's son Nathan?"

When the Terran nodded, Genghis said, "You were a kid the last time we met."

Nathan grinned. "I go by Huxley because my father didn't have a family name so he became a Huxley as well. He died a few years ago ever so thankful the Beings and Biots made it possible for him to have a family and live in freedom for the rest of his life."

Before Genghis could reply, the door to the workroom slid open and the ship's Commander and his ton strode in followed by Ruthie, Humbawloda and a bunch of characters that did not quite look like robots. Then he recalled Octinog's plan for the Hobots.

Genghis eased into a sitting position to greet the newcomers. Ruthie threw her arms around him. "How do you feel? Does everything function alright?"

"I just sat up and have yet to test myself. Your arrival has added many different scents to the room."

Humbawloda also hugged him. "Grandfather wishes to hear your story about the Command Ship. We already have Woodsy's version but want yours as well."

"Woodsy survived?"

"I sure did, partner." At that, a Hobot stepped forward and grasped Genghis' arms. Other Hobots crowded around the pair. "All of us from the shuttle did. We call ourselves Genghis's gang. GG is ready to rumble."

"I like your new shell without the forehead lamps; it turned out better than it looked in the plans."

"We're looking for an appropriate way to thank Octinog." Woodsy raised his arms to reveal a hand with a thumb and three fingers. "Our new bodies are amazing and so much more functional. Nathan and Wxdot enhanced the robot programing better than I could've ever hoped for."

"When the doctors and healers said they couldn't revive you from the coma, Nathan said you were in there and needed help to find the way out," Ruthie said. She leaned against Nathan in the way humans did to show affection. "He shone the bright light on you. His determination made the rest of us believe you would recover. He stayed with you all the time until Woodsy and the other Hobots were able to spell him."

"Saying thank you hardly seems sufficient for rescuing me from the darkness," Genghis said. "I don't know what to else to say."

Still at a loss for a fitting accolade for Nathan, Genghis changed the topic. "How did the robots blow the Command Ship to pieces?"

The robots grinned and one said, "We rerouted its exhaust so it vented back into the propulsion system. Basically it overheated! As you witnessed, it was to be vented externally for a reason."

Genghis shook his head. "My discussions with the entity are all on my communicator."

"We've downloaded them and they are under study along with all the other information from the Command

Ship," the Commander said. "We're analyzing the visuals from your and Woodsy's recorders and communicators and we'll have plenty of questions for you."

"The interior of that ship was a scene from a Terran chamber of horrors. Even an organic without any sense of imagination could not have lasted inside it for more than a minute. On top of that it was disheartening to hear something that twisted." As he talked, Genghis felt more alert. "What's our status?"

"The Fleet is intact and we're finishing our assessment of the state of the enemy ships," *Transformation's* Commander said. "Some appear to be salvageable. The Secunds and Dublos lack the trained personnel for that kind of work and we may have to do it or, more likely, train the Hobots. In their new bodies, they'll be quite capable.

"*Wanderer* is on its way to Hnassumblaw so another part of our mission is complete. However most of us think we've just begun our task here. For now, we need to determine how the entity you encountered gained control of those vessels and what happened to the crews from the Dublo ships.

"We've learned a great deal from the GGs about how the entity hijacked them and altered their programming. Woodsy identified the two controllers you brought from the Command Ship," the Commander said.

"At first we couldn't access them but after the first conversions of the GGs, we were able to work with the ports taken from the sides of their old heads to read the controllers. We've gained some interesting insights into the entity's programming but it's too soon to say what all they could be used for. We hope some beneficial developments will come from it."

"When Woodsy was revived, he identified the robot controller devices you brought from the Command Ship," Nathan said. "From them we're piecing together the way the 18 robots were manipulated by the entity. We're still studying their memories to understand how the devices directed them. We eliminated that programming in them when they became Hobots.

"Meanwhile Genghis needs to fully update himself on what's happened. First, he should try to walk."

Woodsy stood beside Genghis as he eased off the gurney and stepped cautiously about the room. Before long, he was moving at his usual pace.

"That's excellent," the Commander said. "Vasile Stocia and the Elder want you in a peace delegation to the Dublo worlds. Their plan was to leave weeks ago and they'll be anxious to depart now that you're revived.

"You'll travel on the diplomatic shuttle that transported Vasile, Anna and Stocton to Planet 4 to meet the Secunds and attempt contact with the Dublos. Gnoorvants insisted you should be on that mission, which meant it was postponed until the enemy ships were dealt with. While Vasile was a solid military officer, Gnoorvants wondered whether decades of studying the meaning of the original Dome had cut him off from practical concerns. However, he has won the trust of the Secunds."

"Hopefully there's more left than the ruins we saw on the Dublo planets," Genghis said. "What is the status of the Pozzen cruisers?" He thought everyone in the room was staring at him.

"Thanks to your warning, they escaped the worst of the shock waves and are undergoing repairs," Nathan said. "Many Biots were injured when their ships were thrown about, but in time all will be healed."

Kelsey is alive. "Meanwhile send me another communicator and I'll describe everything I can remember about the Command Ship and the lunacy of the entity," Genghis said. "I'll also discuss it with Woodsy and the other members of GG."

"Before we depart, you should schedule a formal vislink session with Admiral Gnoorvants and anyone else who has questions about the Command Ship," the Commander said.

"Meanwhile I have to catch up and answer messages," Genghis said. "Also I need to walk about the ship to fully test my repairs."

He stepped in front of the Commander's ton. "Billions of Secunds and Dublos are dead because the entity resented the way they treated the robots."

"I've not detected any sense of rebellion in the robots I've encountered and that includes the Hobots," the ton said. "They're certainly envious of the status we've achieved."

"We'll leave you be and inform Vasile you'll soon be ready to travel," Ruthie said.

"I would like Woodsy to come with us. There's much about what happened in the Command Ship I need to discuss with him."

"Me too," Woodsy said. "The rest of the GGs are on training and update courses, which should keep them busy for at least a month. Then we have to think of something for us to do."

Genghis grinned remembering his heady days at the end of the Nameless War. "There'll be more than enough for them and all Hobots."

"We like be called Hobots because we're more than robots. The GGs want to select their own names as I did. All the Hobots created so far want to have names and are researching your worlds for ideas."

The room emptied except for Woodsy. Genghis pulled out his new communicator to send a hurried message to Hton promising a full report once he was on route to the Dublo planets. "I doubt I'll ever be able to convey the repulsion I felt facing the entity. I wasn't afraid for myself but what it could've done to all that our worlds have created."

In a separate message, he told Kelsey how glad he was she survived and that he had much to tell her when they next met. "We needed those two laser pistols you sent on the shuttle to *Wanderer* to disable the entity. Without them, it might be still wreaking havoc."

Woodsy was examining the equipment in the lab. "By the way you're touching everything so cautiously, you're still adjusting to the new body?" Genghis said.

"It's so different than the old one that it'll take probably months to fully master what we're capable of. We're still in the adaptation stage; every day we discover new things we can do."

Woodsy stepped beside Genghis. "In the first few days after my conversion, I harbored this intense rage toward the Secunds for putting us in such a limiting shell. Fortunately there were none of them on *Transformation* to vent my anger on. I understand what ignited the hatred in that entity. It had to have been a maverick to start with."

He stared at Genghis. "Then it developed emotions that it could not control. Maybe what was wrong with the programing in the mavericks is that it let us develop feelings without understanding them. For me it was a sense of being wronged by that Secund who stole my ideas.

"I controlled my anger. The entity didn't. There was no logic in the justifications for its actions that it spewed at you. That was simple, unbridled rage.

"I told Nathan and Wxdot about my anger and they watched the other GGs after their conversion. They reported the same sensation so Nathan and Wxdot spent time with each GG after its conversion discussing anger and emotions. *Transformation's* controlling unit Darwin explained to the GGs the development of emotions in the Biots.

"From what I can determine, that helped them comprehend what was happening to them. In the end, it made our transition to the new bodies much easier. This will be an especially important step when the robots on the planets are converted. I suggested to Nathan and Wxdot that perhaps it should be done in a facility well away from the Secunds to avoid any incidents."

"Where will the parts come from if the robots on the Secund world are converted?" Genghis said.

Woodsy shrugged.

"The High Council has placed orders with manufacturers on Terra and Pozzen," the ship's Controlling Unit Darwin said. "Everybody will be involved in helping the robots, and in turn, the Secunds and Dublos."

Genghis looked at the envelope Nathan had given him. Inside were carefully folded sheets of paper. He had never received anything handwritten before and here he was holding the words of Ruth Huxley. He could not imagine a greater treasure.

On the front were printed the words Cogito Ergo Sum. He held the paper up to the recorder in the room. "Darwin, what does this mean?"

"I think, therefore I am. It's a famous phrase advanced by a Terran philosopher named Rene Descartes. Basically, he argued the ability to think and reason is the best test of being alive. It has been much debated on Terra but most agree it's a reasonable standard."

The letter said, "Dear Genghis. That you have received this letter from Nathan means you've survived, which gives me great joy. Humans, Beings and Biots followed your adventure since you boarded *Wanderer*. I'm writing this quickly so Nathan can take this with him on *Transformation*." It went on for several pages. As much as he wanted to read it, he had so much to do. He would save it for the trip to the Dublo worlds.

He resumed walking about the room to test his repaired limbs. "Darwin, what other information do I need to be updated on?"

Kelsey's name came up frequently in the update. Mechanics stopped by every few minutes to ask if he needed anything. Realizing they wanted to help, Genghis waved cheerily and they continued on with their duties. To them, he was a celebrity.

The imager in the room announced an incoming transmission for Genghis. Vasile, Anna and Stocton appeared on the imager from Planet 4.

"Another remarkable exploit," Vasile said. "I look forward to hearing your account of the encounter with the entity. It'll certainly inflame the humans who fear artificial intelligence."

"Anna has a thesis on how the relationship between Beings and Biots runs contrary to what many humans expect of artificial species," Stocton said. "She credits the Beings with creating an atmosphere that allowed the Biots to fully participate in their society."

"True in most ways," Genghis said. "We still haven't matched their creativity."

"Anna thinks the Biots' presence is a major component of Being creativity. They can spend as long as they want studying a problem or advancing an idea because their tons and helpers assist them while other Biots look after everything else. They serve as very helpful sounding boards for new ideas. She calls the Biots the Beings' brain boosters. She experimented with advanced problem solving several times with Stocton." Vasile chuckled. "By the way, she often calls him Annaton."

Not sure what to say, Genghis asked about the status of the diplomatic mission. "I'm ready to leave."

"*Cygnus* and *Perseus* have established contact with communities on a Dublo planet," Vasile said. "They asked for supplies of a medicine to combat a disease that has afflicted them for the last few years. While the Secunds didn't have any, they gave us the information needed to produce it. *Transformation* and several other ships are manufacturing the medicine and we'll take what we can with us when we pick you up in the shuttle. More will be shipped as its ready."

Genghis raised his hand to stop Vasile's explanation. "Someone is approaching this room." When he saw the Hobot, Genghis said, "Come in."

It stepped up to Genghis with its hand extended. "I'm Charlie," it said in hesitant Beingish. "Thank you for the opportunity to receive a new body. It's so much better than my old one. Also for my name. Please finish your discussion with the Terran."

"There's not much more to tell you or Genghis," Vasile said. "The Elder's attendant isn't modified and will travel with us to look after her and let the Dublos see the difference between the original robots and the Hobots."

"I'd like to walk about the ship to make sure I'm functioning properly," Genghis said. "Charlie and Woodsy, come with me. When you're finished explaining the features of the new body, find someone to explain why the Dublos have such antipathy toward robots."

"I doubt even the Elder could tell you that," Charlie said.

"They've little in common," Darwin said. "Displaying visuals of Dublos on the main imager. They're considerably taller than Secunds or Beings with small heads perched on top of long necks. They have narrow legs and a round chest and trunk. Their skin is yellowish brown. They prefer a cooler, less oxygen rich environment than Secunds. They would do okay on Mandela."

"We should walk through the maintenance bay to see how well you can manoeuvre around equipment," Charlie said.

It seemed like a great plan until they stepped into the bay in which hundreds of Biots were packed along with dozens of Beings and Terrans. A booming hip-hip-hurrah ripped through the room, and then the Biots sang *An Ode to the Universe.* It had never sounded finer. Genghis stood motionless, not trusting his voice enough to join in.

Chapter 31
Peace Talks

Before the trip to the Dublo system, Genghis recounted the exploration of the Command Ship for Admiral Gnoorvants, the Galaxyship Commanders and Vasile, Anna and Stocton. Woodsy's version of their time on the ship included frequent praise for Genghis' handling of the demonic place.

The Commanders asked few questions. "We're glad it was you there and not us," Atdomorsin said at the conclusion. Recordings of their accounts were dispatched to Navigation Central, the Being High Council and the United Nations.

With that done, Genghis watched a visual of a robot's conversion. He did not recognize many of the Terrans involved in the process although Nathan Huxley appeared frequently along with a couple of Hobots.

"Since we started, a team of Beings and Biots have undertaken the development of an upgraded power storage cell for the Hobots," Nathan said. "While a thermoelectric generator like in the next-gen Biots would be preferable, the new storage cell will allow us to proceed sooner with the conversion of the robots on the Secund worlds. It'll double their capacity and enable them to recharge both from sunlight and power connections."

The visual switched to scenes of Hobots taking their first steps. Some clearly had problems climbing stairs and co-ordinating the movement of their limbs. "The conversion teams identified design and connection improvements that we'll include in the new Hobots and retrofit in the already-converted ones."

Woodsy narrated the next segment of the visual. "The modifications Nathan made to our programming are as significant as the switch to the new shell. Adjusting to proper hands and more flexible legs takes a lot of time. So does programming that encourages initiative and curiosity. Yet none of us would return to our old form."

When the diplomatic shuttle reached *Transformation*, Genghis and Woodsy toured the craft sniffing everywhere they went. The strongest scent came from Anna's perfume.

Then Genghis went to the recharging station, plugged in and pulled out Ruth's letter. He pondered Cogito Ergo Sum for several minutes. *I think, therefore I am. But what am I?* Ruth's handwriting was clear. She recounted her involvement with the Biots since the moment a co-worker realized the first message to Earth from the Beings three decades ago was intended for her.

"I've given a lot of thought to the questions you posed during our last meeting. For reasons that I can't fathom, Biots don't comprehend they already possess what they most desire. Recall when the medical Biots, after all they did to assist the Nameless, said what they wanted the most was to be creative like Beings. All around them was evidence of their own inventions and imagination.

"Remember the mechanics creating the jets and fighters and beefing up the laser cannons. I could fill many more pages with examples. The leadership that you and other troopers showed during the Nameless War. The work that Biots did restoring Pozzen. I don't have to tell you about the first Biot Galaxyship Commander.

"Biots need to realize they have what they desire and now they must accept the opportunities and responsibilities that it offers, which you in many ways already have. Embrace emotions, don't fear them.

"Don't turn to the next page yet. I want you to think about my message to this point."

Biots think; our organic brains make us living creatures. Ruth is right. We have what we want. We have to decide what to do with our abilities. I'm a living creature. I'm not a machine, I'm an individual with my own ambitions and desires and a member of a species that wants to determine their own fates.

He was about to turn the page when he thought about Woodsy. *He's a robot and even with Nathan's improvements, his actions are dictated by his processor. Yet Woodsy seems to be much like me. Another matter to discuss with Ruth.*

The last page of her letter said, "You're an intelligent species, the same as Beings and humans. That is my message to all Biots. You've more than earned your place beside us. It was obvious to the Biot and Being leaders long before the Alliance contacted Earth. Benjamin Kendo came to believe it most fervently. The time he spent with you only deepened his certainty in the matter. We hope you'll continue to live among us and participate in the affairs of our worlds as you've done successfully so far. They're your worlds as much as ours.

"Hton realized the Biots had to come to a collective awakening as a species. The Nameless War was your beginning. Hopefully this mission will complete the process. Then the Biots' adventure can really begin. You can discuss this with Nathan and Ruthie. They have been part of our Biot study for years."

At the bottom of the page was a stylized Terran heart and Ruth's signature.

Her words reverberated through his mind. He spent 30 years looking for an answer that was always there waiting to be found. Still, his search had been worth every day it took.

Sitting in the recharging chair, he composed a message to send to Ruth. "Your letter brought everything together for me. I'll explain in person." He inserted his rendition of the outline of a heart.

He was sure Ruth would also understand his desire to share the insights with Kelsey.

The shuttle swept past *Cygnus* on its approach to the least damaged Dublo planet. After it went into orbit, radio contact was established with a group on the ground. Woodsy was put in charge of the discussions with the Dublos because of his proficiency in their language. As soon as he mentioned the Elder and the medicine, they wanted to arrange a meeting.

The shuttle touched down in a field near a community of several hundred structures where maybe one in five buildings was still standing. They were mostly round and one story tall with a concrete-like exterior that needed considerable patching and painting.

"While this planet has suffered less damage than the ones *Aurreol* surveyed, it's still in dreadful condition," Genghis said.

The Elder rode on a motorized chair the mechanics on *Enterprise* created for her. It carried the air tank and filter she needed to breathe the Dublo atmosphere. She rolled out of the shuttle and headed for the community. Woodsy and her attendant jogged to keep up with her.

Genghis walked behind sniffing repeatedly as he surveyed the countryside. *Would other planets smell differently than this one?*

A group of Dublos gathered at the Elder's approach. When Genghis arrived, Woodsy was translating her description of the differences between her unmodified attendant and his Hobot buddy. Woodsy then showed visuals of the Biots' discovery of *Wanderer,* the blasted ruins on the Secund worlds and the explosion of the Command Ship.

The Elder pointed out that Genghis and Woodsy engineered the destruction of the lunatic entity ridding the Galaxy of a vicious enemy.

The Dublos said a lot about the visuals. "Let's just say they're mighty impressed and appreciative of what we did," Woodsy said. "None of them can even imagine approaching the Command Ship let alone entering it."

As he talked, Genghis studied the Dublos. Having already seen visuals of them, there was none of the surprise of his first encounter with the Secunds. He did not care for the odors coming from the bodies of either species. Both were ungainly creatures, clearly no physical match for either Beings or Terrans. He grinned at the thought of Secunds or Dublos attempting to brawl like Terrans did.

Yet Secunds and Dublos had independently achieved space flight and spread to other planets. Among the shattered ruins of the Dublo worlds, there would likely be evidence of their technological and other accomplishments, just as on the Secund planets.

Genghis caught the occasional glance at him from a Dublo, who looked away quickly once noticed. *Perhaps he and Woodsy made them uncomfortable, realizing we'd done what they would have never attempted.*

In many ways, the Beings followed the same path as these two civilizations in expanding into space. However the Beings' accomplishments eclipsed both species and were achieved in a shorter time frame especially since the creation of the Biots.

His thoughts were interrupted by the Elder inviting the Dublos to come to the shuttle. When they reached it, Vasile and Anna appeared. The Dublos sounded like chirping birds as they pointed at his face. No one mentioned the breathing tubes in the side of their mouths.

"They can see he was marked by the Ancients," Woodsy said. "If they respect him that much, the Dublos can trust him and those who travel with him."

Genghis and Woodsy helped Stocton unload cases of the medicine that Dublos carted off to their community.

Then Stocton brought an imager from the shuttle to display the visuals of their visit to the Dome. The Dublos watched soundlessly as Vasile explained the first one came from their recorders and the second one was created by Turing. Then he recounted the visit of the envoys from the Dome when the shuttle overflew it during the trip to Planet 4.

When he finished, the Dublo leader spoke. "They have old stories about such a Dome," Woodsy explained. "None of them where it's located but they'll share whatever information still exists that could help us find it. They never heard of any actual encounters with the Ancients."

"The Elder says she hopes both sides have learned the need for a peaceful relationship," Woodsy explained. "She says the Beings have offered to consolidate the Secunds on a couple of planets and are prepared to do likewise for the Dublos."

A Dublo replied at considerable length. As Woodsy translated, it became clear the Dublos were caught as unprepared as the Secunds by the attacks. After centuries of rivalry, they assumed the Secunds were responsible. The Dublos managed scattered communications among groups of survivors on this planet, but not their other worlds.

Genghis interrupted to explain what *Aurreol* spotted on the planet with the mine. The Dublo said two words that Woodsy simply repeated so Genghis concluded that was the name of the world.

At that point, Genghis had the shuttle play the visuals of the exploration of the Command Ship and the conversation with the entity. The Elder and the Dublos shuddered at the gloomy interior of the ship and the vicious arrogance of the entity.

A Dublo said the entity's ranting proved his species correct in not allowing advanced technology. The Elder reminded him the entity was defeated by Genghis and Woodsy, both robots.

During a long discussion among Vasile, the Elder and the Dublo about Biots including their role in the Nameless War, Genghis looked at his companions. Anna sat in-between the Elder and Vasile with Stocton right behind them. Anna regularly typed notes into her communicator and showed them to Vasile and Stocton. Often they whispered among themselves.

The rest of the time she held her husband's hand and stared at the Dublos as if searching for something. Vasile explained the relationship between Beings and Biots, and then his wife's thesis about the importance of Biots to the Being and Terran worlds.

"Both of your societies are badly weakened by the attacks. You've barely survived. Do you wish to start rebuilding? Terra is fully occupied with assisting Mandela and dealing with its own climate degradation and can offer little assistance. While the Beings are too few in number, there are a billion Biots, some of who could come here to assist you. There aren't enough Secund robots and most have yet to be converted into Hobots."

When a Dublo admitted its group did not even know if there were more survivors on this planet, Genghis thought that was the least of their problems. Many were obviously sick with whatever disease the medicine was needed for as well as being on the gaunt side.

"The ship in orbit has been mapping the locations of settlements it can find," Vasile said. "We could transport you to them and you can relate what's happened. We can provide radio equipment so you can be in contact with each other. We could perform the same service on your other worlds."

"The Dublo wants to know why the Beings would bother to help them," Woodsy said.

The Elder spoke to Vasile. "She would like to know that as well."

Vasile looked into the pale blue sky before answering. "It begins with a Being named Humbaw and his curiosity." Vasile spoke in a quiet voice as if delivering a lecture on a topic that he spent considerable time studying. "Restoring your civilizations would be part of his desire to understand the Universe. For more than 200 years, he regularly visited Terra to study our species. He didn't wish to interfere, just to understand. Like all Beings, he'll want to know why your races remained at odds for so long without realizing the benefits of a cooperative relationship."

Dissatisfied with his response, Vasile looked to the sky again for inspiration.

"What he's trying to say is that simply it's the right thing to do," Genghis said patting Vasile on the back. The Terran truly understood Humbaw.

"Think of how much our different species might learn and benefit from an alliance," Anna said. "Or cooperate in exploring the rest of our galaxy. There are enough people in Terra who want to drag us backwards. We must demonstrate the way forward."

The Elder intervened. "She's proposing Vasile as the negotiator for a formal peace treaty between their species and arbitrator of any disputes that could arise," Woodsy said.

The Dublo looked at its own group. "They can't decide for all the Dublos," Woodsy said. "They'll speak in favor of it although Vasile's facial marks are probably the best recommendation."

As the Elder and the Dublos had much to discuss, Anna suggested that she, Vasile Stocton and Genghis "stretch our legs."

They strode down a hard surfaced road covered with enough plant growth to suggest it saw little use. When they reached a couple of hundred meters away from the others, Anna pulled a tube from her pack and clicked it on. "While it's unlikely they possess the ability to listen to us, why take chances?

"From what we've seen of the Secunds and Dublos, I can't believe they ever constituted a threat to each other. The Secunds are slow moving and clumsy while the Dublos, for their size, are weaklings. I'll collect genetic samples of Dublos before we depart so *Transformation* can create a genetic profile of them. It already has done one of the Secunds but I haven't heard any results from comparing it to the Beings or to Earth's reptiles. From what the Elder told me before we left, fighting was rare in either society and unheard of between them. Earth could use those genes."

She took a deep breath. "From what we've learned, the entity sowed the seeds of suspicion about the intentions of the other side and carefully nurtured the resentment the Secunds and Dublos felt toward each other. At the same time, it developed the ability to control other robots as well as Dublo technology and through them took over the starships giving it the ability to attack the planets. It must have fabricated the mines either on a ship or captured planet. Maybe that's what the surface mine *Aurreol* found was used for. As for the Secund and Dublo starship crews, they must have been killed outright or dumped into space. The entity clearly had no use for them."

She took a deep breath. "It's hard for me to conceive robots becoming psychopaths."

"There's a fault in the robot programing," Genghis said. "Woodsy says it manifests itself from time to time. However the independence doesn't usually produce monsters. Most robots stick to what their programing tells them to do."

"While the Secunds and Dublos were manipulated into believing the other side caused the conflict between them, what's most troubling is both societies accepted it without serious questioning of its likelihood," Anna said.

"Eventually the entity would have developed the capability to exterminate both species along with the robots it didn't need. The Secunds and Dublos have a future because of Biot bravery and Being curiosity and technology. It'll take a great deal of time and resources to restore these two species to cohesive functioning societies."

Chapter 32
Eureka

After *Aurreol's* departure from Lavaworld, Gaopod toiled away with the other Biots on upgrading the space station. When the Hobots became capable of assisting, the Biots were able to restore the station's monitoring equipment operation and commence long-overdue maintenance of the rest of the station's systems.

"It's time for you to work full time on deciphering the sounds of Lavaworld's creatures," Amundsen said to Gaopod. "We've enough Biots and Hobots studying its geology and chemistry."

After a couple of days of attempting to distinguish the whistles of the creatures from the cacophony generated by the planet's geological turmoil, Gaopod concluded the din of repairs and upgrades to the space station made his research impossible. He moved his processors to the Conference Center as everyone still called the Secund ship moored to the station. The Hobots from *Wanderer* could operate it because it employed the same flight control system as their old ship, which was on route to Hnassumblaw.

While he enjoyed the solitude of the Center, Gaopod still returned daily through the docking tube to the station to hear the playing of *An Ode to the Universe*. The trips enabled him to acquire additional information from the station's research records.

The short strolls gave him time to mull over the puzzles of Lavaworld's sounds. Distinguishing the creatures' individual communications was comparable to learning Terran from the buzz of talk in a crowded shopping mall where one overheard a few words from a conversation before it was drowned out by others. Gaopod requested information on Terran research into whale and dolphin communications to provide him with other approaches to investigating the sounds.

The station had identified nearly 2,000 sounds; some were repeated more frequently than others. However the robots had made no progress in determining their meaning because they could not identify what they were associated with. Gaopod compiled an oral collection of the whistles based on their pitch and frequency, and then requested Darwin, the Controlling Unit on *Transformation,* to examine it for any patterns.

Next he compared the collection to the sounds generated after the dumping of the Dublo ship, old space suits and station junk on Lavaworld. While he found new sounds from the creatures' sampling of the disintegrating debris, he was struck by gaps in their conversations. An active one would suddenly go mute, and then resume seconds or even up to a minute later. At first he thought they were normal pauses. The more he listened, the more he wondered whether there was another explanation.

Finally, the Biots and Hobots upgraded the station's equipment to the level that Gaopod could directly access the Lavaworld data through his processors in the Center. Gaopod arranged to have *An Ode to the Universe* broadcast so he could hear it.

Five days after the first broadcast, he pulled out of his research to listen to the anthem due in a few minutes. The planet monitors indicated the Lavaworld creatures were quiet. He was checking the status of the equipment when the music boomed through the Conference Center. When it concluded, he checked the planet monitors again. Still silence.

He kept listening and was rewarded when the sounds of the creatures resumed. While discordant and full of gaps, he was certain this was not shopping center chatter. The creatures were making the same sounds in unison.

He struggled for several minutes to repress his excitement and calmly assess the significance of what he was listening to. Then he could no longer repress a bellow of Eureka. Lavaworld's creatures responded to *The Ode* with sounds that seemed to have a purpose. It meant they possessed intelligence and an awareness of an existence outside their realm.

Darwin provided the answer to the gaps in their reply to the anthem. "Your detection equipment must be unable to read sounds above and below the hearing range of Secunds."

Within hours, Gaopod verified that observation. While the station's equipment heard all the frequencies, it only recorded the ones in the Secund hearing range. Gaopod shook his head in frustration at such shortsighted thinking although he was not surprised considering how the Secunds handicapped their robots.

He instructed his processors to examine the incoming sounds on all frequencies. Within minutes, his imager confirmed there were no silences. "Darwin, replay the sounds from Lavaworld after the end of *An Ode to the Universe*. Insert a buzz whenever there is a sound I can't hear."

Within seconds of the final notes of the anthem, a soft buzz not unlike radio static sounded in Gaopod's ears. Then came sounds from the creatures in a rising and falling pattern that covered an immense frequency range. Interspersed throughout it were bursts of static.

Gaopod listened intently to what he became increaseingly certain was a sophisticated response to *An Ode to the Universe*. Double checking the data convinced him it was an arranged pattern. How the creatures could do that surrounded by hot mush added to his puzzles.

He stared at the imager wondering how to determine whether the sounds were the equivalent of words or musical notes. Or both.

His personal analyzer had a copy of Genghis' compilation of Terran classical music. While he listened to it for weeks aboard *Wanderer*, he was certainly no authority on what constituted good musical composition. As with most things, Terrans would probably argue about that as well.

He set two tasks for himself. First, he would broadcast one of Genghis's favorite pieces every hour, other than when the anthem was played. He selected ones with different paces and styles. Hopefully, that would encourage the creatures to share more of whatever he just listened to.

His other task was to arrange the creatures' response to the Ode into a composition completely within the audible range of Terrans and Beings. For the sounds outside their hearing ranges, he would raise or lower the frequency so they could be heard. Then he would adjust the others to ensure their tempo and intervals followed the pattern of the creatures' response and maintained a smoothly flowing relationship to each other.

He hoped this rendering of the creatures' sounds would be good enough for a musical person to turn it into a playable piece the creatures would recognize and everyone else would enjoy. Every note had to be adjusted; a job that consumed nearly two weeks but left him even more convinced the creatures had composed a musical pattern.

When he developed the piece as much as he could, he transmitted it to Darwin to review. There had to be something else he could do. He walked around the Conference Center several times, and then into the station. It finally looked tidy enough to pass Commander Kelsey's scrutiny. One level up Amundsen scrutinized a large diagram of the station on an imager mounted on a wall.

"The Secunds could have easily made this a much more functional facility," his pal grumbled.

Gaopod explained his discovery and his problem.

"No one here will be of any help," Amundsen said without looking away from the diagram. "Genghis once said Ruth Huxley is a good piano player. Maybe she could advise you."

"Why didn't I think of our fairy godmother," Gaopod said.

"What?"

"There are many Terran stories that include magical characters. My favorite character in them is a fairy godmother. That is what Ruth is to all Biots."

Gaopod had taken a couple of steps away when Amundsen shouted, "The creatures responded to the anthem! That means we aren't wasting our time here. Absolutely brilliant work, Gaopod! Your namesake would be proud of you."

Gaopod waved before rushing back to the station. On the way, Darwin contacted him. "While I haven't listened to all of it yet, what you sent me sounds like something Terrans could make music with."

In addition to a long explanation, Gaopod sent a copy of his rendition of the creatures' composition to Ruth.

Then he tuned into the planet. Since receiving the creatures' composition, Gaopod had been broadcasting music at Lavaworld every hour. When he listened to the monitors, Handel's *Musick for the Royal Fireworks* was nearly finished. Would the creatures offer anything in return?

Gaopod was surprised when only scattered bursts of chatter could be detected after the piece finished. He continued to listen and speculate. Perhaps the creatures only had one response. However it had taken five broadcasts of *The Ode* before they responded to it. Maybe he had overloaded the creatures with too many different compositions when they needed more time to assimilate a single piece.

He programmed his processor to play *Musick for the Royal Fireworks* daily twelve hours apart from the anthem. He tuned into the planet after every broadcast of the anthem and *The Fireworks*. Five days later the creatures responded with a new composition. Tomorrow he would present them with a symphony he had not played before.

He hoped no one would ask him for a progress report on figuring out the creatures' language. He still had no idea what they were saying and he now needed to develop a translation mechanism that could include all the inaudible sounds as well.

Having collaborated with Gaopod on interpreting the first response from the creatures, Darwin was able to make an audible version of their next serenade in a couple of days. Meanwhile Gaopod broadcast Beethoven's *Ode to Joy* to Lavaworld.

Gaopod dispatched the second piece to Ruth before setting to work on his compilation of the creatures' sounds. Again Darwin's assistance sped up the task.

They finished listing all the sounds outside of the normal hearing range of Beings and Terrans when Ruth's reply to his first message confirmed her fairy godmother status. It opened with her playing the first few minutes of the creatures' composition on a piano.

While he thought her playing was beautiful, Ruth said, "That doesn't do it justice. I shared the piece with the conductor of the Mandela Symphony Orchestra. You would have enjoyed hearing her humming as she read it adjusting the pace and notes. As soon as the orchestra plays it competently, she'll make a recording for you."

Two weeks later, Ruth's next transmission delivered the symphony and a gift. "The orchestral version will send shivers up the spine of every Being and Terran that hears it. The Mandela Orchestra has already scheduled extra concerts."

Gaopod stood riveted while *The Lavaworld Suite* filled the Conference Center. As it finished, he glanced at the clock. It would soon be time for a broadcast to the planet. How would the creatures respond to this interpretation of their composition?

When *The Lavaworld Suite* broadcast finished, the response from the creatures could only be called jubilant. "I would say they recognize the origin of the composition and are ecstatic to realize their music matches what you have been broadcasting to them." Darwin almost sounded excited. "You should play the other piece Ruth sent you."

After just a few notes, Gaopod knew that as much as he wanted to find a way to communicate with the creatures, he wished to learn to play a Terran organ well enough to match the second version of the Lavaworld Suite that filled the Conference Center.

"This will blow the creatures away," Darwin said.

Chapter 33
Knocking on Heaven's Door

It took months to gather the scattered remnants of the Secunds and Dublos into communities. The 34 billion Dublos on five planets with thriving economies had been slashed to barely 230,000. More than 41 billion Secunds had been beaten down to less than 463,000.

Eventually the Dublos would be relocated to one planet while the Secunds would be transported to two of theirs including Planet 4.

Once the Secund and Dublo fleets were rounded up, the vessels worth preserving were parked in the Lagrange points of unoccupied planets in their systems. Valuable metals and material would be harvested from the rest and the remainder launched into the closest suns. Lavaworld was too distant to justify the cost of towing the debris to it.

In midst of the ruins of a Dublo planet, a team of Biots found an intact library and digital storage facility. "While reviewing the visuals, they discovered references to a Dome, which must be the one the Dublo referred to," Woodsy said after listening to the reports about the discovery.

"It clearly isn't the one that Vasile and Stocton visited. It's described as being on a planet that at first appears to be a second moon to a rocky giant. However it actually orbits independently around the sun of that system."

Inspired by the finding, the remaining Dublo facilities were combed for any further information on the location of Dome2 as it soon became known. After weeks of research, four planets worthy of close-up inspection were finally identified. *Dreadnought* took charge of the search for it while the Dublo planets were combed for any additional information.

With the four possibilities on their star charts, Vasile, Anna, Stocton, Genghis, Woodsy, Humbawloda and her ton Hudaton went exploring in the diplomatic shuttle.

The first planet was a lifeless dud while the second possessed a feeble oxygen atmosphere, which indicated it could eventually be capable of sustaining life. "If we needed a resettlement planet, it could probably be terraformed," Humbawloda said after examining the grey world.

During the search, Genghis found himself closely watching the interaction between Vasile and Anna. They showed their affection for each other in so many ways. He could not decide whether it was spontaneous or learned behavior.

It was in the middle of the night when the shuttle entered the third system. "Did you feel the pulse," Stocton asked Genghis. They were monitoring the sensor data from the planet.

"I sensed nothing."

"This is where we want to be," Stocton said as he stood. "I'll explain later. First I must inform Vasile and Anna."

He knocked softly on the door to their quarters.

"Come in," Vasile muttered. "The Dome is calling us."

Hearing Vasile's words, Genghis reviewed the incoming sensor readings. They showed nothing other than the usual data about the planet's composition.

"We still have to determine the Dome's location on the planet," Stocton said.

"Anna and I'll come to the Command Chamber shortly," Vasile said.

They settled on the Chamber's second bench beside Humbawloda and Hudaton. Genghis, Stocton and Woodsy occupied the front one. They gazed at the image of the planet, a real time feed of what the shuttle's recorders were seeing.

"It has cloud cover and a surface consisting of continents and oceans," Woodsy said. "Is Terra like this?"

"Actually the large continents remind me more of Mandela," Vasile said.

Anna leaned against Vasile. "After all the visuals of planets, it's exciting to see a new one for the first time."

After entering the planet's atmosphere, the shuttle approached its equator. "The scans aren't detecting radio signals or any other evidence of settlements," Woodsy noted. "The continents appear covered mostly in vegetation with some mountainous areas."

The shuttle suddenly banked to the right. "The sensors detected a pulsing light."

Vasile inhaled deeply. "The Dome is signaling us."

The projection on the imager shifted to a longrange view of what resembled a giant frosted light bulb between flashes. "It's circular with a diameter of nearly a kilometer, which is about the same size as the Dome we explored," Stocton said.

As the shuttle headed toward it, the Dome ceased flashing and emitted a warm glow. "The first one didn't react to Stocton and me testing its exterior," Vasile said. "Now it looks like the front and back door lights are turned on to welcome a weary traveller arriving at night."

"It's like they're expecting us," Stocton said. "There's even a flat place to land the shuttle. This is more like a Being world in terms of temperature and oxygen levels."

"Lucky for Humbawloda," Vasile said. "The Terrans have breathers so we'll be fine."

"Must not get a lot of visitors," Stocton said. "While it's hard to see in the dark, the shuttle's descent to the landing area is blowing a lot of dirt into the air. We'll wait for it to settle before exiting the craft."

"Vasile and Stocton should lead the way," Humbawloda said. "Vasile's facial marks and their previous visit might open doors for us."

When Vasile and Stocton stepped toward the Dome, a gravel path emitted a glow to light their way. Even with his hand-held lamp, it was too dark for Genghis to see much of the terrain on either side of path. There was no breeze or sound other than crunch of their boots.

When they reached the Dome, Vasile said, "The exterior looks just like the other one."

"Like ice on a lake," Stocton said.

Vasile faced Anna. "My parents played in a band. The one English song in their repertoire was called Knock Knock Knocking on Heaven's Door. That's what we're doing. They didn't know the lyrics other than the refrain; they just liked the pounding sound of the music."

Anna's eyes widened in surprise and Vasile and Stocton quickly turned around. An open archway in the wall of the Dome revealed a walkway heading toward the center of the Dome. "All that's missing is a welcome mat," she said. The group stepped through and the archway closed. "We should each recount what we can see."

For Humbawloda and Genghis, it was the single story buildings surrounded by brownish plants that covered much of Hnassumblaw especially since the cleanup of the badlands. Anna saw the small Polish village of her childhood while to Vasile and Stocton, the same ordered community from their first visit appeared.

"I see only empty space," Woodsy said.

"Me too," Hudaton said.

"I didn't see anything at the beginning of my first visit," Stocton said. "It'll come to you."

"Look at that shining pillar of light," Vasile said.

"There was nothing like that the last time," Stocton said.

"It must be our host," Anna said as he stepped toward it. When the others followed, the guiding light led them deeper into the Dome.

Vasile took hold of Anna's hand. "Remember I associated the Dome with Bunica's mansions in heaven for angels. When I look at it, the glowing light briefly shifts into a depiction of an angel like I saw in pictures as a child."

"I've seen glimpses of a saintly wizard and a fairy," she said.

For Humbawloda it was a Jerante, a mythical creature that inhabited Hnassumblaw in the time before Beings and whose spirits were said to watch over her species still.

"Now that you've said it, I too spotted a Jerante," Stocton said. Genghis and Hudaton did as well.

"I just see an empty space; no buildings, no countryside, nothing." While Woodsy sounded crushed, he paid close attention to the light as if expecting it to suddenly reveal a shape.

"Genghis, this is what Earth smells like in spring when the flowers and plants come into bloom," Anna said.

"Also the Confederation worlds," Humbawloda added.

Genghis and Woodsy sniffed and sniffed.

They entered a garden full of rock carvings and bushes covered in leaves of many colors. "The buildings around the park look just like the ones in the first Dome," Vasile said.

The guiding light halted in front of a series of busts mounted on round pedestals. The first collection had an image of a Being's head on one pedestal and a Terran head on another. To Genghis, they looked like Humbaw and

Benjamin Kendo. In between them was a replica of a Biot's head.

Nearby were three more pedestals. The center one was empty. On either side of it were busts of Secund and Dublo heads.

A seventh pedestal without a head stood about ten meters apart from the others.

"These busts represent the advanced species in this Galaxy," Anna said. Her eyes moved back and forth among the pedestals as she deeply inhaled the garden's aroma. Her voice lost its usual rise and fall and settled into a monotone.

"The empty pedestal between the Secund and Dublo is for the Hobots when they're ready. The other empty one represents a species in the Milky Way we haven't encountered yet."

The certainty in her voice had everyone staring at her.

"Could it be the creatures on Lavaworld?" Stocton added.

"They'll always be confined to that planet. However, we need to keep attempting to contact them. The Ancients know what the seventh species is but only show me glimpses that suggest the other species' appearance is quite different. We have to find them."

"By inference, the guiding pillar of light is an Ancient," Vasile said.

"It is," Anna said still in her flat tone. "The Ancients date back to the time when the first stars formed, well before the Universe developed the chemicals required for life as we know it." Her gaze fixed on the pedestals. "They witnessed countless stars die along with the planets that collected around them. They watched many species evolve throughout the Universe in the billions of years since. Most are extinct. They were all physically different yet the same in so many ways. Neither the Secunds nor the Dublos are their descendants."

Her focus remained on the busts as if she was in a trance channeling the Ancients.

"The Beings, Secunds, Dublos and other species arose from the conditions on their home-worlds," she said after several more deep breaths. "Humans came well after them, but in a similar process of evolution of primitive to more advanced species. While the Biots were created for a purpose, they've grown well beyond that. Their pedestal should erase any doubts they have about being an independent species."

Spotting Hudaton and Stocton standing behind the others, Genghis flashed them messages in Biot sign language. *"Does the position of the Biot bust recognize our role as a link between the Beings and Terrans?"*

"Anna said our presence on a pedestal signifies far more," Stocton replied with his fingers. *"Like Ruth Huxley, the Ancients regard us as an independent species."*

"It's not just Ruth," Hudaton said. She nodded at Anna whose gaze was coming around to the Biots.

"What's the role of the Ancients in all this?" Genghis said, hoping no one had noticed their conversation.

Anna took several more deep breaths. "While they attempt to inspire species to improve, they can't physically intervene. Their only avenue is to encourage individuals of a species who might improve life for the rest of their kind. The species represented here have figures that fit that role."

"Did the Ancients influence Humbaw and Benjamin Kendo at the crucial moments?" Genghis said.

Anna's smile was all the confirmation Genghis needed.

"Did they have anything to do with the development of religions and belief in a Supreme Being on Earth?" Vasile said. "Or an entity referred to with a hum on the Being worlds and Pozzen?"

"They were part of the inspiration the Ancients attempted to convey. They're meant to encourage us to be better as individuals and species."

Once again, Anna breathed deeply as if inhaling information from the Dome. "We should remain here for a little while longer. For a few minutes, drink in the atmosphere of this place. It'll provide memories to direct and comfort us in trying times."

With those words, the guiding light vanished. Anna stepped carefully to a bench and sat. She cupped her head in her hands and exhaled nosily. Her gaze was fixed on the solitary pedestal. "We must seek the seventh species."

Everyone gazed about and inhaled as if the atmosphere was a tonic. Genghis sniffed repeatedly until he realized Woodsy was as well. "We have to know the scent of a good place," the Hobot said. They kept sniffing.

Then Anna stood. "It's time to leave. Take a last look about in case we don't visit a Dome again." With that, her voice returned to its usual cheerful tone and the shakiness disappeared from her steps.

The Ancient in the form of the pillar of light reappeared and led the group in silence through the Dome, garbed in the dusk that follows a sunny day. The entranceway appeared and they stepped through it. The Dome shone brilliantly.

"It's celebrating," Anna said. "It's telling the other Domes of its contact with us and its message to us about the need to look for the seventh species."

The entranceway closed and by the time they reached the shuttle, the Dome had turned dark like an empty house. "The Ancient allowed me to see it briefly. It appeared to be much like the translucent figures that Vasile and Stocton saw in our shuttle at the other Dome. I could only describe them as an oblong shaped with the ability to extend a limb to touch."

The shuttle started at their approach and lifted off once they were onboard for the trip back to *Dreadnought*. Unable to stop yawning, Vasile, Anna and Humbawloda headed to their sleeping quarters. The Biots and Woodsy plugged in.

"It felt like we were only there for a few minutes but the chronometer says almost 15 hours have passed," Stocton said from the pilot's seat. "Turn on your monitors; the Confederation has been busy while we were meeting the Ancients."

Chapter 34
To Every Thing there is a Reason

Genghis and Stocton read the long announcement while Woodsy waited for them to explain the significance of the Chief Councilor resigning to take on a new task.

"It's not a surprising move on Hton's part," Genghis said. "He's been in that post far longer than his predecessors and has integrated the Biots into the Confederation as much as possible.

"Hton recommended that Gnoorvants succeed him. The Admiral is well respected by Beings, Pozzens and Terrans and now the Secunds and Dublos. Actually Gnoorton told me when I was last on *Enterprise* that Gnoorvants would make a great Chief Councilor if the High Council could ever get him off the ship. His companion hadn't been able to do that very often."

"Even with Hton and Humbaw taking charge of the development of a cooperation agreement with the Secunds and Dublos, Vasile and Anna will remain involved with our new friends, which is fine by me," Stocton grinned.

"This is good news for us," Woodsy said. "If your former leaders are assisting us and Vasile is still helping, then the Secunds and Dublos will have to accept the Hobots have a role among them like the Biots do with your organics."

"There'll be a Hobot bust in the Dome yet," Stocton said.

"That I want to see."

"Gnoorvants will turn over command of *Enterprise* to his Deputy Commander after the ship returns to Hnassumblaw," Stocton said. "*Wanderer* will arrive there soon. About two-thirds of the enemy Fleet is being scrapped."

"What Fleet ships are remaining in the region?" Genghis said.

"*Dreadnought, Transformation* and two other cruisers," Stocton said. "Two transports are bringing gear and will take on the relocation of the Secunds and Dublos. For now, our personnel will remain on the ships and help both sides as they require. Vasile, Anna and Stocton will be stationed on *Transformation*."

"Perhaps the healers will replace the Elder's hips and spine," Genghis said.

"If they can do it, they'll be in line for plenty of business," Woodsy said. "There are many Secunds who suffer from the same condition."

"You didn't mention what's planned for *Aurreol*," Woodsy said.

"It has to take a VIB to Terra," Stocton said. "Then it, *Garzon* and *Tbzor* will be placed in layup. The Beings want to use them to design a new series of cruisers."

"What's a VIB?" Woodsy said.

"A Very Important Biot."

"Who could that be?" Woodsy's gaze was fixed on Genghis.

"A special friend of *Aurreol's* Commander."

"Hah, hah. I was asked to attend the memorial service for Benjamin Kendo." Genghis looked forward to spending time with her on the trip to Kendo's memorial. He would have to find a way to tell her how important she was to him. "What will happen with the crews from the Pozzen cruisers?"

"Many of them are staying behind to restore the ships the Secunds and Dublos want to use," Stocton said. "They'll Hobots to operate them. The others will be integrated into the Fleet. Commander Kelsey will taking command of Transport 27 again."

Genghis discovered what a surge of anger felt like. "After all she's done!"

Stocton burst out laughing. "Gotcha buddy. She's being posted to Hnassumblaw to assist in the rebuilding of the ship into a science and exploration vessel. She'll also be involved in the design of the new cruisers based on her experience with the Pozzen ones. If that isn't enough to keep her busy, there's protecting the intelligence in *Wanderer*.

"When the overhaul of Transport 27 is complete, it'll return to the Secund-Dublo region to assist in the conversion of the robots and possibly building new ones to replace all those that were destroyed. It'll also support *Transformation* in the study of Lavaworld's creatures and undoubtedly participate in the search for species No. 7."

"Maybe they'll name the ship in honor of Humbaw or Hton," Genghis said.

"Woodsy, would you be interested in working with Vasile and Anna Stocia and me?" Stocton said. "I'm sure Gaopod, Octinog and Fleming will want to return to Transport 27 in its new role."

"I would. While it may not be as exciting as breaking into the Command Ship, it'll be a lot more interesting than what I was doing before Genghis arrived. I'm sure the GGs will want to be involved as well. First I wish to accompany Genghis to Terra and Hnassumblaw. They sound like much different worlds and I want to spend some time with *Wanderer*."

"You're invited; you'll be a celebrity," Genghis said. *Maybe he'll become the robots' Hton someday.* "I'm sure Humbaw, Hton and Gnoorvants will attend the Kendo memorial and they'll expect a full recounting of our mission as part of their preparation for their new posts."

"Oh you can count on that," Stocton said. "Look at your monitors." On them appeared a report on the successful mission to retrieve the Biots on *Wanderer*, the discovery of the robots, Secunds and Dublos and the encounter with the berserk entity. Genghis was clearly the star of the show.

"As I said, a VIB," Stocton said.

After a bit of teasing, Woodsy came to the rescue of his pal. "Do Terrans often do what Anna did in the Dome? Her behavior was very different from what I'd seen of her until then. Could she have a connection with the Ancients that no one saw before? They were certainly speaking through her."

"I've known her for 30 years and I've never seen her do anything like that," Stocton said. "Probably she was the most receptive of us to the Ancients, who needed someone to communicate through. She is the least judgmental and kindest human I've encountered.

"The next transmission comes from Ruth Huxley, a person much like her," Genghis said.

Sitting in her lab on Mandela, she related how Gaopod discovered there was music in the sounds of the Lavaworld creatures and that it had been turned into symphonies by the conductor of the Mandela Orchestra. "She's very excited about *The Lavaworld Reflections*. Here's the first one."

Anna announced her presence with a deep yawn. She ran her fingers through her ruffled hair. "I got up when I heard the music. It's beautiful, exhilarating and sad at the same time. The creatures know they cannot leave their world because the lava protects and restrains them. The music is their greeting and offer of friendship to us."

While it was her normal voice, Genghis wondered if she was delivering a message from the Ancients. Maybe she always would be their voice. He would send her message to Gaopod.

The creatures' composition ended all too soon. "Orchestras all over Earth are learning the music," Ruth said in the visual. "It will be featured at special memorial concerts in honor of Benjamin Kendo."

"That would be fitting for without his decision to assist the Beings, we wouldn't have encountered the creatures or come here," Genghis said.

When Stocton explained about Hton and Gnoorvants, Anna excused herself to report the news to Vasile and Humbawloda.

Genghis pulled out Ruth's letter and read it again before passing it to Stocton with an explanation about his session with Ruth. That had been eleven months ago.

Stocton read the letter without comment, and then passed it to Hudaton, who read it and passed it to Woodsy. When he finished, he handed it back to Genghis.

"Hudaton, you said in the Dome you would explain later about Ruth and the others studying us," Genghis said. He almost posed the question in sign language before remembering Woodsy would not be able to follow.

"You would know nothing of this," the ton said. "After the War, Ruth agreed to take charge of a project to track the progress of the Biots in hopes of finding something that might lead us to understand our actual status.

"She attended Hton's taking the oath of responsibility when he became Chief Councilor," Hudaton said. "Before she returned to Mandela, she had a long discussion with him and Humbaw about the Biots. I'll always remember her first statement to Hton. 'When will the Biots realize they're a species just like humans and Beings? Their conduct during the Nameless War proves it.' Genghis was among the Biots she mentioned by name.

"It was obviously a topic previously discussed by Humbaw and Hton. They called it our awakening or self-discovery. Hton said the Biots had to be brought to the point of realizing what they'd accomplished. His very words were 'I could tell them over and over, but it'll do no good. It'll take the actions of individual Biots to make the rest of them aware of their status. While it won't change much in their relationships with Beings or Terrans, it'll likely unleash a tremendous burst of creativity as Biots discover what they are capable of.'"

Hudaton paused when Genghis and Stocton looked at each other and shrugged their shoulders. "In her letter, Ruth's telling you that we've made it, especially with what we accomplished here. Genghis, you were at the center of it beginning with your boarding of *Wanderer*."

Stocton clapped Genghis on the shoulder. "Thanks partner. I would say we Biots are awake. The bust on the pedestal in the Dome confirms it."

The shuttle's Tyson announced a priority personal transmission to Genghis from the Admiral.

Genghis opened it on his communicator. "You'll know by now I'm to take over as the Chief Councilor. Gnoorton can look after the myriad of details connected to that post. I need you to be my advisor on relations with other species."

When he shared the message, Stocton said, "You can't say no to a request like that. Looks like you'll be staying in Hnassumblaw. Too bad. You'll miss all the excitement out here. Interestingly, the Admiral copied Commander Kelsey on this message."

Before Genghis could reply, Woodsy and the Biots were laughing and congratulating him. Vasile, Anna and Humbawloda joined them.

Genghis remembered Ruth's advice to embrace his emotions and happily accepted everyone's congratulations.

Alex Binkley
Humanity's Saving Grace

The first book in the Biot Series

Having barely avoided self-destruction, an ancient race has expanded to eight other worlds. While the Beings explored Earth numerous times during two centuries with their flying saucers, they didn't consider the primitive Terrans worth contacting. That changes when their worlds came under attack from a relentless, mysterious foe. The aliens offer to repair Earth's ravaged environment in exchange for pilots and soldiers to fight their enemy. The First Earth Expeditionary Force battles in space and on the ground while trying to comprehend a link between the enemy and the lost civilization of Atlantis. They're also caught up in figuring out the motives of robot-like creatures that serve the aliens and discovering the origin of centuries old ruins on several planets and a seemingly uninhabited community under a protective dome.

Available from
info@loosecannonpress.com
www.loosecannonpress.com

CPSIA information can be obtained at www.ICGtesting.com
Printed in the USA
LVOW08s0143231016

509661LV00001B/1/P